THE SPAWN OF LAZARUS

A Novel by

Alan D. Henson

This is a work of fiction. Names, characters, places and incidents are either the product of the author's imagination or are used fictitiously unless otherwise noted. Any resemblance to actual persons, living or dead, locales, business establishments or events is entirely coincidental.

Printed in the UNITED STATES OF AMERICA

CONTENTS

CHAPTER 1: VIGIL

The night air was damp in Yaroslavl Russia. It was an unseasonably warm night for November, with the temperature almost reaching the freezing mark. Vigil had reached his own freezing mark some two hours before. He shrugged off the cold and continued to peer through the high-powered night vision scope. It was attached to a custom sniper rifle of his own design. It looked like other sniper rifles in most respects except that the muzzle diameter was very small and fired a projectile that was not much thicker than a toothpick. Gun enthusiasts would have argued that a projectile that small would be ineffective at any distance, but Vigil had designed the shell himself.

The whole cartridge was about four inches long and about as thick as a pencil. The bullet itself was made of a very dense alloy that was much heavier than it looked. It had a corkscrew appearance that unwound when it hit bone, like a broken spring in an old alarm clock. The shell casing, instead of being filled with gun powder or cordite, was filled with a volatile plasma compound that was not available to civilians. Tiny radioactive particles in the primer produced an explosion that was like a microscopic nuclear detonation. The result was a projectile that was faster than anything else on the market and it made a controlled explosion of the target. Because the bullet was so small, it also made the least noise. The downside was that the barrel of the gun had to be replaced after only a few shots had been fired through it. The material stripped away the rifling with every discharge.

Vigil crouched in a small patch of shrubs near the Kotorosl River. The *ghillie* suit he wore made him appear to be just another shrub. Traffic was nonexistent on the nearby bridge, which was not unusual for this time of night. The overcast sky threatened snow and there was a thin layer of fog that formed halos around the streetlamps on the bridge. Vigil looked at the illuminated hands of his tactical watch. It was four-thirty in the morning and his target was late. He had made sure to adjust for the time zone difference when he left the Czech Republic, so he felt as though he had been stood up by his *date*. Then he heard the purr of an engine.

An unmarked delivery lorry had driven down the bank of the river with its headlights off and parked in the darkness beneath the bridge supports. A shadowy figure emerged from the driver's side and went to the back. Vigil could see as clearly as if it was midday through the night vision scope, but he still couldn't be sure if it was the man he was waiting for. The figure was wearing a hooded jacket and his face was hidden. He pulled two bulky trash bags from the back of the lorry and began dragging them to the edge of the river. He slid them onto a skim of ice along the river's bank and waited. It didn't seem as though the man was catching his breath. It was more as if he was saying goodbye to the bundles and relishing the moment. Vigil was pretty sure it was the latter.

After a moment, the man in the hood slid the trash bags into the water where they nearly sank. He had made sure that wouldn't happen for a while. It was not the first time he had done this and it wasn't the first dismembered body he had disposed of here. The body parts would be carried down the tributary and would empty into the Volga River. Were it not for the dams along the way, the body could make it all the way to the Caspian Sea. Some of the body parts might make it anyway.

6

Vigil had followed the man before, but he had not been properly armed the last time he had. That was why he knew where he would dump the body. Vigil knew when he would strike because the killer had a strict timetable that adhered to moon cycles. He didn't know where; but he was pretty sure he knew where the man would dispose of the body. Since the hooded figure was also wanted for international terrorism, Vigil had been assigned to the case. He personally had made sure of that. This was personal. It was as personal as it gets.

The hooded figure watched as the bags floated around a bend in the river. He raised his hand slightly in a final farewell gesture. Then he walked slowly back to the lorry. Vigil waited as the man got behind the wheel and started the engine. Just as he shifted into drive there was a sudden crack that sounded like the snapping of a heavy tree branch. A small pinprick of a hole appeared in the windshield and the interior of the glass was immediately sprayed with blood; making it impossible to see through. The lorry slowly pulled forward a few feet but its progress was halted by a bridge support. After a reasonable amount of time, Vigil approached the driver's side window of the vehicle cautiously. He pulled out a silenced P99 Walther to examine the passenger. The driver's window was also covered in blood and brain matter, so Vigil had to open the door to check his target. The scene inside was sickening, yet satisfying to him. He was unable to identify the body by facial recognition, so he took a blood and tissue sample to run a DNA test later. It was important that he be sure of the individual's identity. He softly closed the door and performed one of the skills he did best. He disappeared into the night.

* * *

The local *politsiya* of Yaroslavl did not know what to make of the crime. They found the body parts of a young woman just a kilometer down river from the bridge. She was identified as a woman who had been missing since two nights before. Evidence in the lorry and signs along the bank confirmed that the driver had been involved. That much had been easy for them to figure out. What they could not understand was what had happened to the man. His head looked as though it had been assaulted with a weed eater fitted with razor wire, but it appeared as though the assault had been done from the inside of his head. A long thin strip of jagged metal was found lodged in the back of what was left of his skull. Other than that, the only other clue that they found was a toothpick size-hole in the windshield. Nothing added up so the police decided to deem the case a murder/suicide.

The official report read that the perpetrator had kidnapped the victim, assaulted her, murdered her and then dismembered her body. Other evidence later suggested that he might not have done those things in that order. She may have been alive as she was being dismembered. The official report also concluded that in a moment of remorse, the perpetrator had placed a gun in his mouth and killed himself; even though no gun was found at the scene. It was easier to have a missing gun remain a mystery than to try to figure out what caused the grisly scene under the bridge, so the case was closed.

* * *

Vigil leaned back in his window seat and watched the scenery speed by. The train would take a few hours to reach Moscow and he was tired. Surveillance always took a lot out of him and he hadn't slept much in the last two days. Vigil had been on the trail of Abimael Hart for a long time. He nearly had him in Libya, but somehow he had slipped past Vigil during a riot. It was two years before Vigil tracked him down. He discovered that Abimael had been travelling around the former Soviet Union; leaving a trail of dismembered bodies in his wake. Old habits die hard it seems.

Vigil would file a report with his contact in Washington but wasn't officially an agent of the United States Government. He was more like an independent contractor...with benefits. He wouldn't even have agreed to work for them except that they could provide him access to other countries with a minimal amount of hassle; but support when he needed it. The assignments he got were the kind that the government would not want to be a part of...officially. That gave Vigil a lot of latitude and that was how he liked it. The money was good, but it wasn't the reason he did the assignments. He liked the covert payment method though. With each assignment he was provided with fake passports, fake identities, credit cards and money in different kinds of currency. He used the credit cards for all of his expenses, and *somehow*, the bills never came due. There was never an electronic paper trail to lead anyone back to the source of his income.

Abimael Hart had not been an international terrorist, but he did deserve to die. Vigil had submitted evidence suggesting his terrorism involvement just so he would be assigned to the case. Travelling to Russia was not that easy for a civilian. Entering the country, executing a target and exiting unseen were harder still. Pursuing an international terrorist put a lot of additional resources at Vigil's disposal. Sometimes he received help and information from the local governments. That had not been the case in Yaroslavl. The political climate was a little shaky there and it was better not to even ask for help. It was better if they hadn't even known he was there. Vigil needed to be invisible for more than one reason.

Disposing of Abimael Hart had been satisfying, but also anticlimactic. Vigil would have preferred to face him when he *resolved* him; or at least have to work harder to track him down. It was almost as if Abimael had given up. Maybe he had. He had been murdering people for a very long time. Maybe it had become dull like everything else in his life. Vigil felt that way sometimes. It was possible that Abimael had just slipped up; but that really wasn't like him. He had always been so careful to cover his tracks. Abimael had been as skillful at entering other countries unnoticed as Vigil was. In a way, watching Abimael die was like watching himself make a mistake and he didn't like it.

Vigil drifted off as the motion of the train lulled him into a fitful sleep. He dreamt of roman soldiers and of generals falling upon their own swords in defeat or disgrace. Bodies were strewn across battlefields by the thousands as a nearly obscured sun set in the west. Vigil stood alone, blood dripping from his own sword. His face was covered in sweat and spattered with the blood of his enemies. He looked at his sword and considered falling on it himself. There had been no honor in this battle. The opposing army didn't have a chance against him. He knew that. He pressed the point of his blade against his breastplate and was prepared to fall on it when he heard a Carnyx battle horn sound. It didn't make sense to him. Armies didn't usually attack at dusk. He looked around and saw no one was left alive. The horn sounded again and Vigil jolted from his dream.

The train whistle announced their arrival in Moscow. Vigil gathered his bags and disembarked at the train station. He took a taxi to the Sheremetyevo airport and checked in. It would be four hours before his flight left and he would spend another eleven hours in the air. Vigil ate lunch in the first café that caught his eye. He wasn't really hungry but knew that he should eat. What he really wanted was a drink and he knew where to get one; *Katie O'Connor's Irish Pub.*

It always amused Vigil to drink in an Irish pub right in the middle of a Russian airport. There was something quirky about the dichotomy of it that he liked. Maybe it reminded him of himself. He never felt he belonged, no matter where he was in the world. He liked the feel of the pub.

Even when it was busy, the pub seemed friendly. A waitress came over to take his order. Vigil resisted calling her a *serving wench* and instead opted to call her Katie, even though she had Alyona (Алёна) on her nametag. She got the joke, but after a thousand times, it wasn't funny anymore. She still laughed and he still tipped her. He drank Irish whisky until his flight was announced, paid his tab and then headed for his gate. Opening his wallet, he gave Alyona another generous tip… and a kiss on the cheek as he left. She was surprised, but not offended. She actually found it rather pleasant.

Vigil hardly showed any signs that he had been drinking, even though the amount he ingested would have put a lesser man under the table. He ordered another drink after he settled in his First Class seat. This time he switched to scotch. An attractive young woman sat across the aisle from him and would have probably been receptive to an unsolicited advance, but Vigil was tired. He was polite to her and made small talk; but after his drink was finished he excused himself, put his seat back and went to sleep. Thanks to the alcohol, his sleep was dreamless. The next time he opened his eyes, he was well within American airspace.

Chapter Two: Ancient History

Vigil never understood how a person could have *too much sleep*. Sleep was a good thing. He loved sleep. It had been explained to him that sleeping too long creates an imbalance in the blood chemistry, but he didn't think things like that applied to him; even when he had evidence to the contrary.

When he woke up, it took him a few moments to realize he was back in his apartment in D.C. Vigil's head was pounding and his mouth was full of cotton. The shadows and his clock would seem to indicate that it was very early, but in fact the sun was going down. He slept most of the way back from Moscow, grabbed a taxi at Dulles and went straight home. He didn't even remember undressing before going to bed. He stood in his bathroom, fumbling with an aspirin bottle. *I am a world-class assassin,* he thought. *Am I really going to be undone by a childproof cap?* The bottle finally gave in, but Vigil couldn't help but think it had a smug look on its face. The jet lag was really getting to him.

Vigil seriously considered going back to bed, but was pretty sure that after a combined eighteen hours of sleep, he needed to stay up. He went to the kitchen to make coffee and discovered he didn't have any; so he settled for tea. He was also out of bread, so toast was out of the question. Grabbing a very stale slice of pizza from the refrigerator, he sat down on the couch and opened his laptop.

His computer had a redundant biometric security system. Not only was his thumbprint required on the security pad, his ring finger had to be placed on an unassuming icon on his desktop screen. Even with those two security measures, a complicated nine-character password had to be entered before access was granted to his files. The password changed automatically every three days.

Vigil failed at the first step of his security protocols. He was about to get locked out of his own system until he realized he had grease on his thumb from the pizza and it was preventing a clear reading on his scanner. He finished the slice and cleaned up before beginning again. While he was up, he made another cup of tea. The second was a little better than the first.

The computer screen glowed in the darkening living room and Vigil looked over the rows of file folder icons until he found the one that he wanted; the one labeled ACTIVE. He clicked on it and several more rows of file folder icons popped up. Each was labeled with a name followed by a cryptic number. He scrolled down until he came to the folder labeled ABIMAEL HART- EG131 and opened it. Pages of information opened up, but Vigil was only concerned with the top of the first one. He highlighted the word ACTIVE next to the name and replaced it with the word RESOLVED and clicked *Save*. Then he moved the folder to another file labeled ANCIENT HISTORY. Vigil looked over some of the files in that folder and sighed. There were not as many in the folder as he would have liked and there were way too many in the ACTIVE folder. Still, this was the job he had chosen and giving up was not an option...not to him anyway.

Vigil considered taking a small vacation, but he had a lead on another target and it wasn't very far away. He made himself a third cup of tea and opened the ACTIVE file once more. He clicked on the folder labeled PASCHAL MIRAHM-CE091. He ignored the data that suggested the last known whereabouts of the target. That intel hadn't been updated in some time, and individuals like Paschal Mirahm didn't stay in one place very long. He was like a shark; if he didn't keep moving, he would die. There were also no updated photos of him, but it wouldn't have mattered anyway. Paschal Mirahm changed his appearance as often as he changed his shirts. In fact, there was only one way to track him that did not involve a lot of invasive procedures; and Vigil always had a number of those in place.

For years, ever since the technology existed in fact, Vigil had used facial recognition software to tentatively identify his targets and retinal scans to confirm them. This was where the government came in. An extremely sophisticated network of security cameras and a bank of dedicated servers were able to *flag* his targets whenever they used an ATM, committed a violation near a traffic cam or simply paid for fuel at a gas pump. The program logged the names they were using at the time and their current locations. Vigil coupled this information with local police reports of murders committed on or around those times. The information gathered the reports provided a fairly accurate map of they were and probabilities on where they were headed. Paschal Mirahm was in Florida...Daytona Beach to be exact.

Vigil checked the messages that had been sent to him through the *shadow web* from various covert agencies. He wanted to see if he could pursue his target or if there was some world-ending crisis he needed to attend to first. There were a couple of military coups taking place somewhere in South America, but they weren't anything standard field agents couldn't handle; so he ignored them. He made flight, hotel and car rental arrangements for his trip to Daytona before checking Paschal Mirahm's file once more. This target had been around for a long time.

Mirahm knew when to lay low and had only recently surfaced. There were no murders Vigil could attribute to him

15

directly that had occurred near any of the locations he had been spotted. This didn't mean he didn't commit any. It just meant he was being very careful. Mirahm probably suspected he was being watched and had always been cautious. Even when he didn't suspect he was being watched, he chose victims who would not be missed for some time; victims who travelled a lot on business or lived in remote locations. As the internet expanded, the world grew smaller and those kinds of victims were harder to find. Vigil wondered what Mirahm was planning to do in Daytona. *Maybe he plans to retire,* he thought. *People move to Florida sometimes when they retire.* A wry smile crossed his lips. *Yeah, as if demons like Paschal Mirahm ever retired.*

Vigil logged off his laptop and placed it in a specially designed case. From the outside, it looked like any other laptop bag; but it was specifically designed to prevent any form of electronic data mining from external sources. It went a step farther by transmitting a data mining signal of its own to the source making the attempt. After it collected all the hacker's data, the case transmitted a virus rendering their devices useless. Vigil then used the information to anonymously report the hacker as a potential terrorist. It was probably overkill in most cases, but he didn't like those types of hackers.

Vigil unpacked his bag from the night before. There wasn't much in it because he had left most of its contents in Russia. It was easier to get another ghillie suit than to explain why he had one to airport security. He had disassembled his custom sniper rifle and stored it in a secure compartment in the lining of the bag. His Walther P99 was stored in a different compartment, equally as secure and undetectable. He replaced the barrel of his rifle and refilled the magazine. Then Vigil went to a large dresser and stared at his reflection in the mirror. To anyone observing him, he would have looked as though he was contemplating his appearance; but an imperceptible retinal scan from the mirror confirmed his identity. The mirror slid into the wall, revealing a cache of high-tech tactical weapons. He considered them carefully and then chose three.

Vigil's flight left at 1:00 a.m., so he showered, shaved and was on his way to Dulles by ten-thirty. He chose a different identity from the one he had used in Yaroslavl, just to be safe. Getting to the airport two hours early was not his favorite thing to do, especially at night. Many of the shops were closed and there wasn't much to do except visit the food courts. Vigil missed the days when one could show up ten minutes before a fight and be rushed right through. That was back when airport security was lax and people were better behaved. It seemed like a long time ago now. *Ancient history,* he thought.

Vigil checked most of his bags, but kept his laptop with him. He was going to need something to do for the next couple of hours. The flight was about four hours long, so he might need a diversion there too. He walked through the concourse and looked to see what was still open in the food court. The Starbuck's was open. *Of course,* he thought. *Starbuck's is always open.* He purchased a venti café mocha and a banana nut muffin. Vigil had only eaten a slice of pizza since returning from Russia. He paid the young man and took his purchases to the lounge area near a wall of windows. As he ate, he looked out at the runway and watched a few planes depart. That never seemed to get old.

Vigil unzipped his laptop case and prepared to do some work. The hairs on the back of his neck stood up and he became aware that someone had sat down directly behind him. Usually this wouldn't have bothered him, but there was no one else nearby and there were plenty of other seats available. Vigil was pretty sure this wasn't going to be an attempt on his life, or even a robbery. No one could be so stupid as to attempt something like that. They were in an airport rife with security cameras and security guards just looking for a reason to cavity check someone.

Vigil placed the case on his lap and opened it. He didn't use his secondary security protocols and simply played a movie. While doing so, he stretched out his arms along the back of the seat in a relaxed pose. In his right hand, he held an object not much bigger than a flash drive. Aiming it behind him, a good view of his unwanted guest appeared in the lower right side of his screen. The kid didn't look twenty-one, but he might have been. He was probably headed to Daytona for Thanksgiving; but maybe not. A warning popped up on Vigil's screen indicating that a signal had been detected. *This might be all this kid does*, thought Vigil. *He sits around airports and steals credit information.* Vigil felt a little sorry for him, but not too much. The damage was done now. After a moment or two, the kid started frantically trying to get his tablet to work. An alert popped up on his screen saying that he had been reported and he should call a toll-free number to resolve the situation. The last part was Vigil's idea. The number was designed to be a *misdirect* to get the hacker to waste his time. The kid headed for the restroom. Vigil suspected he was going to get rid of his tablet, after destroying it somehow.

Now that he was free from prying eyes, Vigil opened the Ancient History file he had been thinking about. The public was aware of a few people in his files; but as far as they were concerned, the crimes they had committed were unsolved and the perpetrators were never caught. Some of the names in the files were well known, but not necessarily for the crimes they had committed. Some of the names were just the opposite. Their crimes had been front page news, but their true identities had never been publicized. That was because they had not been tried and executed; they have been *resolved*.

Vigil's files had never been released to any government agency. Part of his arrangement with the agencies that hired him was he would work with complete autonomy. Another was no one should get in his way. The covert community liked it that way. He accomplished things they couldn't, but they got to take credit for them. They also had plausible deniability if things went south. What no one knew, no one except Vigil anyway, was that they were all related in a way. He coded them all under the umbrella title of *Lazarus*. Vigil came up with the title and had never explained why. No one asked either. As long as the assignments were completed, no questions were asked. Vigil always completed the assignments.

The plane landed in Daytona Beach International Airport at 5:21 a.m. It was nearly six before Vigil collected his luggage at the carousel. The kid who had sat behind him in the airport had not been on the flight. He had been stopped at security and taken into custody. Vigil suspected he would be spending Thanksgiving at Guantanamo. Too bad...for the kid. *Considering what I do for a living*, he thought, *...the kid got off easy.* However, Vigil wasn't heartless. In a week or so, he would send a report to one agency or another to have the kid released; but he would recommend they put him on a watch list. Maybe that would put the Fear of God in him. If not, at least he had tried. Vigil headed over to the car rental office and secured his ride.

Vigil's room at the Marriott wouldn't be ready until two, so he drove along Highway A1A with the top down. He wanted to drive a long way up the coast, but he was hungry. Vigil spotted a restaurant that served breakfast and pulled into the parking lot. While waiting for his order to be prepared – Eggs Benedict and a Bloody Mary pint – he looked out at the ocean through the large rectangular window. The weather was perfect. It was a balmy 74 degrees and the deep blue/green ocean was calm. The fronds from a few small palm trees quivered in the soft breeze. Vigil had seen lots of oceans around the world. They were all similar, but had distinct personalities like the women he had loved. This thought made him sad, so he got back to work.

Vigil had tracked his target to Daytona Beach because Paschal Mirahm had used a credit card to pay for gas. It was a rookie mistake, but after running for so long, it was bound to happen. Vigil pulled up an area map on his laptop and traced a circle around the gas station. Then he looked for any further updates about Mirahm's location. There weren't any, so he ate his breakfast and sipped his Bloody Mary. Large waves began to roll in and crashed softly on the shoreline. He couldn't hear them, but he knew their sound. It had lulled him to sleep more times than he could count.

Vigil closed his eyes and could hear the waves better. He imagined them lapping against the side of a wooden hull. He could smell the sea air and feel the salty spray against his face. The deck began to tilt slightly to and fro, but he matched its rhythm as if he was dancing with the tide. As the deck started pitching at a greater angle, Vigil began to lose his footing. The sea was getting rough and the crew was scurrying to fasten everything down. Shouts from overhead were drowned out by the surf and the wind. It was a warning of some kind, but Vigil couldn't make it out. The clouds lit up with a bolt of lightning and there was a numbing crash of thunder. Vigil grabbed onto the rigging and felt helpless in the raging sea. A shape appeared behind him and he turned to confront it.

"Will there be anything else?" asked the server. She looked at him as if there might be a problem, but she knew better than to ask. This was Daytona Beach after all and she had been witness to a lot...especially during Spring Break.

"No," said Vigil. He was a bit embarrassed. "Everything was great."

"Well, let me know if you need anything. I'll just leave this here." She placed his bill on the edge of the table. He looked at it, took out a twenty...and then another twenty to leave for a tip. Being generous eased his embarrassment a little. He was about to close his laptop when it bleeped softly. Paschal Mirahm had just made another purchase. He was less than three miles from Vigil's current location.

Chapter Three: Paschal's Wager

Vigil knew that Paschal Mirahm would be gone by the time he could get to the gas station. Instead of pursuing him, he logged onto a restricted government site that gave him access to security cameras in the area. The resolution wasn't very good, but he could make out the model of a car pulling onto the highway and there was a fair image of the license plate. The car was a late-model silver Dodge Viper with Florida plates. Vigil couldn't make out most of the number from the gas station footage, so he accessed traffic cams along the highway. The Viper was driving north along Ocean Shore Boulevard. He was taking his time, but not being an obstruction to what little traffic there was on the road. Vigil feared Mirahm would turn off the highway and into one of the many housing additions along the way. If he did, he would be much harder to find.

Vigil closed his laptop and rushed out of the restaurant. The server thought he was doing a *dine and dash* until she saw the tip on the table. The tires of the rental car squealed as he sped out of the parking lot and down the road. He hoped that Mirahm stayed on the highway, but wasn't sure what he was going to do if he caught him. Vigil needed a secluded location to dispose of Paschal Mirahm. He also needed to keep his speed under fifty. He didn't need the added complication of police involvement, no matter how high up his connections went. Vigil realized he was breathing heavily and forced himself to relax. It wasn't going to be easy because he came up behind a Florida *local* driving a green Buick doing twenty-nine miles an hour.

He could tell from the white frosted hair with a bluish

tint that the driver was probably seventy-five or eighty years old. She wasn't in a rush nor should she be. It wasn't her fault that Vigil was in a hurry. She looked like she could barely see over the steering wheel and her hands were placed perfectly at the *ten* and *two* positions. All of her knuckles were white from gripping the wheel so tightly. Vigil smiled. He liked old people. He had good reason to.

A long line of traffic was in the opposing lane. Vigil didn't know where they were coming from, but there didn't seem to be a break in their numbers. Just when it looked as though there might be an opportunity to pass, the lady in the Buick turned on her left blinker. Vigil slowed down to give her plenty of room to turn, but she just kept on driving. After a mile or so, she turned the blinker off. By this time, Vigil had missed his passing window and another endless line of traffic stretched as far as he could see in the opposing lane. Vigil asked his phone if there was some kind of traffic situation nearby. A friendly female computer-voice told him there had been a serious accident on the interstate. He surmised that a lot of drivers decided to take the scenic route to Daytona Beach rather than sit in stopped traffic waiting for a cleanup crew to get there.

The Buick's blinker came on again and this time it looked as though she was really going to turn. The lady pulled to a complete stop in the middle of the highway and waited for an opening in the opposing lane. Vigil couldn't pass her on the right because there was a drop off of about four feet down to the beach. He thought about backing up and driving down the beach until he could get back on the road, but another car pulled up behind him just as he shifted in reverse. Vigil knew when he was beaten. He took the opportunity to put the top up on his convertible and opened his laptop. That made it easier to see in the bright sun. Vigil hoped that Paschal Mirahm had made another purchase. He hadn't, but he had passed another traffic cam. For some reason, he was headed in the opposite direction and on a completely different highway.

Vigil's frustration got the best of him and, with an opening of only four car-lengths in the opposing lane, he screeched across the road and slid crossways, blocking the oncoming traffic. The driver in the front of the line was able to stop just short of hitting him; however, a blast of obscenities and car horns drowned out the sounds of the peaceful surf. Vigil smiled at the little old lady in the Buick and waved her through with a gallant hand gesture. She smiled back and blushed a little. She felt as though a gentleman had just thrown his cloak across a muddy puddle for her to proceed. She would have quite a story to tell her friends that evening when they were on their way to the casino. The lady crossed the road and gave him a noble nod worthy of a queen. Once she had passed by, Vigil spun his tires and sped down the highway. Several middle fingers were extended out of the windows of many cars.

A couple of miles up the road, the traffic thinned out. The accident on the interstate must have been cleaned up. Vigil turned west and drove to the same interstate Mirahm was on and headed south. It was a relief to be moving faster than a sea turtle on the beach; and he was headed back in the direction of his hotel. With any luck, he could dispatch Paschal Mirahm quickly and still have a few days of R & R on the beach. Vigil checked the display that was marked with traffic cam flags. He had a pretty good idea where Mirahm was headed. It was part of his pattern. He had more than one passion...more than one addiction. Not only did he enjoy torture and eventual murder, he had a severe gambling habit. Paschal Mirahm was headed to the dog track.

Mirahm visited casinos and race tracks wherever he happened to settle. He had been a big fan of the casinos in Monte Carlo until his other *activities* started to attract too much attention. Las Vegas had been a decent hunting ground for a while and Mirahm liked being able to dispose of the bodies in the desert; but after a while, it no longer presented him with a challenge. Besides, he was also like the shark. He had to keep moving. Paschal Mirahm had dotted around the country and lived inconspicuously in some of the less desirable areas. His addiction proved that *the house always wins* and his disposable income was disposed of most of the time. Once in a while, he would hit big. When he did, he bought something special for himself. That was probably why he was driving the Dodge Viper. It must have set him back *eighty grand* at least. It wasn't likely that he had stolen it from one of his victims. If he did, the authorities would probably be looking for it and he didn't make those kinds of mistakes.

Vigil drove past the Daytona International Speedway and he could hear a few stock cars practicing for an upcoming race. Personally, he preferred the Formula-1 cars, but NASCAR was pretty exciting to watch when he had the time. The greyhound track was only a few blocks away and Vigil was pretty sure he could find Mirahm's car in the parking lot. It was easier than he thought because Paschal Mirahm was parked in a Disabled parking spot. He had a blue placard hanging from his mirror...probably taken from one of his victims. The man had no shame at all. Vigil parked farther back in the lot and walked between the rows as if he was going in to watch the races. He walked directly up to the Viper, placed his hands on his hips and whistled. Walking around to the front of the car, he knelt down and examined the grill area. Then he did the same thing around the back. A security vehicle pulled up and a man in uniform got out.

"Is there a problem here?" asked the guard.

"I want this," exclaimed Vigil. "I want one just like this! Is this not the most awesome car you've ever seen?"

"I see lots of awesome cars in this lot," said the guard

flatly. "If this one isn't yours, you should move along." The guard held himself in the manner which one with limited authority usually does. He would probably tell his wife about how well he did his job that day by thwarting a potential vehicle break-in. Vigil smiled, gave him a half salute and proceeded through the gates. "Tourists...sheesh," muttered the guard.

Vigil didn't want to be seen by Paschal Mirahm. He bought a *trilby* from the gift shop and pulled it down close to his eyes. He also bought a racing form and held it up, covering most of his face. Vigil knew he was being a cliché, but sometimes the old tricks are the best tricks. He went to the betting window and placed a couple of bets on incredibly long shots. He figured that way he wouldn't need to come back and collect. However, it didn't work out as planned. One of his long shots came in at 60 to 1. Vigil made a little over three hundred dollars on his five dollar wager. *Oh well*, he thought. *I guess dinner is on the track tonight.*

Vigil left the track with his winnings. Thanks to the tracking device he had placed on the Viper, he didn't need to stick around. Mirahm would be at the track until the last race had been run. Then Vigil could track him to wherever he went afterwards. He headed back to his hotel just in time to check in. He took his luggage to his room, changed into a swimsuit and went down to the pool. He took his trusty laptop, just in case Mirahm left the track unexpectedly. Only a couple of the lounge chairs were occupied, so Vigil pretty much had his pick. He sat down in one that faced the pool and looked out over the ocean beyond. Opening his laptop, he placed it on the table next to him and laid back to relax.

A soft sea breeze cooled the slight amount of perspiration on his forehead and the temperature was comfortable and balmy. *If Heaven has a thermostat*, he thought, *this is the temperature it is set on.* Vigil considered his line of work and the appalling things he had done in his life. He was pretty sure he would never get to see Heaven's Thermostat, or even get up to Heaven's gates before Heaven's security wrestled him to the ground. He had made it his mission to eradicate the worst serial killers around the world. These were not assassins or mercenaries who killed for money. Those he could understand. They did their jobs because they were assigned to them.

Vigil's targets were a specific group that killed for the pleasure of killing and tortured just to watch people suffer. Those who he *resolved* deserved what they got and then some. They were part of a brotherhood and they had to be dispatched in a particular way. There could be no doubt they had been killed. Whenever possible, it was preferable that their bodies be completely destroyed. There wouldn't be many mourners at their gravesites anyway.

Vigil was half-asleep when a quiet beep alerted him to movement at the dog track. He typed in a few codes to gain access to the dog track parking lot security cameras. Paschal Mirahm's car was no longer parked in the handicap space. The tracker he had placed under the bumper of the Viper showed him heading north on I-95 at a high rate of speed. Vigil made a few adjustments to his settings to access the security footage. He ran it back a few minutes and saw Mirahm approaching his car.

Vigil needed to get on the move. He folded his laptop and went up to his room. He changed into less casual clothing and armed himself. He hoped he could be finished in time to get some use out of his room, but it could end up being just a place to store his clothes for a couple of days. It didn't surprise him that Mirahm had spotted him at the track. It wasn't the first time they had crossed paths. Of course, that was a different time and they both looked different back then. Still, Vigil hated knowing he was so easy to detect. Maybe the old tricks were not the best tricks anymore. Maybe they were just old tricks. Maybe he was getting too old as well. Either way, there was no point in dwelling on it now. He had a target to acquire. In a few minutes, he was speeding up I-95 in pursuit of his target.

Paschal Mirahm had been careful and he was smart. Placing the tracker on a different vehicle was clever. He was probably laughing at the idea of Vigil pursuing the wrong target. He was picturing his pursuer speeding down the highway after two middle-aged ladies from Jensen Beach. Mirahm had placed the tracker under the bumper of the car parked next to him. It had a license plate frame that said *I'd rather go topless at Jensen Beach*. He had seen the ladies who owned the car. They had been drinking quite a bit and were getting pretty wild. One had been flashing her leopard print bra to people in the stands while her friend tried to keep her under control. Mirahm chuckled thinking of how the encounter would probably go. He wondered if Vigil would dispatch them anyway, just out of frustration or embarrassment.

Vigil chuckled at the thought of Paschal Mirahm. He was headed north on I-95, oblivious to the fact that Vigil was on his tail. Sometimes, the targets made it too easy. He used to hate that, but as the years progressed, he began to appreciate the simplicity of a quick kill. The laptop beeped quietly on the seat next to him. It was going to take some time to catch up to Mirahm. He had quite a head start, but he had slowed down once he was out of the Daytona Beach city limits, probably because of speed traps or increased highway patrols. Vigil had an array of signal jammers that allowed him to skirt most of the authorities. In addition, he had access to advanced satellite feeds which filled in the rest of the information he needed. He caught up with his target near Palm Coast. This was where Mirahm left the interstate and headed up the coast again on Highway A1A. Vigil wasn't sure where he was headed, but he had an idea.

The car with the tracker had headed back to Jensen Beach. The ladies in the convertible had gone to the Dolphin Bar and stayed there for the next few hours. Vigil had seen Paschal Mirahm remove the tracker from his car and place it on theirs. Mirahm didn't realize that Vigil had planted three more trackers on his Viper for just this reason. He had seen the security footage of the ladies as they returned to their car. The way they walked looked like they were having a little trouble with the keys...or even walking for that matter. He hoped the ladies were going to have a good time at the Dolphin Bar and didn't end up in jail.

There had been something about the way Mirahm was looking over the parking lot that tipped Vigil off. His target had known that he was being watched. Kneeling down behind his Viper, he had searched under the bumper until he found the tracking device. Vigil had known that Mirahm had spotted him at the betting window. Once Mirahm found the device, he didn't look for the second one. On the surface it looked like nothing more than the head of a bolt, but he had known what it was. After scanning the parking lot one more time to make sure he wasn't being observed, Mirahm had placed the device under the bumper of the car next to him. Paschal Mirahm was becoming predictable. That was a huge mistake.

Mirahm drove up A1A until he reached St. Augustine. Once there, he pulled into the parking lot of the *Castillo de San Marcos* historical site. Vigil turned off the highway and parked a block or so away. He walked to the ancient fort and suppressed images flooding his mind. This wasn't the first time he had met Paschal Mirahm here. He casually crossed the street and made his way to the entrance. It wasn't too crowded, but it was busy enough that he could remain inconspicuous. Once inside, he paused in a shaded archway to look around. Vigil touched a four-hundred-year-old wall and could feel the history flow into him. He saw Spanish soldiers standing on the walls, looking out over the Matanzas River. Columns of soldiers stood in the courtyard, the sun gleaming off their polished metal helmets. The captain of the guard stood facing them, issuing instructions before dismissing them. As he did, the images of the guards dissolved and a group of tourists stood in their place waiting for the tour guide to begin her presentation.

Vigil spotted Paschal Mirahm at the back of the crowd. When the tour guide began to recite her memorized dialogue, Mirahm disappeared through a darkened doorway on the opposite side of the courtyard. Vigil nonchalantly moved around the edge of the inside wall until he reached the place where Mirahm had been. Then he ducked through the same doorway and waited a moment for his eyes to adjust to the darkness. A figure appeared before him and he reached instinctively for the tactical knife under his shirt.

"Dude! Chill!" A wide-eyed man of about thirty-five held his hands up over his head. He was wearing a baseball cap, cargo shorts, a Hawaiian shirt and sandals with black socks. "I just popped in here to mellow out a little. You wanna hit off this?"

"No," said Vigil apologetically. "I'm good. Sorry for being so jumpy."

"Are you sure?" asked the man. "You look like you could use it."

"No, I'm fine...really. Go on with your...uh, mellowing." Vigil pretended to look at the displays and moved on through another archway. Each of the stone-walled rooms smelled a little of mildew, which was to be expected. The ceilings were mostly high, so echoes were kept to a minimum. Vigil listened for footfalls, but the chambers were silent. He crept cautiously into each room, making sure his own footsteps

31

were unheard. After searching several rooms, he found himself in what had been the soldiers' barracks. To Vigil, it looked more like a dungeon; but compared to the actual brig behind these walls, the barracks looked like a suite at the Hilton. He turned to continue his search when an arm closed around his neck and he could smell the bad breath of Paschal Mirahm. Before Vigil could react, a slim knife plunged into his right kidney. An arm gripped his neck so tightly that it didn't let him inhale the gasp that he so desperately needed. Vigil saw white spots out of the corners of his eyes and he fought to keep from losing consciousness.

"You put more than one tracker on my car, didn't you? I would have bet you that you weren't that clever." Mirahm twisted the knife in Vigil's back. "This reminds me of the last time we were here," he said. "...except back then, you stabbed *me* in the back." Vigil really wanted to respond, but surviving his knife wound was his top priority at that moment.

Paschal Mirahm stabbed Vigil in the back two more times. On the third attempt, Vigil twisted around and plunged his own tactical knife into Mirahm's temple. Mirahm stared at him and started to laugh. He was still laughing when Vigil pushed a small metal button on the hilt of his knife. A cartridge hidden in the handle of the knife expelled frozen gas through an opening in the blade into Mirahm's head. It expanded to 800 pounds per square inch, freezing all of the surrounding tissue. Mirahm's eyes were forced from their sockets and hung like ghastly Christmas ornaments. His skull had fractured in many places as his head expanded, making him look like a gruesome bobble head. Vigil might have found humor in the sight if he hadn't been so gravely injured.

Paschal Mirahm slumped to the floor and Vigil staggered over to a large wooden barrel stored under a stairway. He forced the top open with his knife and stuffed Mirahm's lifeless body into it after removing the dead man's shirt. It too was an ugly Hawaiian shirt, but at least it wasn't bloody; and Vigil needed it to conceal his own injuries until he got back to his car. He made his way back to the courtyard and found his stoned acquaintance from earlier still inside the door. This time Vigil took a hit off of whatever the man was smoking. It did make him feel better and he really needed it. Once he was across the fort's drawbridge, he hurried back to his car. It might have seemed suspicious, but not as suspicious as passing out with knife wounds in his back.

Vigil slid behind the seat of his rental. He was pretty sure he wasn't going to get his deposit back with the amount of blood already pooling on the seat. He thought it might be better if he just disposed of the car in a swamp and reported it stolen. First things first though. He needed to treat his wounds. Then he might go visit the ladies at the Dolphin Bar. They looked like they might be fun to hang out with and he had three-hundred dollars in dog track winnings burning a hole in his pocket. After all he had just been through, he could use some fun.

Chapter Four: *Death Shall Flee From Them*

Vigil stumbled into his hotel room and put the DO NOT DISTURB card in the electronic door lock. The bleeding from his wounds had nearly stopped, but he was exhausted from loss of blood. He had started to get dizzy driving back to Daytona Beach and abandoned his plans to visit the Dolphin Bar. After turning on the shower, he stripped off his bloody clothes and stepped into the tub. The hot spray washed blood down his body and into the drain, looking like a scene from *Psycho*. The pain in his still open wounds was excruciating; but then, it had to be. *Pain encourages healing*, he reminded himself.

Vigil wasn't sure how long he was in the shower because he may have passed out while standing up. One hand was tightly gripping the stainless steel safety rail and the other was holding onto the shower head. It must have been some time because the mirror was completely fogged up and the ceiling was overcast with steam. Vigil dried off and wrapped an extra towel around his wounded back before putting on his bathrobe. He felt a little better, but did not feel good. Lying down on the bed, he opened his laptop and entered his security protocols. The file folders flipped by one at a time until he found the one he wanted. Paschal Mirahm's file was moved to the *resolved* folder and Vigil breathed a heavy sigh. Later, he would send an official report to Washington so they could dispose of the body he had left in a barrel in the four-hundred-year-old Spanish fort.

Before resting, Vigil opened the file labeled *Lazarus Spawn*. If anyone else had been able to look in the file, it would have appeared to be little more than an ancestry chart. Each name had a coded number of which only Vigil knew the meaning. Many of the names were highlighted in gray, while most of the others were highlighted in blue. There were a scattered few in red or orange. Paschal Mirahm's name was highlighted in red. Vigil changed it to gray. He looked back at the names and traced them to their very beginning...to the name *Lazarus*. As he did, he succumbed to his weariness and drifted into unconsciousness.

* * *

Near Jerusalem, there is a town called Bethany. It is mentioned in the Bible as being the place where a man named Lazarus lived...and died...and lived...again. Legends change over the years and some facts are lost while others are embellished. Eventually, getting to the truth is like weeding a garden. One must remove all that is myth to get to the facts. Sometimes, the *weeds* completely take over the garden.

The name *Lazarus* wasn't uncommon during that time in the region, so Vigil's files might be referring to a completely different person than the one depicted in the Bible. It would be oddly coincidental though if they did. The Lazarus in his files also had a close encounter with death and survived...more than once. That Lazarus possessed the ability to heal his wounds almost instantaneously. Whether it was because a man from Galilee had raised him from the dead or because he was born with the gift of instant tissue regeneration, Lazarus lived for a very long time.

The political climate in those days in that area was as charged as it is today. The Romans held authority over Israel and many were unsatisfied with their rule. Religious leaders were often at odds with the Roman military and the political leaders that were appointed by the Emperor. The threats came closer to home and Lazarus thought it might be better to leave the area. In 45 A.D., he and his family joined a trade caravan on its way to Egypt. Lazarus' wife was pregnant and she feared her child would be used as a pawn in some political board game. It had happened before. They got as far as Beth-zur in southern Judea when Lazarus' wife gave birth to a healthy baby boy. They named him Simon after Lazarus' father. After eight days, he was taken to the temple for circumcision following the Jewish custom; but by the ninth day, the foreskin had grown back. They didn't try to remove it second time.

The family stayed in Beth-zur until it was safe to travel before joining another caravan to Egypt. They settled in the town of Ankara and opened a shop to trade goods and services. As far as the rest of the world was concerned, Lazarus and his family no longer existed. Simon grew up as a child of Egypt and excelled in language skills, mathematics and science. Even Egypt was under Roman rule during that time, but the occupation seemed less harsh. By the time Simon was twenty, he had climbed the political ladder and held the position of chief advisor to the Roman governor of Egypt. He felt at home in his role as the power behind the throne and brought much honor to the office. Simon was more than just a subordinate to the governor; they were friends.

Political views were like illnesses in many ways. Just when a *fever* seems to be under control, it comes back more fierce than ever. Simon was with the governor when a group of political zealots moved to assassinate the Roman leader. As one attacker rushed forward with a spear, Simon stepped into its path and was run through. The spear penetrated his entire body, but was stopped by the governor's breastplate. The zealots were taken into custody and sentenced to death. The execution was particularly severe because the governor had loved Simon. The zealots were condemned to be impaled. Not only was it an agonizing way to die, but Egyptian tenets taught that impalement bound the essence (*ba*) and shadow (*sheut*) of the deceased to the ground of execution. This would make them unable to follow their bodies to the afterlife when they were disposed of.

Simon's sacrifice was posthumously rewarded with an honorable Egyptian burial. His body was taken directly to the place of purification (*ibu*) where it was washed with palm wine and then rinsed with water. The chief embalmer wore the mask of Anubis and prepared for the first step in the mummification procedure...the removal of the brain. The priest had just placed a long, hooked rod in Simon's nostril and was preparing to push when he felt a hand grab his in a death grip. He couldn't see clearly because of the mask, but the priest knew it was the hand of the body lying on the table. He began to tremble as Simon rose up on one elbow and looked around. The other servants in attendance dropped to their knees and began to worship him. They had seen people rise from the table who had been thought dead before, but they had died from fevers: not from being run through by a spear. Simon's chest wound was completely healed. The chief embalmer followed suit by dropping to his knees. He didn't want to offend the gods even though he had considered killing Simon out of fear.

Simon got up and walked out of the place of purification into the bright Egyptian sun. His naked body seemed to glow with renewed life and the chief embalmer extended his hand toward him, as if he was trying to take credit for the miracle. He still wore the mask of Anubis to help encourage that suggestion. It didn't help. The attention was focused squarely on Simon. The people of the town began to worship him. They chanted *Ankh...Ankh.* Simon liked that title. From that day on, he called himself Ankh: *the breath of life*. He became part of Ankara's local folklore, but the story became so convoluted over time that it never made it into mainstream Egyptian mythology. *Ankh* didn't mind. He found that reverting into anonymity was more to his liking anyway.

* * *

Ankh had never believed the stories about his father Lazarus rising from the dead until he did it himself. It gave him a new respect for his dad for a while; but that didn't last. The longer Ankh lived, the less respect he had for anyone, especially for *mere mortals*. He thought his father should feel more superior to them too, but Lazarus seemed to feel sorry for them. Lazarus had watched as his friends and family aged and eventually died. Only his own children seemed immune to death and he took comfort in this fact. His first wife had given him six sons and two daughters. He married again shortly after her death and his second wife gave him three more sons. They all seemed to age normally until they reached their twenties. Then the aging process seemed to slow to a crawl. Lazarus stayed with them a while; but he knew the day would come when some would rebel against him. He wasn't sure how he would handle that and thought it better if he simply moved on. Lazarus was between wives when he slipped away during the night. He travelled back to Bethany; then he traveled farther north and then sailed to an island in Greece. He stayed there for a long while and fathered more children with two more wives. The laws about marriage on the island were very lax. As far as the world was concerned, Lazarus was never heard from again.

No matter where one goes in the world, politics are almost always the same. The children of Lazarus found it to be in their best interest not to stay in one place for too long. People would begin to question why they didn't age or how they recovered from mortal wounds. Some scattered to the four winds while others formed caravans and were constantly on the move. Over time, a few became famous artists or inventors, great sages and philosophers. They seemed to be forward thinkers and ahead of their times, mainly because they had been around for so long. It was also because their brain cells regenerated perfectly like all the other cells in their bodies. They were able to use all of the knowledge they had accumulated over the years.

The children of Lazarus were as close to gods as humans can be. Their minor wounds healed instantaneously thanks to their rapid tissue regeneration. More serious wounds, including mortal wounds, took a little longer...sometimes days. Even dismembered body parts grew back within a week. However, the pain was excruciating. Pain is the body's way of telling the cells to regenerate, and with great healing comes great pain. Each mortal wound seemed to age each of Lazarus' children by a month or so. The change was unnoticeable at first, but obvious over time; and they had lots of time. Many of those who had been warriors put away their swords and settled into peaceful, anonymous lifestyles. After they departed, their exploits and adventures grew into legends and exaggerations of their achievements and abilities. In literature, they really were gods.

The children of Lazarus had been witness to an incredible amount of history. A few went to Jerusalem with the Crusades. Some survived the Black Plague that swept across Europe in the 1300s. Several travelled to the *New World* with Columbus and other Spanish explorers. They all watched as advances were made in science, medicine, mechanization and industry. A few were responsible for many of those advances. Then there were the ones who were like Ankh.

The longer some of Lazarus' spawn lived, the less mortals mattered to them. They thought no more of snuffing out short meaningless human lives than a man thinks about swatting a housefly. He doesn't care if the fly had a family or just got a promotion at work. He doesn't care if the fly was about to complete his college degree or was receiving a lifetime achievement award. The fly annoys him and that is enough reason to kill him. Some of Lazarus' spawn had become very jaded with life, so life meant very little to them. The news media over the centuries would report of serial killings from time to time or some mass-murdering dictator's rise to power. Not all of them were children of Lazarus; but many were. Paschal Mirahm had been one of them.

* * *

It was dark when Vigil woke up, but the sky in the east was getting light. His bed was soaked with sweat and he was shivering. He was hardly awake as he stumbled to the bathroom, but he was coherent enough to start the shower. Stepping into the hot flow of water revived him. Flakes of dried blood fell from his back and dissolved in the bathtub drain. The knife wounds had healed over, but were still incredibly painful. He coughed up blood and he was pretty sure there would be blood in his urine. He had come to ignore things like that. It was part of his makeup, part of his training. Some would have considered it an immense form of self-sacrifice. Vigil just considered it another day on the job. He took an elastic bandage from his bag and, using a washcloth to dress the wounds, wrapped the binding around himself as he would have with a broken rib. He donned a fresh shirt and put bloodstained clothing in the complimentary laundry bag provided by the hotel. He would discard it in some dumpster later where it would be less likely to raise questions.

Vigil would have liked to stay in Florida for a few days, but his encounter with Paschal Mirahm had taken the allure out of his trip. He thought once more about going to the Dolphin Bar, but it would be a five-hour round trip and he still needed to dispose of his blood-soaked rental car. He packed a clean towel in his luggage and went down to breakfast. Vigil could have ordered room service, but he didn't like eating in his room. To him, it was like eating in a hospital. It just didn't

41

feel right. The hotel dining room wouldn't open for another two hours, so he walked down the block to an all-night diner. As he slid into an empty booth, he winced with pain and audibly grunted.

"Is everything alright?" asked the waitress. Her name was Antoinette.

"I'm okay," said Vigil. "Just a twinge in my back. The weather must be getting ready to change."

"I don't think so," said Antoinette. "The forecast doesn't call for it. You might have a urinary infection. You look a little flushed. Want me to bring you some cranberry juice?"

"Could you mix it with a couple of ounces of vodka?" asked Vigil. He flashed her a mischievous smile.

"Not *officially*," she said, smiling back.

"Maybe you could bring me an *unofficial* glass of cranberry juice then…and coffee," he said. "Oh, and two poached eggs with dry toast." Antoinette winked and smiled.

"Watching the old cholesterol eh?" she asked. "I get it. I'll be right back with your *juice*." Vigil thought he might hang around Daytona for a while after all. He thought he might find out what time Antoinette would get off work. When she came back, he did just that. She told him she got off in a couple of hours. Her look told him that the rest of his day was already laid out for him. Daytona's allure was back and he was going to need his room for at least one more day.

Anyone else would have gone to the emergency room or, at the very least, tracked down a physician they could trust to get their wounds treated. They definitely wouldn't have made a date that would develop into a twenty-four-hour sex marathon. But Vigil wasn't like anyone else. He too was a child of Lazarus.

Chapter Five: Fallen Angels

Antoinette looked up at the ceiling of the smartly appointed hotel room. After working the breakfast shift at the diner, she should have been getting some rest; but she didn't want to sleep. Vigil was lying next to her; however, his sleep looked anything but restful. She turned to face him and cautiously traced the wounds on his back that looked freshly healed. She touched them softly with her fingers and Vigil's sleep became less fitful. He softly muttered something in a language she did not understand. There were a lot of things about this man she didn't understand.

They had walked back to the hotel after her shift had concluded and he told her to wait in the lobby while he *took care of some things*. She was not aware that the "things" included disposing of bloodstained towels and cleaning up dried blood from the bathroom tile. He also had to order fresh towels, have housekeeping change the linens and do a quick once-over of the room. Vigil cursed himself for not taking care of it before going out, but he hadn't planned to bring a guest back. He got careless; and in his line, he couldn't afford to be careless.

Their lovemaking had been like something from the movies. He had been considerate and patient. She had been daring and innovative. Vigil had been careful to wear protection and she was on birth control. All in all, it had been a carefree and fulfilling morning. It had also been exhausting.

Antoinette wondered what time it was. She had lost a contact lens during one of the more acrobatic moments of their romance session. The red LED numbers on the clock across

43

the room merged together because of the difference in her levels of focus. The heavy curtains had been closed and the room was nearly dark. She liked for it to be dark when she was naked. There were a number of body issues she wasn't proud of.

Vigil had found no flaws with her at all. Norms had changed over the years; he had seen fashion trends come and go. In the late sixties, *Twiggy* had been popular and girls tried to look like her. Back when the Titanic sailed, being more *Rubenesque* was the style and it was a fashion Vigil liked. Antoinette was kind of a blend of many styles over the centuries. Her hips were wider than she would have liked and she would have loved to have bigger breasts; but those were things she could live with. She was not a fan of her stomach. Having a child had wreaked havoc with her muscle tone and her skin didn't quite snap back. Childbirth left her with a look around the bikini line that she couldn't do anything about without some expensive cosmetic surgery. Vigil had told her it didn't matter, but she didn't believe him. She thought he was making fun of her when he said that he even liked it; but he really did. He said it gave her character, and he loved character.

Antoinette quietly slipped out of bed and rummaged around in her purse for her cellphone. She could make out the numbers if she closed one eye. Scrolling down her contact list, she hoped she got the right name when she dialed the number. The voice on the other end was flat and judgmental.

"Who was it this time? That worthless ex of yours?"

"First of all, it's none of your business," whispered Antoinette. "…and no." She took a moment to compose herself. Antoinette loved her mother, but she hated talking to her on the phone. Her mother never had anything good to say about her, or *to* her for that matter. The choices her mother had made with her own relationships in the past were anything but stellar, so she seemed to think it was alright to come down on her daughter for making similar mistakes.

"Can I speak to Brodhi?" she asked.

"Why would Brodhi be here?" her mother asked harshly. "She won't be home from school for another two hours. Are you high again?"

"No, I am not high!" Antoinette was getting fed up with all the judgment. "I just lost track of time. It happens sometimes you know."

"Not to decent people. Decent people know when their kids get home from school." There was a hint of self-pity in her tone. She was pretty consistent with playing the *martyr card*.

"I am not playing this game with you again mother," said Antoinette. "Have her call me when she gets home."

"As you wish, your Highness," replied her mother. Antoinette hated her sarcasm most of all and hung up without saying another word. She turned to see Vigil standing next to the bathroom door.

"Is everything alright?" he asked. "I didn't get you in trouble, did I?" Antoinette started and froze. Vigil had moved from the bed to the bathroom as quietly as a shadow. She wasn't sure what to do. The room was brighter than before and she was standing there on display fully naked. Her first instinct was to cover up, but that would have embarrassed her more. She tried to act casual, which wasn't working either. It wasn't like she had never been naked in front of a man before. She had been married once and had moderately long-term relationships after. It was just that Vigil was different somehow. She couldn't put her finger on it, but she wanted him to see her the way she wanted to be seen.

45

In an action seeming as though he was reading her mind, he moved toward her in a casual manner of his own. She tried to maintain eye contact; however, she couldn't help but marvel at his body. It wasn't that he was an Adonis or anything. His appearance was a little above average as was his physique and *physical attributes*. There was just something about him. He wasn't like other men she had slept with. Vigil had a kind of confidence she had never experienced. There seemed to be a sort of wisdom and worldliness in his eyes that his age did not suggest. In fact, his age was hard to pin down. Her estimates ranged between twenty-five and fifty-five, which made him even more intriguing. Their bodies brushed each other as he moved behind her. She involuntarily shivered and gooseflesh rose up on her arms and breasts. Her soft sigh ended with a shudder and she blushed.

"It's alright," said Vigil. He pressed close to her and kissed her softly on the neck. She shivered again and forgot all about her judgmental mother. She turned around and held Vigil tightly. This had been a one night…or more accurately, a one *morning* stand; but she wanted it to go on forever. She backed up slowly until the backs of her knees touched the bed. Then she fell backwards holding Vigil in what she had hoped would be a romantic scene from the movies. Instead, it was more like a romantic comedy. Their mouths were pressed together as they fell and their teeth clicked. This caused Antoinette to start laughing uncontrollably. Vigil followed suit. There is nothing like a little slapstick to relieve the tension and make one forget that they are naked. When they finally stopped laughing, they embraced again and resumed their erotic workout. Vigil and Antoinette ran out of condoms that afternoon and chose to depend on her birth control pills the last time they made love. Just as they were about to bask in the afterglow, Antoinette's cellphone rang.

"Mom? You wanted me to call?" Brodhi's voice

seemed a little concerned. No doubt Antoinette's mother had been badmouthing her and painting her in the most unflattering light possible. She wrapped herself in a sheet as if her daughter was in the room with her. She looked over at Vigil who was lying back with his arms behind his head. He was uncovered and looked as though he was ready for yet another romance session. Antoinette felt embarrassed by him and covered him with part of her sheet. The resulting "tent" made her begin to laugh uncontrollably again and she struggled to tell her daughter that she would have to call her back. Brodhi was ten, but was pretty sure she knew what was going on. She feigned innocence for the sake of decorum. Once Antoinette got control of her emotions, she decided to take advantage of Vigil's *mood* one more time.

* * *

Antoinette kissed Vigil goodbye in the lobby of the hotel. She wanted to walk back to the diner alone. She was pretty sure she wouldn't be able to talk with her heart in her throat and she needed to process her feelings. She didn't think she would ever see Vigil again. She hadn't asked for his last name. She didn't even know if he had a last name. He was a superstar in her book, so he didn't need one. Their time together had been special and it would get more special as time went on. Memories tend to do that. Either the events get better each time they are recalled or they get worse. Seldom do people remember things exactly as they happened. Antoinette stifled a sob. *At least we have the Marriott*, she thought. She felt as if her life had changed. It really had, but she didn't know how much.

Vigil packed up his belongings and prepared to dispose of the rental car as he had planned. Halfway to the gator-infested swamp where he planned to dump the car, he changed his mind. Instead he drove to a Publix market and bought a gallon of bleach. It would be just as easy to explain the accident and a police report wouldn't be necessary. He splashed it liberally all over the front seat and erased all of the bloodstains. He didn't think he would be back to Daytona anytime soon, so it didn't matter what the rental agent thought. He caught an earlier flight back to D.C. and took the next few days organizing his weapons, equipment, and repairing or replacing his wardrobe.

* * *

Things always got quiet for a while when Vigil made a special kill. There was some kind of information network that told others in the *Lazarus* community to lay low for a while. It happened even when Vigil didn't let the government dispose of the resolved targets; so it was less likely there was a leak in one of the organizations he contracted with. A couple of those times, paid killers took the opportunity to come after him; but that didn't happen too often. When it did, he dispatched them just like the others. Vigil had a lot of security measures in place, so he always managed to keep the upper hand.

Vigil opened his laptop and checked to see if there were any assignments waiting for him or if there were any intelligence notifications about any of his *most wanted* targets. One came up as an Instant Message, encrypted as always. He decoded it and took a deep breath. Two targets had come up, and not just any two. They were twin brothers who were known by Interpol as the *Fallen Angels* because of their names.

Adriel and Zuriel Van Der Holt had committed atrocities across Europe since the reign of Charlemagne. In the days before global communication, slaughter had been easy for them. Sometimes they were able to kill whole families and assume their properties and fortunes. In the time of the Black Plague with so many deaths, it was an easy thing to do. When life got too dull or the surrounding population got too large, they moved on. As the centuries passed, they had to be more

48

discrete about their murderous ways. The last time they were investigated, they had settled down in Switzerland. This was where they adopted the name Van Der Holt. There they lived as the adopted sons of a wealthy banker and were content to spend his money and exploit his name. They kept their homicidal extracurricular activities away from where they lived and usually used false identities when visiting other countries. However, even the most cautious of individuals can make stupid mistakes sometimes.

One of the brothers, probably Zuriel, really wanted to purchase a thick gold neck chain in Vienna Austria. Not only did he use a credit card to make the purchase, he and his brother visited the Hofburg Palace to see the supposed *Spear of Destiny*. They found it fascinating that history, myth and legend could become so convoluted over time. It was that convolution that kept them safe throughout their lives.

One legend held that Longinus, a holder of the spear, had been condemned to spend eternity in a cave with a lion. Each night, the lion would maul his flesh and each day he would heal. Adriel and Zuriel knew that part of the legend was true, just not the dates or other facts related to it. *That* Longinus was another of their brothers from a different time period. Vigil thought there might be a chance that someone would show up to view or possibly even steal the spear; so he set up special surveillance in the area. He accessed surveillance for other religious relics around Europe and the Middle East as well. Austria was the one that got a ping.

Adriel and Zuriel Van Der Holt were no longer in Europe and they were probably not going by those names anymore. Their last known whereabouts had them travelling to a small burg in Scotland. That move made sense to Vigil because in a little town, there would be less electronic security. They could travel by train to nearby or faraway locations and continue murdering people. Vigil thought it might be best to give them a chance to settle in, even though it would probably cost a few of the locals their lives. He couldn't help that. If he lost track of them, their savage slayings could continue for decades. Clicking on a few computer links secured him plane tickets, hotel accommodations and a travel itinerary. When Vigil posed as a casual traveler, he always made straightforward arrangements that would be easy for someone stalking him to trace. Then he would use alternative means of transportation to throw them off his scent. Better safe than dead. He would arrive at Heathrow International at 4:37 a.m., London time. Once there, he would check into one of the hotels favored by business travelers and see the sights as an average tourist. That would give him an opportunity to establish if he was being tailed and deal with the pursuer if need be.

One problem with using public forms of transportation was they were sometimes unpredictable. Vigil's flight to London was delayed and he wouldn't arrive at Heathrow until 6:45 a.m. It wasn't like he had anything to do during the two hour period, but it made him feel vulnerable to be out in the open for so long. Dulles was pretty busy for some reason. That meant a lot of faces to watch, so he kept his back to the wall. Already tired when he checked into the Rosewood Hotel, he was glad that his room was ready. He was anxious to take advantage of the king-sized bed in the *Executive King* room...but not before placing security devices around the doors and windows. They were proximity sensors linked to a passive alarm program on his laptop. The computer would in turn send a signal to Vigil's watch. The subtle vibration in it had always alerted him.

Vigil slept until 3:30 in the afternoon and thought about having afternoon tea in the dining room. Instead, he showered, dressed and went out for a walk through the scenic cobblestone lanes. The streets made him think of London some time back:

a long time back in fact, during the time of Jack the Ripper. *That had been an unusual turn of events*, he thought. Vigil knew things about the case and those murders that no one in the world knew; even those who were there at the time.

Vigil's walk took him to the Lincoln's Inn Fields which was not far from the hotel. The sky was overcast and the trees had littered the ground with a beautiful array of leaves. The wrought iron gates seemed to keep a bygone era captive inside. One could easily imagine what the fields looked like when Lincoln's Inn was just one of the *Inns of the Court* in the 1400s. Vigil didn't have to imagine.

It wasn't a very long walk to the tube station at Chancery Lane, so Vigil decided to go a bit farther on his sightseeing tour. He had, in fact, spotted a tail and wanted to see how far the individual would go. His intent was to lose his pursuer in the *underground* since it was likely to be busy this time of day. A large group of businessmen crowded onto the escalator to the transit system below. Vigil blended in with them and slid deftly to the side as they reached the bottom. He made short work of the lock on the door of a utility room, slipped inside and waited. It wasn't long until the person who had been following him appeared. The long, sandy blond hair was styled in a perfect blend of waves and curls. It was Jillian. She worked for one of the agencies that gave him assignments from time to time. Like Vigil, she didn't have a last name. That would have been a waste of time because their last names changed so often.

Jillian's hair was something of a trademark and for anyone else would it would have been a liability; but, it wasn't a hindrance because of her appearance. Even though she was probably in her late twenties, she could change her look to range from an adolescent to that of a teenager. In certain circles, this made her disarming and deadly. She was one of the most effective assassins the agency had. Her typical targets

51

never saw her coming because she looked so young. However, Vigil was not a typical target. He waited until the train pulled up and passengers exchanged places. The crowd thinned and he could see Jillian trying to be invisible next to a concrete support. She looked mildly puzzled by his absence, but all the more determined to find him. Never had a target eluded her, but Vigil planned to be the first.

Three more trains unloaded and loaded passengers before Jillian finally considered the possibility that Vigil had boarded a train unobserved. She cursed loudly as she went back to the escalator. It caught a few people off guard because of her apparent age. She had to fight past a fresh group of individuals pouring onto the platform. Vigil took the opportunity to blend in and moved as far away from the escalator archway as possible. His feet were on the yellow safety line next to the tracks as he heard the rumble of the next train. As the train approached, he felt something press against the small of his back. He knew it wasn't a gun or a knife. He had felt those before and was pretty familiar with their feeling. Yet somehow he knew what it was. It was the curved handle of an umbrella. The train had almost reached the station when the umbrella handle dug into his back and forced Vigil over the side and onto the tracks.

Chapter Six: Sleep of Death

O'Hanlon lay on the roughhewn table in his finest clothes, which wasn't saying much. He didn't own more than two garments to begin with. The other jerkin he had was for work in the fields and was only slightly more frayed than what he was laid out in. To say that his death came suddenly would be an out-and-out lie. He'd been drinking for nearly three days straight and had shown no signs of slowing down when he keeled over as dead as the night. The owners of the *Graces Three Pub* were his friends and had allowed O'Hanlon to sleep it off in the back room more than once. Gavin McHughes, the proprietor, liked him and seemed to owe him a deep debt of gratitude. They never spoke of what it might have been, but it must have been substantial. Gavin tried to hide his feelings, but he was severely grief-stricken.

All of O'Hanlon's friends – which was to say the entire village – sang and laughed...and drank. Seeing the *dearly departed* die from imbibing too much alcohol seemed less like a cautionary tale to them and more like a challenge. Some were so drunk, they were drinking to the health of the dead man. A couple of the mourners were so caught up in the moment that they kissed O'Hanlon square on the lips, and then hit him in the jaw to regain their manly status. Gavin's wife Siobhan took it all in stride by refilling their pewter tankards and fending off their advances. She never allowed herself to get too close to anyone in the village. Her troubled past caused her to keep a wary eye on strangers and a closer eye on friends.

O'Hanlon had not been born in Cork. He arrived on a trade ship from Europe a decade or so, after the Black Plague had reduced much of the population. He wasn't immediately accepted in the community until he proved himself. He did so by supporting the plot to overthrow Henry VII of England. O'Hanlon would have joined the rebellion, but he broke an arm and a leg in a brawl at the pub and wasn't able to fight. It turned out to be better for him. In England, the rebellion collapsed and everyone involved was executed. No one was quite sure how O'Hanlon managed to break both his arm and his leg since everyone was fairly drunk at the time that he did it. It saved his life though and he still got credit for supporting the rebellion. In the end however, the drink got the better of him. So he lay there on the roughhewn table: the guest of honor at his own wake.

"'ere's to O'Hanlon," said Mayor Lavallen. "'e was a patriot and a gentleman...well, 'e was a patriot by any callin'. May there be a generation of children on the children of 'is children."

"I don't think he had any children," whispered Sour Bob, the tanner. Siobhan rapped him on the back of his head, but he hardly noticed. The mayor continued.

"If e'er there was a man who could hold his ale, it was O'Hanlon...well...until the end." The mayor hoisted his tankard and took a healthy quaff. He paused for a moment, having a little difficulty focusing his eyes.

"Take it easy, your honor," said Siobhan. "We don't want you to be laid out there next." She smiled at him wryly; but her smile turned to a sneer as she turned away. Siobhan was not fond of Mayor Lavallen.

The wake continued until the wee hours of the morning when everyone fell silent. That is to say, everyone had passed out. Most were asleep on or under the tables, but Sour Bob had passed out standing up, supported by a wooden beam. Siobhan and Gavin had left the crowd to fend for themselves and retired for the evening. A cock crowed well before dawn and a lot of cursing and spitting could be heard in the pub. Gavin rose from his bed, dressed and went about the room collecting from each man what he owed for the ale he had imbibed. Some of them were not awake yet, but Gavin was a fair man and only took what he deserved. He was so preoccupied with collecting his remuneration that he didn't immediately notice the body had been moved. A stillness fell over the pub like a calm before a storm. Then Gavin's booming voice thundered to the rafters.

"I am not going to stand for this type of mischief! I have a reputation to uphold here!" Those who were not awake suddenly regained consciousness. Many looked around for their disapproving wives. They were slightly relieved to see that it was only Gavin who spoke.

"I want to know right now! Where is O'Hanlon's body?" The men in the bar looked at the empty table and then to each other. All of their gazes eventually lit on Sour Bob. His eyes were wide open, but he was still using the wooden beam for support.

"I saw him," he said nervously. "...got up from the table he did, just as big as life." He began to chuckle at the irony of his statement. Seeing that no one else found the humor in it, he continued. "...'e gave me a nod and walked right out the door!" Someone threw a wooden bowl at Sour Bob that hit him square between the eyes. He hardly noticed. Bob was a notorious teller of tall tales. The men in the pub were about to pounce on him when Siobhan shouted at them. In the commotion, she had risen from her bed and wrapped herself in a woven blanket.

"Can anyone explain *this*?" she asked. Outside the threshold, there were fresh footprints in the soft clay, leading away from the pub. Two of the bolder men went to investigate. The prints led down a fog-shrouded lane in the direction of the sea. Brave as they might be, no one wanted to follow a dead man into the fog. They were all much too sober for that. Instead, they sat down and fought off hangovers by ordering more ale.

"We should make a marker anyway," said the mayor. "A man should be buried with a name. If not, his spirit cannot find rest and will haunt the village."

"Did he even have a name?" asked Gavin. "I only knew him as O'Hanlon."

" 'e told me once," claimed Siobhan. "I wasn't sure I believed 'im. Drinking 'e was. Told me 'is name was Vigil. I started to laugh, but I could tell 'e was dead serious."

"Vigil O'Hanlon...right; someone should make him a marker, straight away." Mayor Lavallen made his statement sound like an official decree. The job fell to Carrick O'Brien. He worked with wood and knew how to write. They toasted O'Hanlon one more time, to help keep the spirit at peace.

"To Vigil O'Hanlon," they all said in unison.

* * *

Vigil released his grip on the train's brake cables after the car came to a stop. He rolled over the protected electrified third rail and climbed out on the other side of the platform before anyone noticed. There was another utility door that he slipped into and found an access ladder to the surface. He didn't know why his memory had returned to Fifteenth Century Ireland. The flashback may have been triggered by the scent of oil under the subway car. It was hard to tell. Vigil remembered he had been poisoned back then.

Back in that time, consuming too much lead from the pewter tankards would sometimes lead to blindness or death, but he was immune to those. Someone had slipped him something much stronger. He wasn't sure who it had been, but he was confident it was another of Lazarus offspring...or one of his descendants. *Same bloodline; different vintage*, he thought. Since he had become the prey, he decided to leave Ireland and head to Spain. Years later, he would voyage to the New World to elude those who would seek to kill him. Being nearly immortal, death was not the worst thing that could happen to him.

Vigil hailed a taxi and had the driver take him to the *Alexander McQueen* store. It was one of the finer clothing shops in London. His clothes were in a terrible state after being pushed under a subway train. His shirt, trousers, zip-up leather boots and black lambskin bomber jacket set him back just under four thousand pounds. He couldn't say money was no object, but his ensemble scarcely made a dent in his expense account. The person assisting him hardly blinked an eye when Vigil told him to dispose of the clothes he wore into the shop. People buying new clothes and discarding the old ones must have been something that happened more often than he thought.

It was no longer necessary for Vigil to keep a low profile. Vigil's cover had been blown somehow and it was going to be risky to return to his hotel room. Still, he needed some things there. He was leery about using the underground again, so he hopped on an open-top double decker bus heading near his destination. He chose the bus because it had multiple escape points just in case he needed them. The open half of the upper deck was nearly empty. Most of the sightseers chose to ride in the enclosed half near the front of the bus because of the weather. In the distance, Vigil could see the *London Eye* turning ever so slowly. He always marveled at the giant Ferris wheel, but never rode it. He would have been exposed and vulnerable for far too long in one of its enclosed capsules.

Vigil stepped off the moving bus a block from the hotel. He used his momentum to guide him directly into an arched doorway where he could determine if he had been followed. He focused very hard and his skin tone began to darken. One of the physical traits of the children of Lazarus was their ability to cosmetically adapt to their surroundings. It happened naturally over a couple of weeks; however, they could force a change in a couple of hours if they concentrated hard enough. When Vigil felt he had reached the desired level of pigmentation, he joined a cluster of tourists and businessmen headed up the block. When he got to his hotel, he slipped around to the side entrance where trucks were unloading supplies for the kitchen. Grabbing a box of produce and keeping his head down, he infiltrated a line of kitchen workers and delivery men. People do not seem to care where you came from as long as you are easing their workload. Once inside, he placed the box on a steel counter and ducked around a corner to the service elevator. He took it down to the basement.

If anyone was spying on him, Vigil knew they would be watching the elevators, stairs and fire escapes. That would be what he would be doing if the roles were reversed. The basement gave him access to the elevator service door. Inside, he found a pair of rawhide work gloves he thought he might need. An inspection panel gave him access to the top of the elevator. Now all he had to do was wait for someone to push the button and see which floor it went to. This part didn't matter much. He didn't need to go to his own floor...just a floor near it.

Vigil thought he might be on top of the elevator for some time. He opened the maintenance trap door in the roof just a bit and cautiously looked down into it. He knew the elevator was still empty, but he had to check just to be safe. He thought about jumping down and pushing some buttons, but that would be careless. It was too late in the game to make stupid mistakes. Patience would be the rule of the day. As it turned out, he didn't have to wait long.

The service elevator jolted and the well-lubricated pulleys began to turn. The car sped up inside the shaft and then dropped ever so slightly when it got to the sixth floor. The momentary weightlessness caused by the sudden drop made Vigil's stomach tickle. He let out a soft and uncharacteristic giggle like a toddler. Of course, they didn't have elevators like this when he was a toddler. *They barely had wheels*, he thought. The doors opened and a person from housekeeping pushed a large canvas cart filled with linens into the elevator and pushed the button for the basement where the industrial laundry equipment was. Vigil had counted on this. He gripped the ledge behind the doors as the elevator dropped down from under him. The rawhide gloves had come in handy. He gave the elevator a chance to reach the bottom of the shaft while he hung suspended six stories above. Then he pried the door open slightly to make sure no one was in the hallway. A black nose pressed up against his.

Raleigh was a Pembroke Welsh Corgi who had slipped his collar and was leading his owner on a merry chase around the hallways of the sixth floor. Vigil could hear a woman calling the dog's name while she tried to catch her breath. Raleigh licked Vigil's face as if they were old friends. Animals liked him for some reason. He never got close to them for the same reason he didn't get close to too many humans; they never lived long enough. It hurt when he lost them. He eased the door closed just enough to see Raleigh's exasperated owner finally catch up to him and slip the collar back over his head. Raleigh didn't want to leave Vigil, but the lady promised the dog a treat so he reluctantly went with her. Checking both ways, he pulled himself up out of the elevator shaft and closed the doors behind him.

Vigil passed a mirror as he quietly crept to the stairwell. The dog had made him lose his concentration and his complexion was returning to its former state. He just looked like a well-tanned version of his former self. It didn't matter now. If *they* were after him, how he looked wouldn't change anything. *They* were agents. Not just any agents, but agents who did mercenary work on the side. They came from a number of covert organizations around the world including MI-6, several from the United States and a few from the Middle East. Their actions were seldom sanctioned...officially anyway. One of them was hiding just inside the door leading to the fourth floor where Vigil's room was. *He must be new at this*, he thought. *Rookie mistake.*

Vigil continued his descent to the fourth floor from the outside of the stairway. He held onto the bars of the railing and dropped down, narrowly catching the railing at the next landing. He hoisted himself up on the railing and performed a spindle as if he were on a Pommel Horse and landed directly behind the agent at the door. Before the man could react, Vigil asserted pressure on an artery in his neck, causing instant unconsciousness. The man was dead within a few seconds. Without an autopsy, it would appear the man had suffered an aneurysm while climbing the stairs. Vigil relieved him of his weapons and anything else connecting him to a government agency: friendly or otherwise. He then placed the agent on the steps in such a way as to suggest his unfortunate physical condition had caused his death.

Vigil stepped out slowly into the hallway. It seemed to be clear, so he continued to his room. He didn't need his keycard because the door was slightly ajar, but only by a quarter of an inch. That was out of character, even for rookie agents. There was no indication the door had been wired with an explosive and it was possible, however unlikely, that the cleaning staff had neglected to fully close the door. Vigil wasn't willing to take a chance. Still, there were things he needed in his room; so caution was a luxury he couldn't afford at the moment. He pushed the door open with his foot and entered the room with a forward roll, terminating in a crouched position on one knee and his gun aiming straight ahead.

The room was dark, which was also suspect because the cleaning staff usually opens the heavy curtains when they work. In the corner was a chair; and in the chair, a silhouette. It was a familiar shape, but Vigil didn't lower his weapon.

"Hello Vigil," said the intruder.

"Hello Jillian," said Vigil.

Chapter Seven: Frenemy

The intense glow from the viridian green laser sight sparkled in Vigil's eyebrows. He knew that Jillian's Belgian-made FN Five-seven pistol was trained directly between his eyes. While the weapon's lead-free copper projectile might not kill him, its rapid expansion could scramble his brains long enough for him to be *resolved* in a number of more effective ways.

"You know those shells have a lot of penetrating power," said Vigil calmly. "You could end up killing people in the next three rooms."

"Collateral damage only means more paperwork," said Jillian. "...and I've got people for that. Speaking of *collateral damage*, I assume you dispatched the agent in the stairwell."

"You know I did," said Vigil. "Was he working with you?"

"I work alone," Jillian answered. "You know that. I thought you would have recognized him. The agent was Stapanski, former KGB."

"That was Stapanski? Wow...he lost quite a bit of weight," said Vigil. "...and to be fair; I only saw him from the back."

"Then I guess he must have suffered an *aneurysm*," Jillian said. Vigil could see a trace of a smile in the dim light.

"I take it you were not a fan," he said.

"He was an idiot," said Jillian. "...always playing by the book and screwing things up. He didn't know how to improvise. To tell you the truth, I wonder how he managed to survive as long as he did."

"As much as I enjoy our talks," said Vigil. "...I am guessing you are not here to kill me. If you had been, I think you would have done it when I came through the door."

"I was sent to keep an eye on you," she said. "You have been doing a lot of *off-the-books* missions lately which makes some of the higher-ups nervous. They fear you might be going rogue."

"Is that what you think?"

"I know better," she said. "I've studied the cases and the files. I know the patterns of people going rogue and you don't fit that pattern. It would probably have been possible to convince your superiors of that on my own, but I *really* wanted a paid trip to London. Recent budget cuts make it so hard to get travel approved anymore; let alone, get a nice hotel."

"Well, since we are not planning to kill each other," Vigil suggested, "...maybe we could put our guns away and act like we are civilized."

"Fine with me," said Jillian. "You first." Vigil cautiously lowered his weapon; but he was prepared to spring into action if the need arose. The green sparkle disappeared from his eyebrows and Jillian opened the curtain just enough to let a little light in. Vigil sat on the edge of the bed, angled so he could keep an eye on her, and on the door.

"I don't mean to be rude," he said. "...but I need to get some of my things and relocate."

"That won't be necessary," said Jillian.

"Uh...it kinda will," said Vigil. "I still have someone

64

after me; maybe several *someones*."

"Actually, you don't," she said. "I took care of the *umbrella man* in the tube and three other agents here at the hotel. You took care of Stapanski. Those were the only four who knew where you were staying. So I took the liberty of arranging for you to check out and register at another hotel across town. This room is in *my* name now; well, one of my many, many names. It's amazing what one can accomplish using a smartphone and a little help from headquarters."

As Vigil's eyes became more accustomed to the light, the less his conversation with Jillian seemed normal. She had the look and demeanor of someone who could be no older than fourteen; but she was a seasoned field agent with numerous kills under her belt. She was especially effective working undercover busting human trafficking rings. Jillian could look older if she wanted to or if the occasion called for it; but she preferred to give people the wrong impression. She liked having them believe she was innocent and vulnerable; but that made it difficult for Vigil to address the *elephant* in the room.

"So...are we supposed to stay in this room...together?" He tried to ask the question in a way that wouldn't seem suggestive. With anyone else, he might have; but with Jillian, it just felt perverted.

"What? I'm shocked!" she gasped. "You are *way* too old for me." Then she began to laugh...like a schoolgirl. Vigil breathed a sigh of relief. He *was* too old for her. If she only knew how much too old.

"I secured the adjoining room," she said. "I'll be staying in there, but that doesn't mean we can't have a little fun."

"What?" Vigil's nervousness was back.

"Not THAT kind of fun, sicko," she said giggling. "I

was thinking we could go to a pub and try to get them to serve me alcohol. You can be my daddy and I'll be your little girl. It will be hilarious."

"I can be your daddy? Now who's the perv?" Vigil spoke as he reset his proximity sensors. "Besides, I would prefer to keep a low profile right now. A father/daughter combo in a bar might draw too much attention I think."

"Maybe you're right," said Jillian. "So, what are you up to these days?" Vigil was glad she was asking the right questions. It made him more confident that the purpose of his trip wasn't public knowledge.

"I have acquired a target and I am zoning in on it," he answered. "That's probably all I should say."

"I may not be able to help you if I don't know the details," she said.

"You have eliminated the ones following me which has been a great help already. You should just enjoy the rest of your company-funded paid vacation." Vigil was more relaxed, but took a pricey bottle of scotch from the minibar.

"Would you like a drink?" he asked.

"Are you trying to contribute to the delinquency of a minor?" she responded with an indignant but adolescent tone. "Actually, I thought you would never ask. I would like a vodka please, straight up."

Vigil handed her the drink and sipped his 12-year-old single malt as he looked around the room. It wasn't like Jillian to be inaccurate, so he was puzzled by something.

"You said you arranged adjoining rooms. This room doesn't join with any others. Did you mean that they are just next to each other?"

"I always mean what I say," said Jillian. "Apparently

you haven't been briefed about some of this hotel's special features." She walked to an unassuming blank wall, touched a hidden switch in the molding and a door-size panel slid to the side. It revealed a typical adjoining room door Vigil had not been aware existed.

"That's been there the whole time?" he asked nervously.

"See? This is what happens when you don't attend briefings," said Jillian. "Do you think you are the first operative to stay here? They have a few of these hidden doors in some of the rooms. By the way, one of the agents I dispatched was the desk clerk who assigned you to this room. I guess there is a job opening now if you are looking for employment. It's a good thing you didn't actually sleep here yet."

"Maybe I should put in an application," said Vigil. There was a trace of perspiration on his forehead. "I might be getting too old for the assassin game."

"Noooo…" laughed Jillian. "You're still in your prime. What are you, a hundred?" Vigil answered back with a sarcastic, "You're so cute. Shouldn't you be in school or something?"

"Okay," said Jillian. "I have a couple of Public Service Announcements. First, don't try to use this door without telling me. I have security monitors and traps set up on the other side. They could ruin your day."

"What's the other announcement?" asked Vigil.

"I'm starving! Can we please go get something to eat?" she pleaded.

"Okay," said Vigil. "…but I am not sure where we can go that has a children's menu."

"You know what? This is going to wear thin really quickly," said Jillian.

"I'm sorry," said Vigil. "Let me make it up to you. Dinner is on me."

"Damn right it is!" she said. "…and drinks."

"Alright…how about the Hawksmoor?" he asked. He already knew her answer.

"Nice! Elegant, yet informal," said Jillian. "I won't have to wear my prom dress."

"You brought a prom dress?" Vigil raised one eyebrow.

"You really don't get the concept of humor, do you?" asked Jillian.

"I don't think either of us does," said Vigil smiling.

"I should go get ready," she said. Jillian rose from the chair and left by way of the main door. Vigil set up more security protocols on the newly-discovered access point to his room and closed the secret panel. Fifteen minutes later, there was a light knock at the door. Jillian stood in the hallway looking every bit like a slightly spoiled American teenager. She wore what looked like a vintage high school letter jacket, a cream colored turtleneck, boot-cut jeans and western boots for the full effect. Her curls cascaded over the shoulders of her jacket and there was glitter in her hair. Her makeup was obvious but tasteful.

"Am I going to have to keep the boys away from you?" asked Vigil.

"Not if I can help it," said Jillian. Vigil liked her semi-cryptic responses. It was easy to forget that she was less innocent than she looked.

They took a cab to the *Hawksmoor Seven Dials* and requested a table on a far wall. They both instinctively sat on the same side of the table...not to be intimate, but to keep an eye on the patrons and exits.

They both ordered the same thing, which surprised Vigil. They had the Chateaubriand with Béarnaise sauce, roasted tarragon potatoes and asparagus with lemon butter. Vigil let Jillian order the wine, and of course she ordered the most expensive one on the menu: a 1990 Krug Champagne, costing a little over £700.00.

"You don't mind, do you?" she asked. Jillian used a disarming mock sheepishness which Vigil couldn't help but find adorable. That was dangerous. He was sure many of her targets had fallen prey to the same charm.

"No," he answered. "That's fine. Nothing is too good for *my little girl.*" The sommelier hardly flinched, but his left eye twitched slightly. Vigil was pretty sure he was being judged by the wine steward. After all, if she was there as his date, she looked way too young for him; and if she really was his daughter, he was not being a very responsible parent. Vigil winked at him knowingly, just to reinforce his wrong impression. Jillian shook her head slightly, chiding his behavior. He shrugged and winked at her as well.

Their entrées were prepared to perfection. Vigil had expected no less. The Krug had been a good pairing. The bottle was empty and was resting upside down in the ice bucket in no time. Jillian considered ordering a second bottle, but Vigil cautioned her against it. She really didn't want one. She was just testing how much he would be willing to spend. If money had been the only consideration, he would have ordered it himself; but he was afraid their charade had already attracted too much attention. There was no evidence to back up the suspicion; he just had a feeling.

Their dining experience ended, as it should, with dessert. Vigil had the plum tart with vanilla ice cream. Jillian had the passion fruit sorbet. Watching her lick the spoon after each bite reminded him of just how old he was. He didn't feel old, but he did feel weary. The profession he had chosen seemed to be never-ending. Vigil felt that he could never have a *normal life*, nor did he really want one. A few hundred years ago, he and a girl of Jillian's apparent age could have been romantically involved and people would hardly have noticed. Now he felt conspicuous, even though his intentions were honorable and she was of legal age. Staying at the hotel or choosing a less high-profile restaurant would have been preferable and safer. But Vigil owed Jillian. She had saved his life, or at the very least saved him a large amount of difficulty.

The waiter brought the check and Vigil didn't even look at the total. He filled in a generous tip, even though the custom of tipping was fading in and around Europe. Old habits die hard and he left a gratuity anyway. He wanted to leave the staff with at least a modicum of a good impression. Because of Jillian's appearance, he was pretty sure several considered him to be a pedophile. The waiter barely smiled as he took Vigil's credit card along with the check to process it. He returned shortly and wished them both a good evening.

There is a common ritual most people perform when leaving a restaurant, especially a nice one. They stop, look up at the sky, breathe in the night air...and smile. Vigil and Jillian did all those things, except smile. Their senses were on high alert and their practice of surveying their surroundings was automatic.

"We're being watched," Jillian mentioned nonchalantly.

"I know," said Vigil. "We should walk for a while. I don't want to lead anyone back to the hotel. As much as I hate the idea, maybe we should take the underground. Only this time, I'd like to ride on the inside of the car."

"That's probably a good idea," agreed Jillian, smiling. "There's a tube at Covent Garden not far from here. Well, it's a little far, but there are a lot of twists and turns to get there. We should be able to shake a tail."

The narrow streets would be nothing more than alleys in many large cities, but Jillian thought they gave the area an authentic charm. However, they made the hair on the back of Vigil's neck stand up. Every turn was blind and he constantly had to keep watching in all directions. The buildings were not very tall. He and Jillian could just about be taken out by a couple of well-placed concrete blocks dropped on their heads. They stayed under overhangs and ledges wherever possible. Vigil did his best to keep a 360-degree view of the streets. He had goggles that would have let him do that, but he didn't bring them. As they reached the Covent Garden Square, he thought they might just have been paranoid. That is, until a large man in a ski mask grabbed Jillian around the throat. Another man placed a cold metallic object next to Vigil's spine.

"You know," said one in a raspy voice. "I could snap your little girl's neck like a pencil. How 'bout you hand over your valuables and wallet?"

Jillian winked at Vigil and asked, "Like a pencil? Do you even know how to write; or do you just use it to pick your..." She twisted in his grip until she faced him. Her palm came up sharply, breaking his "...nose?" The assailant's knees buckled, bringing his crotch down to a manageable level. Jillian's knee met it with much more force than her small frame would have seemed to contain. She completed the routine with a sharp strike to the throat with the tips of her fingers. He crumpled to the ground, writhing in pain and struggling for breath.

71

Vigil's assailant stood dumbfounded. He had not expected the little girl to be a match for his partner, who had been nearly three times her size. During the man's momentary lapse in concentration, Vigil turned, disarmed him and shoved the weapon into his attacker's mouth. At first, he thought it was a gun. Instead, it was a length of pipe...probably lead.

"What do you think, sweetie? Should we turn them over to the proper authorities or just deposit them in the rubbish bin?"

"Oh, daddy," said Jillian. "I'm tired. I don't want to answer a lot of questions. Can't we just throw them down the sewer?"

"Anything for my *little girl*," Vigil replied. He removed the pipe from the man's mouth and said, "Sorry about this." He dropped the pipe and placed his thumps on each side of the man's fat throat, just below the barely perceptible jawline. The attacker's eyes widened and then glazed over as he lost consciousness. He slumped to the ground next to his partner, who had also passed out. Jillian arranged their arms in an embrace and placed their lips together. Then she then stood back like an artist admiring her work.

"You are so bad," said Vigil.

"...and you must be getting soft," added Jillian. "There was a time when you wouldn't think twice about erasing these two from existence."

"I know," said Vigil. "...but I'm tired; and that would mean paperwork and phone calls and...well, you know."

"I think it's cute," said Jillian mischievously.

"Don't get smart, young lady," said Vigil. "I will have to ground you."

"See? An old softy...just like I said."

The subway wasn't too crowded and Vigil did indeed ride on the inside of the train this time. It was late when they arrived back at the hotel. There was also a light fog hanging low which threatened to get heavier. Vigil couldn't shake the feeling they were still being watched. Jillian felt it too, but kept it to herself. He stopped and made one final check of the streets. Jillian grabbed him by the collar of his leather jacket and looked him in the eyes.

"We are being paranoid," she said. "We should get some rest. We have a lot to do tomorrow." She smiled at him with her childlike face. Vigil heard the cough of a silenced weapon and a spot of blood appeared directly in the center of Jillian's forehead. Her eyes widened as a trickle of blood ran down her face. Vigil heard two more coughing sounds in the darkness. Then everything faded.

Chapter Eight: Bloody History

In 43 A.D., during the reign of Emperor Claudius, the Romans invaded Britain. When they did, they built a bridge across the Thames River. Seven years after that, they determined that the area was an excellent place to build a seaport. The water was deep enough for seagoing vessels, but was far enough inland to protect the port from raiders. The area was named London. Some say the name originated from the Celtic word *londinios*, meaning *place of the bold one*. The history of the area was turbulent and bloody, but the Romans retained control for 300 years. After that, the city was abandoned and the Dark Ages began. A new city sprang up outside the main walls on the site of Covent Garden. It was much smaller than Roman London with less than 10,000 residents. Monks arrived in 597 A.D. with the goal of converting the Saxons to Christianity. A mint was established there to produce silver coins; and the rest, as they say, is history. Lots and lots of bloody history.

* * *

Vigils left eye opened slowly. The right one was crusted with dried blood. The pain in his head was intense. His pain was always intense. Intense pain was a by-product of rapid tissue regeneration. It didn't last long, but it was crippling. He raised his head cautiously and assessed his situation. Jillian lay under him; her angelic face and flowing hair glowed in the light of a streetlamp. He closed his eyes for a moment and then raised himself off of her. *This is why I work alone*, he thought. He hated to lose people, especially when they were so young.

Vigil bared his teeth and looked around for their assailant. He was prepared to extract the most pain possible from him before sending him to Hell. But there was no one to be found. Fog surrounded the streetlamps making them look like dandelion spheres preparing to disperse their seeds in a summer wind. He found traces of blood leading off down a narrow lane, but had no idea why it was there. He would have followed the trail, but he didn't know how long ago his assailant had fled or if it was even his blood. Vigil took a deep breath and prepared himself for what he had to do. It was important that he contact Jillian's agency and have them collect her body. They had only spent a short time together, but he liked her. She had a charming personality that had not shown up in her profile. Personalities seldom do unless they are psychopathic. Her death would be a terrible loss to the agency.

The fog grew thicker and Vigil became disoriented. The fact that he had been shot in the head didn't help. At least it would be harder for passersby to see her body lying on the sidewalk. But then, he was having trouble finding her himself. He moved to the edge of the building and retraced his steps. The darkness and the fog seemed to be working in conjunction with each other to conceal Jillian's body. The same fog and darkness was probably protecting him from their attacker's return. Vigil managed to return to the spot where the shooting had occurred but still couldn't find Jillian. There were bloodstains on the sidewalk, so he knew he was in the right place; however, her body was gone. That didn't make any sense...unless.

"Did you lose something?" Jillian's voice from the darkness startled Vigil. He had already concluded that the assassin had been from her own agency and had claimed her body. He had not been prepared to hear her voice.

"We should get out of the street," she suggested.

76

"I don't understand," said Vigil.

"Well, that's two of us," said Jillian. "There are some questions to be answered, but not here."

They took the elevator up two floors and then took the stairs the rest of the way. Vigil's security protocols had not been tripped, so they slipped inside his room and reset them. Jillian cautiously checked the windows, took off her jacket and kicked off her boots.

"What are you doing?" asked Vigil.

"I am going to wash this blood off," answered Jillian. "...and after I went to all the trouble to get my hair just right."

"Shouldn't you do that in your own room?" he asked.

"It's *your* blood. So I am using *your* shower. No peeking," she said. She left the bathroom door open slightly so they could continue to converse. She was much more shaken up than she let on. That was another trait that made her such a valuable agent.

"Okay," she said from inside the shower stall. "How did you take a bullet to the head and still be here to talk about it?"

"It just grazed me," said Vigil. "The bullet didn't penetrate my skull."

"That's not what it looked like," said Jillian. There was skepticism in her voice. "It looked like it came straight out of your forehead. If I had been taller, it would have hit me too."

"I thought it had," he said. "It looked like it had."

"That was *your* blood...as I said," said Jillian. "...and don't try to change the subject."

"I just have a hard skull," said Vigil.

"It must be made of Kevlar," Jillian said.

"Maybe," said Vigil sheepishly. "What happened after I was shot?" Jillian quit trying to interrogate him. She knew it wouldn't work, so she had no reason to believe Vigil would give up information if he didn't want to.

"When you fell on me, I fired into the dark," she said. "I had a vague idea where the shooter was. I must have seen the muzzle flash in my peripheral vision. He didn't come over to finish the job, so I must have hit him."

"I found a blood trail leading away from here, so I guess you did." Vigil collected his essential items. Most of his clothes he would leave behind. He could always get more clothes and changing his look would be a good idea. Jillian emerged from the bathroom. She had her hair wrapped up in a towel and was wearing Vigil's luxurious bathrobe provided by the hotel. It hung all the way to the floor on her.

"Are you going somewhere?" she asked.

"London seems a little crowded," said Vigil. "I need to get on about my business."

"So where are we off to next?" Jillian asked as she helped herself to the minibar.

"*We* aren't going anywhere," he said. "It's too dangerous. I need to work alone."

"Well...first, I have an assignment to complete," said Jillian. "...and second, you would probably be dead right now if not for me." Vigil couldn't argue with that. If she had not put a 5.7mm slug into his attacker, the man would probably have finished the job. Still, he felt she was a distraction. The fact that she looked like a kid made him feel as though he should protect her as one.

"You know you can't stop me," she said. "I could even

make it more difficult for you if I wanted." Vigil knew when he was beaten. He could stop her of course, but that would mean doing something he really didn't want to do. Besides, he was going after two targets this time. He might actually need a little help.

"I need to get dressed, get my things packed and fix my hair," she said. "...I should be ready in..."

"Two and a half hours?" Vigil's tone was humorously flavored with a hint of sarcasm.

"Twenty minutes," said Jillian indignantly. "My mom used to be a stylist. I know some tricks." Vigil removed his security protocols and she left by way of the front door. He showered quickly after she left. His own blood washed down the drain. He stared at the crimson whirlpool as it began to clear and wondered how much blood he had lost over the centuries. He began to drift off, so he shook himself awake and finished up.

Vigil sighed as he looked in the mirror at the nearly-healed wound in his forehead. He wasn't sure he was going to be able to style his hair to hide it. If Jillian stayed around him much longer, he might have to tell her the truth about himself. Vigil didn't like to let people into his confidence. It was risky; it made him vulnerable and put them at risk as well. There was no point in worrying about it now.

Vigil stepped out of the bathroom only to find Jillian standing there. He felt fortunate that he had been holding the damp towel in front of him as he did. He hurried to wrap it around his waist as discretely as possible.

"Whoa..." exclaimed Jillian. "A perv *and* a flasher. Stranger danger! Stranger danger!"

"Okay...that will be enough of that," said Vigil. "You left with my robe. Besides, you said twenty minutes."

"I know, right? Eleven minutes and twenty-two seconds. A new world record." Jillian had her hair pulled back into an adorable ponytail. She wore a tartan skirt, a white silk blouse and a waist-length jacket. On her head was a tartan Tam o' Shanter that matched her skirt.

"We are going to Scotland, right? I do my research." Jillian curtsied ever so slightly.

"You look like a schoolgirl in that outfit," said Vigil.

"Good," said Jillian, smiling. "That's what I was going for."

"Yes," Vigil said under his breath. "You won't be a distraction at all."

"Excuse me?" she asked. "Did you mumble something?" Vigil shook his head, but Jillian knew what he had said.

"You know," she said, looking in the mirror. "There are lots of websites dedicated to this look."

"You aren't going to make this easy, are you?" asked Vigil. He really was starting to feel like a parent.

"Okay," said Jillian. "I will quit. Hurry up and get dressed."

"Are you going to at least turn around or something?" he asked.

"When did you get so shy? Okay," she said smiling. "I have to check the exits anyway. What a prude."

"I thought you said I was a perv."

"Prude...perv...toe-may-toe, toe-mah-toe. Just hurry." Jillian left and Vigil dressed hastily. With anyone else, he wouldn't have been self-conscious; but with Jillian, he felt like he would have to explain things to her mother. He knew he needed to shake that to be an effective assassin, but the experience was kind of new to him. Hopefully, he would become accustomed to it by the time they reached Scotland.

Jillian was standing at the end of the hall when he came out of the room. He had two bags with him: one for his clothes and one for his ordnance. Jillian had just one bag and it was slung over her shoulder.

"One bag? How do you make all those wardrobe changes?"

"This girl knows how to pack," she said.

He shook his head as they took the stairway to the floor above. From there, they took the elevator to the lobby. That maneuver wouldn't fool a seasoned professional, but they had probably exterminated all of the *seasoned professionals* for the time being. Once outside, they hailed a cab and went to the Kings Cross train station. They booked a sleeper car on a train headed to Edinburgh, even though it was only about a four-hour trip. Vigil didn't like being exposed for too long and a sleeper car seemed the best way to remain concealed. From there they would rent a car, perhaps two, to continue on to Lochgelly.

Vigil and Jillian settled into their berth and looked out the window as the train pulled out of the station. They were both tired and Vigil pulled out the bench seat to form the lower berth. His head still hurt terribly from the bullet wound and he needed to lie down. Head wounds always took a little longer to heal...at least on the inside. He didn't know how such things worked and he wasn't about to let anyone experiment on him to find out. There had been some procedures done on a few of his lineage during the Second World War, but most of those findings had been *lost* during the Allied liberation of a notorious Nazi extermination camp. In reality, some of the experiments performed there had been done by a couple of

Vigil's own relatives.

Jillian removed her tam and her shoes. Instead of using the upper berth, she snuggled in next to Vigil. He made her feel safe, even though she was probably in more danger being with him. He placed his arm over her like the protective father he was pretending to be. Vigil felt content and nothing more. It was a feeling he couldn't allow himself to get used to. It wouldn't last. Nothing ever lasted.

A lone figure stood in the shadows of the platform and watched the train pull out of the station. His shoulder still ached from the 5.7mm projectile that had pierced it. The exit wound had been as big as a golf ball. The bullet had been designed to expand when it hit bone and expand it did. Ankh didn't like how rapidly technology was advancing. He felt as though his advantage of being nearly immortal was slipping away. He missed the old ways and the old days. It was possible to survive anything back then. One time, he was revered as a sorcerer. Another time, he was burned at the stake as a warlock. Ankh had a plan to maybe return the planet to the Bronze Age, but it was going to be tricky. He wanted to do it without plunging the world into thermonuclear war.

* * *

Ankh had been partially responsible for the U.S. involvement in World War II. It was at his urging that Admiral Yamamoto gained authorization to launch a full-scale attack on Pearl Harbor. Even back then, Ankh feared technology was increasing at an alarming rate. It wasn't until the atomic bombs were dropped on Hiroshima and Nagasaki that he thought he might have overstepped his boundaries by encouraging war. Had he been present in or near one of the targeted cities, he would have been literally erased from existence.

There was another close call during the Cuban Missile

Crisis, as the world took a step closer to nuclear devastation. It was narrowly averted or nearly caused by the President of the United States, depending on who one talks to. Just to be sure, Ankh was in Dallas Texas the following year to make sure it didn't happen again. He didn't need to pull the trigger himself; he was very good at convincing people to do his bidding.

During the 80s, he helped convince certain government officials to reduce the stockpiles of nuclear weapons to manageable numbers. Instead of being able to engulf the world in radioactive flames, specific targets could be eliminated...leaving much of the world intact. Even that proposal was risky. Ankh's next plan was to eliminate the risks altogether.

* * *

The train pulled into Waverley Station in Edinburgh nine minutes ahead of schedule. Vigil felt as though Jillian had dissolved in his arms. She had slipped out of his embrace a few minutes before and was freshening up in the W.C. She looked as fresh-faced as ever when she came out. Vigil was pretty sure he looked like a homeless transient. A look in the mirror confirmed that he was right. Fortunately, Jillian was there to rescue him...again.

"We should probably get a room here in Edinburgh and then continue on tomorrow. You are a wreck."

"Thanks," he said. "You give me such confidence."

"I know," said Jillian. "It's a gift. No, really...you need to be better rested before we go to Lochgelly. Both of our lives may depend on it." Vigil knew she was right. Besides, he needed to add to his wardrobe and Edinburgh would be better than Lochgelly for his purchases. They arranged for a room at the Cairn Hotel because it was near downtown, but had a much lower profile.

Vigil and Jillian took a cab to the hotel, keeping an ever-watchful eye on their surroundings. Jillian didn't know whose *feathers* Vigil had ruffled, but she didn't know how he could live like this. She felt like a goldfish in a bowl. They arrived at the Cairn and checked in. Instead of adjoining rooms, they opted for the twin room. It had twin beds and a few amenities, but they could watch each other's backs. While checking in, Vigil acted his part as a doting dad.

"Look sweetie," he commented, looking at a brochure. "The Royal Botanical Garden isn't far from here. We could go see that."

"Oh, daddy," Jillian whined. "I want to go to a bar. Can't we go to a bar?" Vigil gritted his teeth.

"Now sweetie...remember what your parole officer said." Jillian stamped her foot like a defiant teen. Vigil looked apologetically at the desk clerk.

"Nae tae fash yerse sairrr," the clerk said. "Ife got a body at haem jist loch 'er." Jillian had a puzzled look, but Vigil was much more familiar with the dialect.

Vigil leaned close and whispered, "He said, 'Not to worry, sir. I've got a body at home just like her.'" Jillian's eyes narrowed and she gave the clerk a look that probably made his blood chill. Even though she was just playing a part, she played him for all it was worth. The clerk's hand was shaking when he handed Vigil the keycards to the room.

"Don't worry," he said. "She's only mean when she *doesn't* drink." The desk clerk appeared to believe Vigil.

"Mebbe ye shoods gie 'er a wee somethin' 'en," he suggested. "There's a pub nae far frae haur. Ah can draw ye a map." Vigil smiled and turned to Jillian.

"See sweetie...he just wants to help."

"I didn't understand a word of that," said Jillian. Her arms were folded and she was tapping her foot.

"He said there is a pub near here...and he is willing to draw us a map to get us there. You must be making quite an impression."

"Maybe later," Jillian replied. "I want to go to the room right now."

"Anything you say princess," said Vigil. He thanked the desk clerk, who was visibly relieved as they went to their room on the second floor. Jillian was playing her part by skipping behind him.

"Aren't you laying it on a little thick with the skipping?" he asked as they got to the room.

"I blame you, daddy...you shouldn't have let mummy drink while she was pregnant with me." Jillian's eyes twinkled as she spoke. Vigil looked around the hallway to make sure no one had heard her. He ushered her into the room quickly and secured the door.

"It is no wonder you are the most effective assassin ever," he said.

Vigil couldn't help but admire her. Her disarming childlike behavior must have made it easy for her to slip under the radar of most people. Bars were the only places where she would look inappropriate, so she made herself up to look older and blended in. They were a refuge of sorts to her. She didn't have to be who she really was; the person inside Jillian was a stone-hearted killer. That was the person she needed to get away from once in a while.

Jillian liked playing the role with Vigil. She liked keeping him on his toes. He had a reputation as an elite killer himself and she might need the advantage of keeping him off-guard. She pranced around the room touching things, the way a curious child would. She looked in the bathroom while raising one leg up behind her like a ballerina. Then she went to the bed and took the foil-wrapped mint chocolate from the pillow. Vigil was putting his bag down when he noticed her.

"Jillian! Stop!" he shouted.

"What?" she asked as she bit down on the candy.

"This hotel doesn't put chocolates on the pillows!" Vigil raced to her as she swallowed involuntarily.

Chapter Nine: Night Terrors

Europe's dark history is full of gallantry and cruelty. Its pages are filled with tales of victories and defeats, ultimate truths and treacherous lies. The problem is that history is often recorded by the winners. This means the stories are often skewed in a particular direction and may not contain actual facts. One could think of history as a vast game of *Chinese Whispers*. That game is also known as *Russian Scandal, Whisper Down the Lane, Grapevine or Broken Telephone*, as well as other names. For every historic event chronicled in books, there were thousands of other eye-witnesses who had their own version of the stories. Those accounts were passed down by word-of-mouth and gave rise to legends and myths.

One of those myths strongly influenced the people of a 13th century principality. The people of the area had strong superstitious beliefs. Those beliefs saw them through difficult times and helped to explain those things for which there were no explanations. Ankh had settled there for a while in the Southern Carpathian Mountains. He had actually grown tired of war for a while. He and four of his brothers--Yachin, Uzziyyah, Peleg and Izevel--had participated in the Second Crusade beginning in 1247 A.D. None of them had any great loyalty to the cause. The crusade was just another excuse to kill people randomly without troublesome consequences. The advantage of having rapid tissue regeneration was that war held no horror for them. Of course, there was pain; but they were used to pain. However, after a while the thrill of killing wore off and the brothers left the battlefield. They headed north for no reason in particular and were satisfied to stay in a region that would one day be Romania...more accurately,

Transylvania.

While the name Transylvania has come to bear a sinister connotation, its etymology is simply Medieval Latin for *on the other side of the woods*. The Carpathian Mountains were home to an abundance of wildlife, vegetation and several natural mineral springs. As villages cropped up throughout the region, they gave Ankh and his siblings ample victims for their insatiable lusts. They developed reputations as malevolent beings who could not be killed by conventional weapons. Legends circulated that they could fly and change their forms at will, but could not tolerate direct sunlight. It was rumored that they drank blood and imprisoned souls. They were said to commune with demons and perform bizarre rituals. Some of it was true, much of it wasn't. The brothers did nothing to mitigate the rumors, so the rumors grew into legends. But sometimes, the truth is more fantastic than the legend.

Ankh and his brothers did avoid the daylight, but it wasn't because they couldn't tolerate it. They committed their atrocities at night so they wouldn't be recognized. That way, they could walk among the villagers during the daytime unnoticed. Their unique metabolisms allowed their appearances to adapt to their surroundings and look like those native to the region. Of course, typical weapons couldn't hurt them...not permanently anyway. As for changing their forms at will, those stories were started by individuals who had too much to drink or were not getting enough attention. Ankh preferred to be a legend, even an evil legend. Mortals didn't matter to him anyway.

Even though the villagers did everything in their power to thwart the brothers, they were superstitious people and usually paralyzed with fear. Locking themselves in at night proved to be a useless security measure; but they locked their doors anyway. They used every superstitious charm, remedy and incantation they could think of, but they would still find the bodies of loved ones in the milky light of dawn. Usually, it was that of a young maiden. She would be left near the center of the village with her throat torn out. Often, she would be naked with obvious signs of being raped multiple times. Occasionally, cryptic symbols would have been carved into her body. The brothers did that just for effect. The symbols meant nothing to them, but the villagers cowered in fear.

Feeling their own beliefs had abandoned them, the villagers sought out help from a higher power. The village elders selected a messenger to take a letter to Pope Boniface VIII in Rome asking for his blessing and help. The courier did not make it as far as the other side of the mountains. A few days after he left, his head was found in the village square with the parchment letter stuffed into his mouth. His dead eyes were still wide with terror and the villagers were certain that his soul was being tormented by the inhuman brothers. After the macabre visage was left for the people to see, it was difficult to secure volunteers to take another message to the pope. In addition, the attacks against the village became far more frequent and cruel. Victims now found in the square after that were seldom dead. Both males and females were found there...maimed and bleeding, but still alive. Limbs had been amputated, tongues cut out and genitalia mutilated in retaliation for the villagers having been so bold as to send for help.

After those atrocities, most villagers hardly ventured out of their homes. But three men came forward to volunteer with a plan. Their names were Cyprian, Andrei and Neculai. Cyprian was the father of a girl who had been taken and returned with her arms amputated and the wounds cauterized. Neculai had been engaged to her. Andrei was the father of a young boy who would never be able to produce heirs because of the atrocity committed on him. The three men were grief-stricken and felt they had little to lose. Their plan was for two of them to attempt to cross the mountains in hopes of making it. Meanwhile the youngest, Neculai, would venture south in an attempt to get through unnoticed. The southern route would take longer, but the village elders thought the prolonged time might give their attackers the impression that they had given up.

The fears of the townspeople were realized one morning when the torsos of Cyprian and Andrei were discovered in the village square. Identifying the bodies had to be done by family members and even then they couldn't be sure. Then each day following, different appendages were left near the village well, until all but the heads had been delivered. It was obvious from the condition of the torsos and limbs that horrible torture had been involved: the worst tortures possible. The hopes of the villagers sank. They were sure that Neculai's body would soon be delivered in a like manner. As if the horror was not intense enough, a woman drawing water from the well one morning found herself face to face with Cyprian's decapitated head in the wooden well bucket. One of his eyes had been gouged out and the other hung from its optic nerve like ripe fruit from a tree. The resulting panic and hopelessness of the situation nearly drove many of the villagers insane.

Neculai was unable to deliver the letter to Pope Boniface VIII, but not because he had been captured. He managed to barely elude one of the brothers, Uzziyyah; but not before receiving a mortal wound. He was practically dead when his horse reached the Adriatic Sea near a small coastal fishing village. Neculai was barely able to tell his story to local fishermen and he pleaded for someone to continue with his message to the pope before he expired. Neculai died with a permanent expression of despair and failure on his face. Those who had found him were also superstitious people and buried him using their own ceremonies and traditions to ward off evil. They did however try to keep their pledge to deliver his message; but during that time and with the instability of Europe, the pope could have been in any one of several cities. The best they could do was to send the message across the Adriatic Sea to Rome and hope for the best. That was how it came to be in the hands of someone who was familiar with Ankh and his brothers.

Vigil had been searching for two of the brothers since Damascus. He had used a significant amount of his money to buy a ship and sail to Europe. Figuring he could recoup the amount he spent by selling the boat once he was there, Vigil had docked near the fishing village to pick up fresh water and supplies and had opened the letter even though he wasn't supposed to. Yachin and Izevel weren't mentioned by name in it, but he recognized their torture and mutilation methods. He had seen it before in Jerusalem during the Crusades. Individually, the methods might have gone unnoticed, but in conjunction with one another, they were like a signature.

Vigil ordered that the ship sail across the sea without him, deliver its cargo and then sail back to the village. After that, the sailors should wait for him until he returned. He had a loyal crew and was confident that they would follow his orders to the letter. Purchasing a horse and supplies, Vigil rode east to the Carpathians. The letter said there were five brothers who he must deal with. That was not going to be easy. A battle of the gods was about to ensue and he would need to be at his very best. He began to formulate a plan as he rode.

* * *

Jillian lay on the twin bed, her lips blue and her tongue swollen. She was shaking violently and only the whites of her eyes were visible under her lids. Vigil had flung himself across the bed and forced his fingers down her throat when he saw her begin to put the candy into her mouth. He had been able to get a small amount of the chocolate out of her mouth. She threw up the rest on the carpet, but not before a bit of poison seeped into her system through the walls of her esophagus. Vigil didn't know if the amount would be enough to kill her; but considering she wasn't dead yet, he thought she had a fair chance of surviving. He had not been cautious enough when he initially scanned the room. Vigil feared that he was becoming too reliant on Jillian. He hadn't expected her to eat the chocolate either. The mistake was one a rookie would make; but then, Jillian was playing a part. It was her practice to fully immerse herself in a role. Still, he blamed himself.

Vigil probably should have taken Jillian to the hospital, or at least arranged for her agency to extract her. The severity of her poisoning was impossible to gauge. Her symptoms suggested a poison he was familiar with...one he had used himself from time to time. It was probably a cicutoxin derived from Water Hemlock. There was no real antidote for it if that was what it was. One could only treat the symptoms; and recovery (if the victim recovered) could take up to two days.

Vigil left Jillian long enough to find an apothecary nearby. He didn't want to raise suspicion by talking to the pharmacist about the poisoning. Instead, he purchased a water filter and a case of bottled water. The man at the checkout looked at him curiously because it didn't seem like the two should go together. However, it wasn't his job to judge, so he rang the sale up anyway. Vigil headed back to the hotel and found a young lady manning the front desk. He took a moment to stop and ask her about the man who had checked them in.

"There won't be anyone else working until later this evening," she said. She had a trace of a Scottish accent, but nothing as thick as one the man had. Vigil asked her to describe the man who would be there later and his description was nothing like the person they had talked to. Vigil took a deep breath. He was getting sloppy and that was going to get Jillian...or himself...killed. He thanked the girl and then turned and asked, "I thought people from Scotland all talked with a heavy Scottish brogue?"

"Many of us do, but not around tourists. Hae a braw day," she said smiling. Vigil smiled back and hurried to the room. Jillian was having another seizure and he worried that her airway would close. He took a bottle of water and the filter into the bathroom. It was necessary to break open the insert inside the filter so the activated charcoal could be spread out on the counter. Vigil crushed it into powder with the butt of his gun and used a cardboard placard to form it into a neat line. Then he scooped it into the water bottle and shook it up. The powder dissolved sooner than he had suspected, so he breathed a little easier. The trick would now be to get Jillian to drink it.

Jillian did drink it, but gave him trouble at first. It was to his advantage that she was a bit delirious and she gave in after a few seconds. At first, Vigil thought she was going to throw up. She gagged a couple of times, but then finished it obediently. He didn't know if the charcoal was fast acting or if Jillian was just experiencing a placebo effect, but she stopped shaking and seemed to breathe easier. She drifted off into a peaceful slumber and snored ever so slightly. Vigil found it adorable, but realized he was getting too close again. She was so good at playing her part; she could literally do it in her sleep.

Since Jillian seemed to be out of danger for the moment, Vigil pondered the problem of how the poisoning had happened. Whoever had attacked them in London could possibly have raced ahead of them to Edinburgh, but he had no idea how they knew the hotel they would choose or which room they would get. Then he thought about the man who had checked them in. He was familiar in some way, but Vigil had seen so many people over the centuries, everyone looked familiar in one way or another. Still, old memories seemed to come to mind for no apparent reason. He pulled a chair next to the bed and placed a cold compress on Jillian's forehead. Vigil brushed back her curls and stroked her hair softly. She smiled and opened her eyes slightly.

"You're a good daddy," she said hoarsely. Her voice was weak and she sounded a little dehydrated. Vigil gave her a sip of water. The more that she could drink, the sooner the poison would flush from her system. She drifted back to sleep and rested for an hour or so until her sleep became uneasy. She was dreaming and whatever she was dreaming about terrified her. Her face contorted in a way that gave Vigil chills. She tried to cry out, but a scream seemed to be frozen in her throat. She stiffened, paralyzed with fear and neurotransmitters. He reached over and softly stroked the space between her eyes with his thumb. He didn't know why it worked, but her muscles relaxed and her face softened once more. Vigil continued to move his thumb in tight circles and didn't notice that Jillian's eyes had opened.

"Who...who did this?" she asked softly.

"I don't know," said Vigil. "I will figure it out. You need to get some more rest." Jillian smiled and snuggled beneath the covers. She felt safe around Vigil even though she probably shouldn't have. It had been a long time since she had felt safe or trusted somebody enough to let her guard down.

"Go back to sleep," he said. "I will keep watch tonight."

He spoke absently as he struggled to capture memories dancing around the periphery of his consciousness. He remembered riding a horse. In the distance were mountains. He remembered urgently riding through the night. Lights began to flicker in the recesses of his brain. Disjointed memories tried to form a coherent pattern. Faces came into view. The face of the desk clerk stared at him and then melted into something monstrous. Darkness surrounded him and he heard a howl in the distance. It was joined by others until the night was filled with the howling of wolves. The beat of the horse's hooves against the soil quickened and the wind was biting Vigil's face. He suddenly remembered why the face of the desk clerk was familiar.

* * *

Vigil had arrived at the small village just as dawn was breaking over the Carpathian Mountains. Cold somber shadows painted mocking designs on the humble walls of the dwellings. The entire village was silent and Vigil began to fear that everyone there had been slaughtered. It would not be the first time he had witnessed a scene like that; and it would probably not be the last. He desperately needed sleep but rest would have to wait. He heard the slightest creak of a window shutter and then a whispered curse in a language he was barely conversant in. He went to the dwelling, knocked respectably and waited. A man came to the door quicker than he expected. Monsters do not knock, the occupant had concluded. He ushered Vigil inside and they sat together at a roughhewn table near the fire. After a few minutes, Vigil was nearly fluent with his language. That was one of the advantages of living such a long life. Most languages stem from the same roots; and part of being able to blend with a new culture was picking up the language quickly.

Vigil told the man of Neculai's fate. The villager bowed his head and made a sign on his chest. Vigil wasn't sure what it was, but didn't question it. Then the man raised his head and looked Vigil in the eye. His look was one of hope and hopelessness at the same time. It was the look of a man facing the executioner, but still hoping for a reprieve.

"I appreciate your journey here," he said. "Neculai was a fine young man...brave and hard working. He still planned to wed Cosmina, even after what those monsters did to her." The man whispered the rest to Vigil so that his children would not hear the awful details. Vigil bowed his head, but mostly out of rage. He recognized the horrific pattern and knew he was close to his targets. Their way had been not to just destroy a life, but all chance of future generations in a family line. In many cultures, it was worse than death.

"We know there is nothing you can do," said the man. "...again, thank you for telling us of Neculai's fate. We shall resign ourselves to ours now."

"Do not be so quick to dismiss me," said Vigil softly. "I know things that others do not. I may be able to help. But first, I could use something to eat and then a place to rest for a little while. I need to speak to the village elders later. Could you arrange that?"

"I will do it," answered the man. "This afternoon will be okay?"

"That will be perfect," Vigil replied.

The man's wife had come down and heard much of the conversation. There was more hope in her eyes than there had been in his. She brought Vigil a chunk of hard cheese in a wooden bowl and a piece of bread that was only slightly softer than the cheese. He thanked her and finished it quickly. The woman unfurled a large animal fur and laid it down in front of the fire. Then she bid Vigil to lie down on it. He didn't remember doing it, but he was asleep immediately. He began to dream. He dreamt of battlefields and of facing Yachin and Izevel. They were his brothers, but he had never met them before that battle. Vigil had many brothers he hadn't met...sisters as well. Maybe they had been born with a lack of humanity or maybe evil had just developed over many years; but they were ruthless. Their cruelty knew no bounds and even their own comrades feared them. It was never enough for them to merely vanquish their enemies. The brothers felt compelled to torture and humiliate them. Macabre trophies had hung from their belts in battle...usually tokens taken from their enemies' loins.

Vigil dreamed of other battles and other wars. One individual always appeared in the distance. It was another brother whom he only knew by reputation. It could be said that this brother was the worst of all the brothers. He had wanted more than to just conquer his foes. He also wanted to conquer his friends, as if anyone could truly be his friend. This brother wanted more than just the destruction of their bodies. He wanted to destroy their very souls. His name was Ankh.

Chapter Ten: A Cry in the Night

Ankh wasn't stupid, and he didn't make stupid mistakes. He could have taken Vigil out any time he wanted. He was toying with him the way a cat toys with a mouse. Jillian was just a bonus. Vigil actually cared for her and Ankh was enjoying exploiting that vulnerability. Whether Ankh was a sociopath or a psychopath was hard to tell. He might most accurately be described as having an advanced case of *Dissociative Identity Disorder*. Of the personalities that inhabited his brain, a couple of them were sociopathic, while others were psychopathic with a ton of narcissism mixed in for good measure. He cared little for what Vigil did to or for other people, unless it affected him.

Ankh had no feelings for humanity at all. Their fleeting mortal lives made them no more than insects to him. He even felt he was doing them a favor by *extinguishing their flames* while they were young. The sensation of hunting and killing them was the closest he ever came to feeling joy. In the late sixties, he spent some time in Northern California. The climate was pleasant and there were a lot of remote areas where he could hunt his prey. Over thirty murders were attributed to him during that time, but not all of them were committed by him. Copycat killers rode his coattails for a while and some of them made Ankh extremely angry. He didn't want to be associated with the killers who left victims alive. He wasn't that sloppy. But it didn't stop him from sending cryptic taunting letters to the authorities. He figured the notes would confuse them even more and make him harder to track. He was right. No one was ever identified as the killer.

Getting to Edinburg ahead of Vigil had not been a problem. Ankh hired a small plane and pilot to fly him to his destination. He landed in Turnhouse well before Vigil's train would arrive and secured a car for the twenty minute drive to Edinburgh. Once there, it was only a matter of setting up the trap at the hotel. He had remotely cloned Vigil's phone while they were at the restaurant in London. Jillian had been just enough of a distraction to allow him to do it. He suspected that they would stay at the Cairn hotel because of the online booking Vigil had made with his phone. Arriving well ahead of them, he used an altered version of benzodiazepine of his own design on Cassie, the girl manning the front desk. A small scratch on the back of her hand rendered her unconscious for nearly an hour. While she was out, Ankh had time to find the perfect room for Vigil; place the poisoned candy on their pillows and be back at the desk to check them in.

Under normal conditions, Vigil would probably have recognized him, but over the years Ankh had become an expert in theatrical prosthetics and make up. Much of what he learned, he picked up while he was in California. For a while, he worked at a major motion picture studio. Ankh could also alter his appearance at will, just as Vigil could. The thick accent could have been a giveaway, but Vigil was immersed in his role too; and part of being believable involved a fair amount of suspension of disbelief. When Cassie came out of her stupor, she had no memory of Ankh or even of being unconscious. In fact, there were no ill-effects from the drug at all. Waiting nearby at a fish and chips café, he saw Vigil walk briskly to the apothecary and he knew the candy had not done its job. That pleased Ankh. He really didn't want his cat-and-mouse game to be over. It would have been a simple task to go back to the hotel and dispatch Jillian, but he had other plans in mind. Simply poisoning her would not be nearly satisfying enough.

* * *

The medieval village of Zothmara in the Southern Carpathian Mountains existed in the shadow of fear and dread. It could be said that the villagers were blessed and cursed at the same time. They were cursed in that death was always near at hand because of the monsters that lived in the mountains. They considered themselves blessed in the sense that they never failed to show those close to them how much they were loved.

Vigil met with the elders of the village as had been arranged by his host, Anton. Grief and foreboding lay heavy on them because the other villagers were looking to them for salvation. Vigil quietly and assertively let them know what they were up against, while he skillfully avoided informing them how he knew. Eradicating the threat was not going to be easy and it was certain that some of them were going to die. A few of the villagers felt they had little to live for anyway and volunteered for whatever dangerous tasks might be asked of them.

"The monsters you seek to destroy are brothers," said Vigil. "They will not fall easily or without sacrifice." He bowed his head and took a deep breath. "If there was any other path, it would be the one I would choose. One of the brothers will need to be parted from the rest. What can you tell me about their activities?"

"We know little," said Anton. "They only come to our village at night. We don't even know what they look like." The elders of the village dropped their heads and beat their chests. Despair and disappointment were old companions of them. Then a small voice behind the men spoke up.

"I know what they look like," said a timid maiden as she came forward.

"You are not to be here," exclaimed one of the elders gruffly. "This meeting is for the elders of the village only. You shall be beaten for this!"

"Let her speak," said Vigil. "...and she will NOT be beaten. Not if you want my help." The girl, who could have been no more than twelve, stood in the circle formed by the elders.

"I have seen at least one of them at dawn more than once," she said meekly. "The one I saw was no monster as we imagine monsters. He was just a man. He looked like any other man in the village, except..."

"Except what?" asked Vigil softly.

"Except for his eyes," she responded. "His eyes were full of hate...and lust. Blood trailed from the corners of his mouth; and that day, my friend Betta was found in the square. Terrible things had been done to her."

"Go on," said one of the elders, remembering his obligations to the village.

"The man loaded sacks of supplies on his horse," she continued. "That didn't happen every time; only when they came on the night of the new moon."

"What need would monsters have of supplies," asked one of the other elders. "Are we to believe what this child says?"

"As she stated," said Vigil. "They are men; exceptional men, to be sure, but men nonetheless." Then he spoke to the girl in a soft whisper. "Why were you out of your house at dawn? The village streets are perilous in darkness." The girl leaned close to Vigil's ear and spoke very softly.

"Sometimes I meet with a friend," she whispered. "Our kind of friendship is forbidden." Vigil nodded, touched her face and then turned to the elders.

"She has spoken truth," he declared firmly. "Her word is not to be doubted." A few of the elders started to protest, but halted when Vigil held up his hand. "It is a time for action; not debate." The elders didn't like that they were being upstaged by a girl and they liked it even less that Vigil had not shared what she had said to him; but they were at a loss as to how to handle the problem, so they gave in. The meeting with the elders was concluded and Vigil spoke to each of them privately in their own homes. Some were given specific instructions, while others who were less trustworthy were given passive tasks to perform. One of the less trustworthy was Petru.

A couple of the elders had confided in Vigil that they did not trust Petru. He was given the task of keeping watch on the north road out of the village. As soon as he was out of sight of the village square, Petru ran into the woods to where he had tied his horse earlier. Two of the men from the village were waiting for him there. After extracting a confession from him, they left him there...buried in a modestly marked grave. His head had been removed from his neck and placed between his feet. That was done to prevent his body from rising from the grave and vexing the village. He wasn't suspected of having a supernatural nature, but the villagers weren't taking any chances.

They returned with Petru's confession. It had been his intention to inform the brothers of Vigil's plan in hopes of receiving a huge reward. Vigil had suspected as much. Several hundred years of dealing with people had taught him how to read the signs of betrayal. It was no great loss to the village, or even to Petru. Had he reached the brothers with the plan, they would have killed him themselves; and the villagers were much more merciful than the brothers would have been, but only by a little.

The night of the new moon brought one of the brothers into town; right on schedule. Yachin road to the edge of the village and tied up his horse. He was an exceptionally large man with a grip of iron. He preferred to ravish young girls with tiny frames. No one knew how Yachin tracked the girls down, but he always came to the right house when they were at their most vulnerable. Vigil had counted on that. As large as Yachin was, he moved as silently as a cat. The villagers who accompanied Vigil were not aware the man had even entered the house until he was almost upon them. Vigil had heightened senses and watched as the big man crossed the humble dwelling toward the place where the girl was sleeping. One of the villagers panicked and darted too early. Yachin grabbed him by the neck and crushed it in his hand. The villager's head fell over like a thistle with a broken stem.

As Yachin turned to face another villager who had come forward, Vigil brought an axe down on Yachin's head, splitting his skull. Two of the remaining villagers cheered and one of them fainted.

"We are sorry that we lost Tiberiu in the trap," said an elder. "…but at least, it's over."

"It's not over until we do what needs to be done," said Vigil gravely. "There is a ceremony that needs to be performed."

Vigil knew that Yachin's wound would heal. He didn't know for sure how long it would take. Some of his brothers healed faster than others. Two of the most trusted elders helped Vigil carry Yachin outside and throw him over the back of a horse. His blood had already clotted and did not leave a trail on the ground. Vigil bound his hands and feet just in case he would revive and brought his own horse around from behind the house. He and the two elders rode off into the forest to the south of the village. There, deep in the woods, they found the grave they had dug earlier. It was very deep and surrounded by a few fairly large rocks. Vigil unrolled a skin on the ground and handed tools to the elders.

"First," he said, "We must sever the head from the body." Vigil swung his axe just as Yachin's eyes opened. The elders fell back, frightened by the sight. They would have run off blindly into the dark forest had it not been for Vigil's courage. He held up his hand to reassure them and then continued. Yachin's eyes glazed over as his head was lifted from his shoulders. Vigil laid it upon the ground and placed a wedge of silver in Yachin's mouth. Then he drove the wedge the rest of the way in with the flat side of the axe.

"The next step is to make sure he doesn't rise from the grave," said Vigil.

"He is strigoi?" The elder's voice was broken and weak.

"You could say that," said Vigil. "Help me drag him into the hole." One of the elders helped Vigil drag Yachin's body by the arms while the other elder carried his head in outstretched arms. He was being careful to avoid the mouth at all costs. He did not want to become one of the undead creatures himself. Vigil smiled when he saw him. Nothing was going to turn the elder into what Yachin was, or what Vigil was for that matter. Still, he played along.

"Place the head between the feet. Now for the most important part," said Vigil. He took a long iron stake, about four feet in length, and drove it into Yachin's chest just above his solar plexus. Then, using the flat side of the axe again, drove it through his body and two feet into the ground below. Just to be safe, he drove a similar stake through the head. Then the men pushed the heavy stones into the grave, crushing the body. The final parts of the task were the fill the grave in with dirt and cover it with fallen leaves to conceal it forever.

The three men rode back to the village in silence. None of them regretted what they had done, but they knew the others would be coming. The brothers would torture the villagers until they got the information they wanted. The elders and Vigil were committed to their tasks. The only way out now…was through.

* * *

"I haven't seen an extraction team, so I guessing the little tart is still alive." Ankh spoke softly but menacingly into his cellphone. Calling Vigil's room had not been part of his plan or even recommended; but his twisted nature wouldn't let him do otherwise. "I had hoped you would be the one writhing in agony as the poison coursed its way through your system; but I guess that would have been too much to hope for."

"I knew it was you," said Vigil over the phone. "I recognized the poison you used. I should have finished you in the Carpathians."

"Now, is that any way to talk to your brother? Besides, I went on to make quite a reputation for myself there. The Turks never knew what hit them." Ankh loved to gloat.

"As I recall, they put an end to your reign there," said Vigil.

"I let them think they did," said Ankh. "I was getting bored; impaled people are such whiners. It gets old after a while."

"So why the visit? You have usually kept your distance from me since Romania."

"Why don't you call it by its proper name?" asked Ankh. "Transylvania."

"Two reasons," said Vigil. "One, that wasn't where we were; and two, I won't give you the satisfaction."

"Quibbling over trifles. That's SO Vigil," said Ankh with a terrible schoolgirl impression. "I was very proud of the impact I had on history…and the cinema. Oh, and to answer your question: you were getting too close. Zariel Hart and I were closer than the others. We were like-minded in many ways. Seeing him killed was like watching myself be taken down. And yes, I saw the whole thing."

"Why didn't you do something about it then?" asked Vigil.

"Because it would have been too merciful," said Ankh. "Have you learned nothing from the stories? I really like to make my enemies suffer."

"As well as innocents, from what I have read," said Vigil.

"There are no innocents!" Ankh took a moment to collect himself. "People fall into two categories. They are pawns or obstacles. Either way, they are expendable." Ankh waited for a response, but didn't get one. He was bored anyway. So he finished with, "Enjoy your little treat while you can. We'll see each other again soon. Or rather, I'll see you!" He resisted laughing maniacally and hung up.

Vigil had used his laptop during the call to triangulate Ankh's location. He was less than a block away, but there was no use chasing him. Ankh was a skilled runner and even qualified for the Olympics a few decades ago. He may or may not have been a member of the Black September group in 1972. Vigil didn't hate a lot of people, but Ankh was an exception.

Vigil watched the blip fade on his laptop screen like a shadow in the fog. He rested his arms on his knees and dropped his head. *Maybe it's time to quit*, he thought. *They are getting worse and the world is getting worse with them.*

"Who was that?" Jillian's voice was childlike even when it was raspy. Vigil thought it was adorable, but he didn't show it.

"That was the piece of... That was the individual who left the chocolate on your pillow." Vigil pulled the chair back over to her bedside and sat down. "How are you feeling?" he asked softly.

"Better," she said. "...but my throat is still sore. Can I have some ice cream?"

"In the morning," said Vigil. "Right now, you can have some more water."

"How about some ice chips?" asked Jillian.

"That I can do," said Vigil.

The night was long and sleepless for Vigil. He started every time Jillian softly cried out and could only imagine what she must have been dreaming. He knew all too well of the pain she was experiencing. He had been poisoned many times before. Several times, when poison had attacked his liver, he had been reminded of Prometheus in Tartarus. Vigil wondered if Prometheus might have really existed and was one of his kind.

The stories about Scotland's inclement weather seemed to be myths to keep tourists away as the sun rose on a bright morning. Jillian tapped Vigil lightly on the forehead with her index finger like a child waking a parent on Christmas. She didn't want to startle him because he might kill her by accident. He had fallen asleep just before dawn and could barely make his eyes focus as he forced them open. Jillian's angelic face was once again framed in glowing ringlets of blond hair.

"You promised me ice cream," she said. Her words were stern but childlike.

"For breakfast?" Vigil rubbed his eyes and looked at his watch. His head fell back on his pillow, so Jillian continued to poke him in the forehead, harder this time.

"Okay, okay...I'm up." Vigil sat on the edge of the bed. Under his breath, he reminded himself of what Ernest Hemingway said. *Always do sober what you said you'd do drunk. That will teach you to keep your mouth shut.* He hadn't been drunk the night before, but the saying seemed to apply anyway.

"You knew Hemingway?" Jillian thought she was joking.

"I met him a few times," said Vigil. He wasn't joking. "Let's go get that ice cream."

They found Jillian's ice cream in a Turkish restaurant of all places. Vigil thought it was just a little ironic and a bit disturbing, considering his recent chat with Ankh. She had Italian *Creme Glacee*...strawberry and chocolate. Vigil had the Mediterranean breakfast which consisted of eggs, spicy sausage, tomatoes and cucumbers with feta cheese. The restaurant usually didn't serve ice cream at such an early hour, but they made an exception for Jillian. People always made exceptions for Jillian it seemed.

Ankh didn't usually keep *mortals* alive for very long, but he too had made an exception for Jillian. Vigil had become attached to her, so she had ceased being an obstacle and had been promoted to pawn. From his perch on top of a low building across the street, he positioned the scope of his sniper rifle so that the crosshairs were perfectly centered on Jillian's temple. As she licked the strawberry ice cream from the back of her spoon, Ankh pulled the trigger.

Chapter 11: Crosshairs

Ankh was an old hand at measuring wind speed and had made the proper adjustments to his high-powered scope. He held his breath and smoothly squeezed the trigger as he let it out. There was a sharp report from the barrel of the rifle. Shattering glass created secondary projectiles as the jacketed hollow-point found its target. The exit wound was as large as a fist, and the wall of the restaurant was transformed into a Jackson Pollock painting. There was a momentary pause in the restaurant as the realization of what had just happened sank in. The young girl flew back and then forward in reverse momentum, smashing her head on the table before toppling it over. She involuntarily convulsed on the floor as her brain functions erupted with synaptic overloads before shutting down. The patrons of the restaurant panicked as a second louder report was heard from across the street. The young girl's companion fell over backwards as the projectile penetrated his skull.

Ankh quickly disassembled his sniper rifle and packed it away in its unassuming briefcase. He would have done the job for free, but he was getting paid for this one. The second victim was just a bonus. The girl was his real target. She was the daughter of a South American Ambassador who was being uncooperative about releasing certain classified information; information Ankh didn't need to know about. He had been hired to do a job and the details were unimportant to him. It didn't even matter if the action was effective in precipitating the desired result. The regime would probably change in a year's time and there would be a whole new roster of players. By then, he would be in another part of the world looking at someone else through a sniper scope. It would get more difficult to travel with a rifle in later years, but in 1979 it wasn't a problem. Ankh would adapt. He was very good at adapting.

* * *

Ankh held his breath and smoothly pulled the trigger as he let it out. There was a light machine click as the firing pin plunged into the empty chamber. Killing Jillian from across the street would be too easy. He had considered firing a rubber bullet just to make a point, but he didn't want his targets to be that cautious. Just because he wanted a challenge and satisfaction didn't mean he wanted the job to be too hard. The little girl had ripped his shoulder to shreds and the healing hurt like hell. He was whole again, but he was going to make her pay dearly for that eventually. Ankh wanted to get Jillian away from Vigil and take her up north to a desolate area he was familiar with. This time of year, the trees would be devoid of foliage and a layer of fog would be resting just above the ground. Color would drain from the landscape at certain times of day and everything would mimic scenes from *The Hound of the Baskervilles*. Her terror would be exquisite; Ankh would see to that. So would her long agonizing death.

* * *

Vigil didn't like feeling exposed, and he hated having any sort of vulnerability. That was one of the reasons he avoided relationships. Another was that it was getting harder to lose people he loved to the ravages of time. Several times, he held women he had loved as old age took them from him. Vigil had loved them for decades and would not have traded their time together. But having to watch them die was something he no longer was willing to do. Jillian was more like the daughter. He might have had a few offspring around the world, but he had always tried to be careful. Still, accidents happen. He knew about four boys who

112

were his sons. Two led unassuming lives somewhere in Europe and Indonesia the last he heard. They were born with Vigil's unique regenerating ability and coped with it well. One son did not inherit it and died during the Battle of Hastings in 1066. That was a dark time...both for the world and for Vigil.

His youngest son, Aristide, took the dark path. He didn't start out that way. Early in his youth, he followed strong religious beliefs and would have been a great philosopher in his own right. However, he began to stray from the straight and narrow when his beliefs were ridiculed by the clergy. One of his discourses sought to define the real meaning of *good* and *evil*. The Church believed in a literal translation of the *Tree of Knowledge*, while Aristide took a different view. He professed that the story was allegorical for how intelligence developed in man. He believed morals and the interpretation of good and evil came about as a result of man learning that there were consequences for his actions. An act that was committed for the sake of an individual without consideration for the impact it would have on others became the definition of Evil. An act that took others into consideration in a positive way defined Good. The Church opposed the ideas because they removed any form of deity from the equation and elevated man to the level of God. Aristide was burned at the stake for heresy. He barely survived, but he was changed.

Aristide made it his mission to vanquish the self-serving false teachers of organized religions. His actions were calculated and surprisingly just. He began to hunt down those clergy members who placed moral or religious burdens on the people for their own gain. The richer the church, the more likely they were to show up on Aristide's list. Of all the parables in the New Testament, he followed one specifically:

> *The kingdom of heaven*
> *is likened unto a man* that *sowed*
> *good seed in his field: but while*

*men slept, his enemy came and
sowed tares among the wheat,
and went his way.*

*But when the blade was
sprung up, and brought forth
fruit, then appeared the tares
also.*

*So the servants of the
householder came and said unto
him, "Sir, didst not thou sow
good seed in thy field? From
whence then hath it tares?"*

*He said unto them, "An
enemy hath done this." The
servants said unto him, "Wilt
thou then that we go and gather
them up?"*

*But he said, "Nay; lest
while ye gather up the tares, ye
root up also the wheat with them.*

*Let both grow together
until the harvest: and in the time
of harvest I will say to the
reapers, Gather ye together first
the tares, and bind them in
bundles to burn them: but gather
the wheat into my barn."*
— Matthew 13:24-30

Aristide's interpretation was that the wheat in the story
was the honest word and the tares represented the deceit of
organized religions. He made it his mission to remove as many
of the *tares* as he could find. Sometimes he followed the
scripture to the letter and bound them in bundles to burn. The
irony always made him smile.

Vigil couldn't bring himself to *resolve* Aristide. While his actions may have been somewhat skewed, his motives could be considered noble in a demented sense. In Aristide's clouded view of justice, he was doing the world a favor and defending the meek. When he was able, Vigil did what he could to deflect Aristide's assaults on the churches and restrict his movements. Aristide vanished in the early twentieth century and Vigil could only hope he had given up his crusade. He didn't allow himself to believe that someone had eliminated Aristide. For all his faults, Vigil still loved him.

* * *

Vigil had seen the shadowy figure on top of the building across the street. He knew he and Jillian were in no immediate danger. That wasn't Ankh's style. He thought he detected the reflection of sunlight off of a sniper scope; but if he did, it would have been intentional on Ankh's part. Ankh didn't make mistakes like that. There were too many ways to remain concealed. No, he was just reminding Vigil that he could have killed Jillian any time that he wanted and there would be no way for him to prevent it.

Vigil had eaten only a few bites of his breakfast and sat staring into his small cup of rich Turkish coffee. It was practically strong enough to chew, but Vigil enjoyed it. He wanted Jillian to go away so she would be safe, but didn't know how to approach her about it. Technically, she was on assignment. That would mean making a lot of explanations to her superiors when she went back. Jillian sat eating her ice cream in a contemplative way. She too was deep in thought and observers might have guessed that the couple was embroiled in a father-daughter spat that had stalled. She put down her spoon and placed her childlike hand on top of Vigil's.

"I can't go with you to Lochgelly," she said softly. Tears were forming in her eyes and Vigil was a bit puzzled.

115

He didn't know how to react. This was exactly what he wanted, but he hadn't been sure how to approach her about it without sounding mean.

"Why is that?" he asked. "I thought part of your assignment was to keep an eye on me."

"I am causing you more trouble than good," she answered. "Things have gone downhill since the *tube* in London. You can't protect yourself while you are trying to protect me. Besides, I have a plan."

Vigil let out a slow imperceptible sigh of relief before speaking.

"What is your plan?" he asked.

"It's best if I keep that to myself," said Jillian. "Let's just say that according to my reports, you are headed to a major metropolitan city in Europe and I have to observe you there. After a few days, you will give me the slip and I will have to return home."

"I appreciate what you are doing," said Vigil. "…but I have to ask why?"

"I am not frightened by very much," said Jillian. "…but I am not used to being the victim. It is important for me to always be in control of a situation. I no longer think that I am and I feel as though I am being hunted. I am even getting paranoid about it. I was sure I caught a glimpse of a sniper a few minutes ago. I need to shake it off and I can best do that by changing locations. I would ask you to come with me, but that wouldn't do any good. We would still be stalked. Besides, I know you have a job to do."

"If that is what you feel you need to do," said Vigil. "…then I am fully in favor of it. I will miss you though."

"Oh, come on," said Jillian. "You can't hit on the ladies with me around. I have been cramping your style. I know how you are."

"Now wait a minute..." Vigil stammered. Then he stopped. She was kind of right. It wasn't as if he was on the prowl for companions, but he didn't turn them away very often either. That is, unless there was something suspicious in their behavior. Vigil was a little saddened by the prospect of parting from Jillian; but he knew she was right and it was exactly what he wanted. He could handle the brothers in Lochgelly...and he could handle Ankh; but even if he couldn't, it would still be easier than having Jillian around as a distraction. With her in Europe, he would have a level playing field, which was the only advantage he needed.

"I have something for you," said Jillian. "It's kind of a going away gift."

"But I didn't get you anything," said Vigil. Jillian never failed to puzzle him.

"This is work-related," she said. She slid her linen napkin across the table to him. When he felt the weight of what was wrapped inside, he lowered it under the table before looking at it.

"This is your gun," said Vigil. "It's the Five-seveN you used in London. Why are you giving it to me?"

"It has a feature your gun doesn't have," she said. She slid an unmarked box across to him as well. "These shells have been specially designed to my own specifications. They contain tracking chips that activate when they have been fired. There is a small drive in the box for your phone. The app will allow you to keep track of people you shoot if they don't die. You seem to have a problem with that."

"I don't know what to say," said Vigil.

"You don't have to say anything," said Jillian. "Just stay alive."

"I will do my best," he said. "…but what are you going to do for a gun?"

"I have more guns than I let anyone know about," said Jillian. She flipped her hair to the side like a *valley girl*. "…and I know lots of places to get them when I need more. I'll be fine."

"I know you will," said Vigil.

They finished their breakfast and Vigil was much more relaxed for the rest of the meal. He paid the check and they went back to the room to collect their things. They paused in awkward silence for a moment before Jillian stood on her tiptoes and kissed Vigil on the cheek. They embraced for a long time as if she were his daughter going off to college. Then she picked up her bag and left without another word. Vigil had no idea how she would make her travel arrangements or where she would go, but that was the way she preferred; and it was how he would have done it. He collected the rest of his own things and prepared to leave. He checked the room three times to make sure he didn't leave anything behind. No matter how little he brought with him, it was something he always did.

Vigil checked out of the hotel even though he didn't really have to. There was no way they would ever be able to trace him, but he did it as a courtesy. Rather than rent a car, Vigil chose to buy one. Dealerships usually had salespeople who had been with the company for a long time and were less likely to be imposters. He found a previously owned black BMW for just a little over £7,500, but Vigil was able to talk them down to £7,000 even. Money really wasn't an object, but he didn't want to stand out by paying the asking price.

The distance to Lochgelly from Edinburgh was only 37 kilometers, but Vigil filled the tank in Queensferry anyway. The last thing he needed was to be stranded on the side of the road. Once there, he would find a place to stay without making a reservation. Hopefully, there would be an inn or bed & breakfast where they wouldn't ask too many questions.

The drive took considerably longer than anticipated due to congestion on the Forth Road Bridge. Vigil sat in heavy traffic and was glad he bought a vehicle as comfortable as his BMW. As the traffic slowed to a stop, he stared out the window at the Firth of Forth: an estuary of the River Forth that emptied into the North Sea. Technically, the waterway is a fjord formed by the Forth Glacier during the last glacial period. The Vikings called it *Myrkvifiörd* when they crossed the North Sea to raid and pillage monasteries located there. Vigil was not part of any of those raiding parties, but his relatives had been. Many of the stories he had heard told of brutal psychotic behavior. Vigil knew enough about Vikings to know that most of the stories were made up. While they were brave and sometimes vicious warriors, they possessed a code of conduct and pride. He lived with a tribe a long time ago and admired their ways and belief systems.

In the distance, Vigil saw a boat crossing the Forth. He wondered if it was the proposed hovercraft passenger service that was supposed to ease traffic on the bridge. He suspected by the lack of progress he was making that it was not. He leaned back in his seat and closed his eyes. A car horn would surely alert him if traffic began to move. In his mind, he imagined the glacier slowly cutting its way through the landscape...carving out the coastline as delicately as Michelangelo carved blocks of marble into masterpieces. Vigil liked warmer climates, but cooler climates had their charms. The BMW's heater made the interior of the vehicle toasty warm. He nestled into the plush leather seat and shivered slightly with contentment. He folded his arms and began to dream. He felt the soft animal pelt that seemed to clothe him and was transported back in time.

Vigil looked to his left and his Viking hunting party

was crouched low, preparing to take down a stag. The stag was beautiful...nearly white with a twelve-point rack of antlers. It seemed a shame to kill it, but the Vikings would make sure it would have a noble death. Nothing would be wasted, and their feast would be fit for Valhalla. The stag must have heard one of them. It straightened up and put its nose in the wind. Something had alerted it. It sprang for the woods and was gone before a single arrow could be nocked. Then Vigil heard what had startled the stag. In the distance, a battle horn sounded. His own village was being attacked. He turned to run and many of the hunting party were already ahead of him. As they got closer, the horn sounded again. Then there was a tapping.

"Haur, wake up an' move yer crease, thes is nae parkin' lot." A tall man in overalls tapped on Vigil's window again. He wasn't completely sure what the man had said, but it probably had something to do with his choice of rest areas. He waved back at the man and shifted into drive. The man continued to talk in his heavy brogue with words that Vigil suspected were mostly obscenities. He thought of Jillian's reaction to the dialect when they checked into the Cairn hotel. He was reminded that the hotel clerk had been Ankh. Vigil drove on with greater purpose.

Chapter Twelve: Plunder and Pillage

Adriel and Zuriel were also sons of Lazarus. They were twin brothers, but nowhere near identical. Adriel was tall and thin. One's first impression of him would be that he resembled a stereotypical undertaker in the Old West. His drawn face seldom smiled except when he was exacting some form of torture on an innocent victim.

Zuriel was much shorter and had a stocky build. His legs were too short for the trunk of his body, so his clothes had to be tailored to his frame to be stylish. Most times, he didn't worry about it. He wore a long black leather duster that concealed his lack of style; as well as a wide selection of weapons.

They had been a part of a Viking clan about the same time that Vigil was in that part of the world. Vigil's clan was some distance from theirs and their paths never crossed back then. There was so much carnage going on during that era, Vigil had no reason to suspect they were in the area at all. In addition, news travelled slowly back in those days and it would have been difficult to distinguish their particular *modus operandi*, even if he had been looking for it.

As the traffic thinned and he continued across the Forth Road Bridge, Vigil knew the brothers had been among the Viking raiders who came to the Scottish shores several centuries back. In his mind, he gave them nicknames in order to make it easier to *resolve* them when the time came. Not that it would be difficult anyway, but he needed every edge he could get. Applying nicknames was a way of depersonalizing them and keeping his conscience clear. If he started to feel good about the killings, he believed he would be just as bad as they were. From that point on, he only referred to them as

Plunder and *Pillage*.

Lochgelly was a quiet little town with a quaint ambience. It could easily be mistaken for a movie set on some Hollywood back lot. Vigil liked it, but his hope of finding a bed and breakfast or some other kind of lodging was quickly waning. Lochgelly wasn't a popular tourist destination and most of the residents liked it that way. It had been a mining town for over a hundred years, but that all came to an end in the Sixties. If there were any hotels in town, they didn't advertise very well.

Vigil found a pub on one of the town's main streets. It was a decent looking place and seemed friendly. He ordered a pint of Guinness at the bar and sat down in a plush leather seat next to a low table. The pub might have had a long history, but looks can be deceiving. The heavy wooden beams that decorated the ceiling looked like many he had seen over the centuries. It didn't matter if they were authentic or not; Vigil sat back and enjoyed his pint.

The pub wasn't very busy, so Vigil struck up a conversation with the barmaid as he ordered a second pint. Her name was Leslie and she had raven hair and ruby lips...just like in the song. Her eyes were the color of emeralds and her complexion like ivory. He was lost looking at her for a moment because she reminded him of someone from his distant past. No matter how hard he tried, he couldn't think of who it might be.

"I know," she said. "I remind you of someone, right?" She only had a hint of the Scottish brogue, so Vigil was pretty sure she had labeled him as a tourist. He didn't mind. He felt like a tourist no matter where he went in the world. Nothing was the same as it used to be and wouldn't remain as it was.

"Would there be a place nearby where I could get a room for a few nights?" he asked.

"There are a couple of establishments a few miles away," said Leslie. "...but if you are looking for someplace within crawling distance of the pub, I am afraid you are out of luck."

"That *is* what I was hoping for," said Vigil. He smiled at Leslie and her expression softened ever so slightly.

"I don't know why," she said. "...but you strike me as a trustworthy fellow. I may know someone close by who might be willing to take in a boarder for a few nights."

"That would be excellent," said Vigil.

"It might be expensive," said Leslie. "...and you would have to be on your best behavior."

"I swear," said Vigil. "Solemnly." Leslie looked skeptical, but amused.

"Alright then, come back here around two and we will go over the details," she said. "And don't be getting too drunk or mother won't let you stay."

"Mother? You are talking about your mother's house?" Vigil controlled an impulse to stammer.

"Didn't I mention that," said Leslie. "...must have slipped my mind. Yes, my mother's house. Actually, it's a *semi-detached*. I think in America, you call it a *duplex*. It's on a lovely quiet street not far from here. We can walk there if you like."

"That sounds perfect," said Vigil. It wasn't exactly what he wanted, but he didn't have a lot of options at the moment. He took her hand gallantly and thanked her for her help. She held on to his a little longer than seemed normal. Once he paid his tab, he left to explore the town until two o'clock.

Lochgelly was much less rural than Vigil had imagined.

The streets were relatively busy and there was a lot to see. He wondered where *Plunder* and *Pillage* had found lodgings, but then he considered their natures. Most likely, they murdered some poor woman on the outskirts of town and were occupying her house. With as big as the town was, it wasn't going to be as easy to find them as he had thought.

Vigil had mixed feelings about staying at someone's home. The lack of privacy was one concern and another was the danger his host might be in. As he walked along the sidewalk and smelled the delicious aromas coming from the Chinese *takeaway* restaurant, he considered driving to one of the nearby towns where a regular hotel room might be secured. He decided to think it over while having a bite to hold him over until later. The Chinese noodles were just as delicious as they smelled and he wished he had ordered more. Vigil got a couple of curious looks as he walked down the sidewalk eating his noodles with chopsticks. *Maybe people here don't eat out in the street,* he thought. *Or maybe they are just wary of strangers.* He smiled, nodded politely and continued to eat...purposely making a slurping sound as he did.

By two o'clock, Vigil had made up his mind to commute back and forth to Lochgelly. He returned to the pub to inform Leslie of his decision. Her eyes sparkled when she saw him and his resolution began to wane.

"Are you ready to go?" she asked as she folded her half-apron and placed it behind the bar.

"Well, I..." Vigil said.

"My mother is going to love you," said Leslie. "...and she makes the tastiest haggis you have ever eaten."

"Oh, yum..." said Vigil. "Haggis." His fake enthusiasm was pretty obvious. That fact wasn't lost on Leslie, but she played along. She hated haggis herself.

"Come on," she said. "It's not far." She took him by

the hand and led him out the door like a toddler. Vigil couldn't bring himself to protest and thought he might as well go along with it for a while. Anyway, what could it hurt to stay one night? He could always leave in the morning.

Leslie led him down a few twists and turns onto a street that seemed to have no place to park his car anyway. Some of the houses on the block had small garages, but only a few. Still, it was quiet and pretty charming. They stopped in front of a semi-detached with a low white picket fence. The small yard in front had another short fence separating it in two. Leslie led Vigil to the left side of the duplex. Once inside, she turned to face him and pressed her lips hard against his. His eyes widened and he was taken aback for a moment. That hadn't happened too many times in the past and he needed a little time to process it. While he did, she pulled his coat off his shoulders and tossed it on a chair.

"You said…your mother…here…" Vigil tried to make coherent sentences between copious amounts of kisses.

"Oh, yes," said Leslie. "We have to be quiet so she won't hear us."

"Your mother is here?" There were just too many unexpected things for Vigil to take in. "Where?"

"Not *here* here," said Leslie. "She lives in the other half of the semi-attached. But we share a wall; and if we make too much noise, she will hear us. Trust me. That makes for some uncomfortable breakfast conversations."

"I can imagine," said Vigil.

"And that works both ways," added Leslie. "There have been times when she has gotten a bit randy with her fiancé. They've been engaged for seven years or so; but they still go at it like teenagers sometimes. It's embarrassing; that's what it is."

"I will do my best to remain quiet," said Vigil. "...but I have to ask. Do you usually bring men home who you have just met?"

"I have done it before, yes," said Leslie. "...but no, I don't *usually* do it. I have a gift, you might say. I can instantly tell things about people. I can tell that you have a good heart. I can tell that people don't want to get on your bad side...and I can tell that you have an old soul. Plus, you are pretty easy on the eyes, if you don't mind me sayin'."

"I must say, I am flattered," offered Vigil. "...and you are right on most of your observations. I am not sure about having a good heart though."

"Having a good heart is not always something you can see in yourself," said Leslie. "Others have to recognize it in you. Then maybe you can see it." Leslie kissed him on the cheek and whispered, "Now...I have to be back at the pub by six and I expect great things from you." She turned and walked toward the bedroom, dropping her clothes to the floor as she did. Vigil was paralyzed by her beauty for a moment and her aggressive sexuality. Then he pulled his own shirt up over his head and obediently followed her. He had been with many women over the centuries, but this was one he would definitely remember. The two of them failed terribly at keeping quiet; and breakfast the next morning would indeed be awkward.

* * *

Vigil awakened to the aroma of hot tea. His eyes were closed and the feel of the comfortable sheets kept him in place. He imagined Leslie standing over him with the tea, wearing nothing but her inviting smile. As he opened his eyes, he was met with the inviting smile, but it belonged to a woman he hadn't seen before.

"I apologize for my daughter's lack of hosting skills,"

126

she said. "...but it was imperative that she return to work and she didn't want to wake you."

"You must be Hazel," said Vigil. He tried to keep his composure in spite of the fact that he was in Leslie's bed...and that he was naked.

"You needn't be embarrassed," Hazel said. "My daughter and I don't have too many secrets." After the romance session he and Leslie had just enjoyed, he doubted that was entirely true. Vigil took the tea that had been offered to him and thanked his gracious hostess. The china cup was floe blue and was probably vintage. The tea was just the way he liked it, with just a squeeze of lemon. Leslie's mother must have been a little psychic as well.

"This is very good," he said. "I am sorry to be an imposition."

"Yer not an imposition at all," said Hazel. "I enjoy playing hostess to Leslie's gentlemen callers."

"So there have been a lot of those then, I guess..." Vigil said.

"Not as many as you would think," said Hazel. "My daughter is pretty selective. That speaks very highly of you. I must say, you are a bit more, uh...well...um, *proportioned* than her usual beaus." Vigil squirmed a little uncomfortably under the quilt covering him. He wondered how psychic she actually was.

"I'm not psychic," she said, creating a bit of a paradox. "You were uncovered when I came in. I discretely covered you up...after a few moments." Her wide smile made him feel at ease, even though he was sure she was probably being honest.

Hazel was an attractive woman who really didn't look old enough to be Leslie's mother. Her light blonde hair was very long and a thick braid hung down over her right shoulder. It was easy to see Leslie's facial characteristics in her, but she had a personality all her own. Vigil wondered if she was going to hit on him and how he should handle it. Hazel sat down in a comfortable chair and waited for him to finish his tea. He sipped it slowly and the conversation awkwardly lagged.

"Well, this was delicious," said Vigil finally. "...and I thank you very much. I guess I should get dressed now and make my way back to town."

"You don't have to leave so soon on my account," said Hazel. "You might at least want to take a shower. You had quite the marathon session this afternoon from what I heard. Not that I mind, of course. I enjoy the scent of a good manly musk."

"I wouldn't mind taking a shower," Vigil agreed. "I am a bit self-conscious at the moment."

"Well," said Hazel. "Come this way and I will show you where the clean towels are." She stood up and waited at the door. There was another long pause as Vigil waited for Hazel to leave the room. It became apparent that she was not going to leave anytime soon, or even turn around. He wasn't too concerned. Some of the cultures he had lived in over the centuries hardly wore clothes at all compared to the current standards. He stood up and waited for Hazel to direct him to the shower and fresh towels. She paused for another moment to admire his physique.

"Have you ever thought about shooting a crossbow?" she asked absently. Vigil smiled. He knew her question was in reference to a character on a television program.

"I have shot a few," he said. "...but that was a long time ago. Even then, I preferred a long bow."

"I'll bet you did," said Hazel. Vigil was sure she

thought he was employing a double entendre, but he was talking about the *Middle Ages*.

"Well," said Hazel, snapping out of her trance. "We best be on about it; this way to the towels." Vigil followed her down a short hallway to a tall rattan wicker shelf. Various colored towels were neatly folded on the bottom three shelves and there was a selection of toiletries on the top. There was a variety of wrapped toothbrushes and razors as well that made Vigil wonder just how often Leslie had overnight guests. He didn't really care. It wasn't his place to judge, not with his own past.

"Take as many towels as you like," said Hazel. "I do the laundry around here, so I have the final say." Vigil took two large bath towels, a green toothbrush, travel toothpaste and a disposable razor. He turned and Hazel already had the shower running in the next room. By her mood and suggestive behavior, he half expected her to be undressed and in it. That thought had crossed her mind, but she had reminded herself that she was engaged. However, it didn't stop her from fantasizing about the prospect.

"There you are," said Hazel. "I'll leave you to it...unless you'd like some help with those hard to reach places."

"You are very kind," said Vigil. "...but I think I can manage." He smiled at her as Hazel gave him one more admiring glance, up and down. Then she left, closing the door behind her.

The hot water cascaded down Vigil's body, rippling slightly over his well-defined muscles. He bowed his head under the showerhead and let the water rinse his hair. The water swirled down the drain between his feet. He imagined the water becoming muddy; and suddenly he was wearing tan rawhide boots. Color drained from his mind and the scene took on a sepia tone like in old time photographs.

* * *

Vigil's blood mixed with the muddy water on the battlefield as rain continued to fall. The sky was as dark as predawn or late twilight, even though it was midday. Vigil struggled with the arrow that had penetrated his chest and dropped to his knees with the effort. An English soldier advancing through the battle line sought to finish him off by plunging a long pike into his side. The pain Vigil felt was incredible and he passed out just long enough for the soldier to conclude that the wound had been a mortal one. When he regained consciousness, the *Battle of Flodden Field* appeared to be over. Dead or dying soldiers, both Scottish and English littered the landscape as far at Vigil could see from his limited vantage point.

Once he was sure he would not be observed, Vigil gripped the arrow still protruding from his chest and ripped it out with a tremendous effort. A fresh flow of blood turned the muddy puddle where he lay into a scarlet pool. The sight, as well as the pain, caused him to nearly lose consciousness again; however, the wound healed quickly and his pain began to subside. Lifting himself up on one elbow, Vigil could see that the battle was still raging to the east. He feared for the life of the king, whom he had sworn to defend. The sky was still dark, but the rain had stopped some time before. Struggling to get to his feet, Vigil took a pike from a fallen Scotsman and used it to support himself while he recovered from his wounds. He skirted the edge of the battle in hopes of finding his commander and king...James IV of Scotland.

Vigil had advised the king against attacking England, but James was a man of uncommon bravery and honor; and had a strong sense of duty. Henry VIII had invaded France and James IV was their ally by treaty. He had hoped to take advantage of Henry's absence on the battlefield, but things hadn't worked out that way. James was determined, but reckless. He had rushed headlong into battle before giving his troops their orders. He thought it better to teach by example and would always put himself in harm's way before expecting his men to do the same.

A figure stood on a small rise, defending himself and some of his men from the advancing English soldiers. He seemed to pay no attention to some of the wounds his enemies had inflicted. His defense was so fierce that the English soldiers seemed to be reluctant to attack him. It even looked as though they were about to retreat when an arrow pierced the king just above the right kidney. James IV dropped to his knees and the English soldiers, encouraged by the attack, continued their advance. Distracted by their goal of slaying a monarch, the English didn't see Vigil slip up behind them and begin to reduce their numbers until it was too late.

With his pike under his right arm, he ran two English soldiers through while decapitating three more with a sword in his left hand. Even though the Claymore he wielded was a two-handed sword, he wielded it in one hand like a Roman gladius. Vigil was proficient with many weapons. Before the other soldiers could turn and mount a defense against him, he had dispatched most of their number. The rest elected to initiate a strategic retreat. Vigil knelt beside the king, who did not have long to live. James looked Vigil in the eye and thanked him for his advice and his service. He never admitted that Vigil was right, but he did whisper that things did not go as planned. He expired there on Flodden Field. Vigil secured a horse and removed him from the battlefield. Enemies often took the bodies of fallen leaders as trophies and he wasn't going to let that happen to his king...whom he flattered himself to say was also his friend.

The history books would say that the body of someone thought to be James IV was recovered from the battlefield.

The site of his actual resting place is still a point of contention and there are many rumors that are supposed to be true. The king had gone into battle without his royal surcoat to show his men he was willing to fight as one of them. Vigil took the body of the king to a castle northeast of the battlefield. There, he placed it in a small cave with the simple respect and dignity the king would have wanted. He had intended to remove an iron chain from around the king's waist, but knew the reason it was there; so he left it.

Vigil returned to the battlefield and heard the news that the conquering English army led by Catherine of Aragon (the Queen of England and wife of Henry VIII) had taken James' bloodstained coat back to England as a trophy. She was pregnant during the battle and went into labor prematurely. The baby boy was stillborn...once again leaving Henry VIII without a male heir.

Vigil had seen the outline of the man who had fired the fatal arrow into King James IV. It was an outline he was familiar with. The man had not been alone. The two men were nearly naked and their upper bodies as well as their faces were decorated with elaborate markings. They wore helmets of brass and one carried a round shield in his left hand and a fifteen billhook pike in his right. The other man carried a longbow and had a quiver of arrows bound around his waist. Vigil recognized them as *picts;* and their unusual markings seemed to go unnoticed in the heat of battle. Their appearance was concealed by their markings and they had adapted to the Scottish climate since the time they had arrived with Viking raiders. Still, he knew who they were. He was sorry to say that they were family. They were Adriel and Zuriel: *Plunder* and *Pillage*.

Vigil stood with a dark furrowed brow. He had hoped the brothers had given up their malevolent practices, but there they were. James IV was not the first monarch they had killed and he would not be the last. The two of them had recognized Vigil as well. They had smiled condescending smiles which seemed to place hot coals on Vigil's head; he had burned with rage as the two ran whooping and screaming away. It would only be a matter of time before he would see them again. Rain had begun to fall. It was a cold, unforgiving rain.

*　*　*

"Sorry luv," said Hazel. "...but we only have a wee water heater. I'm afraid the water's gone cold on ye." Vigil blinked back to the present. Hazel was right. The shower was downright icy. He turned the knob and stepped out onto a thick bathmat. Hazel stood there admiring him before reluctantly handing him a towel.

"Well," she said. "There's no damage done as I can see. Everything seems to be the same...uh, size as before."

"I do what I can," said Vigil. He was always flattered and a little amused by harmless flirting. He decided to throw some flirting back at Hazel. Instead of wrapping the towel around his waist, he dried his hair with it and hung it around his neck.

"Did you see my clothes around here anywhere?" he asked.

"Indeed I did," said Hazel, blushing slightly. "I took the liberty of laundering them for you. I'll fetch them from the dryer."

"I'll go with you," said Vigil. Hazel didn't know how to take his open attitude about nudity, but she didn't hate it.

"R..rright this way," she stammered. "Maybe you should go ahead and I will guide you."

"You just want to look at my butt," said Vigil.

"Well, of course I do," said Hazel. "I'm breathing,

133

aren't I?"

"Yes," said Vigil. "...and heavily."

"You're a bit of a cheeky monkey, you are," laughed Hazel.

"I can be," said Vigil. "Now, if you've had a good look...where is that dryer?"

Vigil dressed and kissed Hazel on the cheek as he left. He was no longer certain breakfast would be uncomfortable, but it would surely be interesting. His clothes were toasty warm from the dryer and his jacket had been on the back of a chair where he left it. The weight of the concealed weapons in it was almost unnoticeable. Vigil told Hazel not to wait up as he left. She gave him a shrug and a smile that he couldn't interpret. He retraced his steps back to the pub without a problem. Vigil had a way of making maps in his head. It had served him well over the centuries. His car was right where he had left it...except there was a parking ticket on the windscreen. He didn't see any posted signs, but thought it best not to make any problems. He would pay the fines tomorrow with no complaints.

Leslie was busy behind the bar and didn't see Vigil come in. The pub was busy and he suspected it was always hectic around the same time each evening. He would let Leslie know he was there in a few minutes and hoped the rush would die down soon. Vigil sat in a corner booth to wait and looked out over the pub patrons. Many of them could have stepped straight out of a Robert Burns poem. He could imagine Burns himself sitting at the bar and writing a sonnet about Leslie as she tended to the taps. She smiled at every customer as if she had known them her entire life. Some of them, she may have. She had that way about her. That was why he was alerted when the smile left her face. Two patrons had made their way to the bar and she waited on them the same as the rest; but her smile was gone and there was the slightest hint of concern in her eyes.

The two men turned from the bar in a way that prevented Vigil from seeing their faces. Leslie seemed a little relieved as they left the serving station. He would have liked to have questioned her about the incident, but the pub was too crowded. He would ask her later during their return to her semi-detached. The two men settled into a booth at the far end of the pub and huddled together. It wasn't as if they huddled in fear. It was more as if they were conspiring. Shadows covered their faces and the crowd obscured Vigil's view. He finally went to the bar to order a pint and to see if he could get a better vantage point to check the two out. Leslie seemed relieved to see him and touched his hand softly when he reached for his glass.

"Are you okay," he asked. The din of the crowd muffled his words, but Leslie read his lips.

"I'll be okay," she said softly. Her words were also lost in the cacophony of conversations. "I'll tell you about it later." Vigil looked subtly over at the two who had raised his concerns. Only one was still at the table when he did. It was possible that the other was in the WC, but Vigil didn't want to take that chance. He took his drink back to his booth where he could keep his back protected and his eye on their table. He was pretty sure who the men were. They were his targets...*Plunder* and *Pillage*; but he didn't want them to know he was on their trail. They had been easier to find than he thought.

Chapter Thirteen: Pleading for Death

Even though Vigil nicknamed Adriel and Zuriel *Plunder and Pillage*, they might have been more accurately named *Rape* and *Plunder*; but that less alliterative title didn't have the same ring to it. The title also left out a few other depictions of their atrocities. Rape, pillage, plunder, murder, torture and dismemberment were all part of their repertoire.

They had never required payment when they were hired to slaughter innocents; instead, the brothers financed their lifestyles by stealing from their victims and from plundered treasures they could find. Often, entire villages would be massacred and burned to the ground with only a few silver pieces to show for it. That didn't bother the pair. Money was only a side benefit for them. Their real satisfaction came from the deaths of the village men and the cries of the women as they satisfied their perverted lusts. The women were eventually put to death, but not until they begged for it. On rare occasions, the two would allow some of their victims to live; not because they were showing mercy, but because they had maimed them so viciously, and made them watch as their children were butchered before their eyes. Those women eventually died of their wounds later anyway. Those who did not usually wound up taking their own lives or asking someone to do it for them.

Adriel took no part in the rapes. It wasn't that he objected to it morally. It just didn't provide him with any kind of carnal satisfaction. If he gratified himself later, no one knew about it. It might have been possible that he experienced gratification during the act of mutilating or disemboweling a victim. If he did, he never admitted it. It was almost as if torturing a *lowly mortal* was a very personal, if not spiritual thing for him. He made a very effective interrogator during the Inquisition.

Zuriel, on the other hand, could have been nicknamed *Rape* or *Rapist*. However, neither of those monikers would have fully expressed the depths of his depravity. First, there was no victim who was off limits to him. He cared nothing for gender, age or body type. He would be just as likely to violate an elderly grandmother as he would a young child. Zuriel didn't even require his victims to be breathing. Often they would die during his attack and he would continue on violating them until completion. Sometimes, he would revisit some of his victims hours after they had expired. It was not unusual for him to violate a child in front of their mother, while the father lay spilling his lifeblood on the ground before them. Zuriel's behavior went well beyond hate. It was rooted in frustration and self-loathing, but no one would ever get him to admit that. In his mind, he was like a man incinerating insects with a magnifying glass.

When the two brothers came to Scotland on a Viking Long Ship, they came less as raiders and more as exterminators. The monks in the monasteries were the first to go...slowly and horribly, of course. Then, nearly anyone who resembled able-bodied men had to die. With the women, children and elderly unprotected, they took more time and tortured them more thoroughly. It didn't take long before their own Viking clan cast them out. They believed that Adriel's and Zuriel's actions were without any form of honor and that the gods would descend upon them. *Plunder* and *Pillage* believed their destiny was their own to make and that mortals invented gods to compensate for their own helplessness. They didn't mind leaving the clan. There were many villages to be ravaged in this new land. Eventually, they joined the *Picts* and acted as mercenaries after a fashion. Usually, the only thing about them that they ever changed was their garments. Their behavior was as depraved as ever.

* * *

Vigil wanted to separate Adriel and Zuriel so he could *resolve* them individually, but he made him nervous that they were separated now. He couldn't keep an eye on them when they were apart. He really hadn't expected to run into them in the same tavern he had become so *familiar* with. From time to time, Leslie would glance over at him with a worried look. Vigil wanted to give her a reassuring look back, but he didn't know if he was being watched. He thought it might be best to distance himself from her as he did with most people. But for the time being, she was probably safe in the crowded pub...as safe as anyone can be with two immortal monsters on the loose.

The FN Five-seveN that Jillian had given him rested snuggly in the concealed pocket of Vigil's leather jacket. The pub was far too crowded to guarantee a clean shot and that type of attention from the locals would virtually eliminate his chance of getting the other brother. His own P99 Walther was in another jacket compartment. The silencer was detached but could be added in a fraction of a second if need be. His tactical knife was safely sheathed in a pouch under Vigil's left arm. It hadn't taken long for him to install secret compartments in the lining of his jacket; and the light weight of his weapons made them nearly undetectable.

Vigil finished his pint of Guinness and went to the bar for another. There was another long awkward pause as he waited for a chance to submit his drink request. He used his cellphone to covertly capture a video of the pub and its patrons, stopping long enough to get a better look at his target at the far end of the room. The man sat at the table with his head bowed, almost as if he were in a state of meditation. Vigil was pretty sure it was Adriel. His brother had not returned and therefore must not have been in the W.C., or was experiencing quite a bit of trouble in there. More likely, he was out scouting for another victim in an attempt to satiate his demonic lust.

"What will it be luv," said Leslie. "...another Guinness?" Her eyes darted to the far end of the pub nervously.

"That would be excellent," said Vigil. "I expect this night to turn out very nicely." He tried to reassure her without being too obvious. She must have caught on because she softly touched his hand again as she handed him his glass.

"Expectin' to get lucky, are ye?" She smiled, but there were tears in the corners of her eyes.

"If the lady is receptive to my charms that is," said Vigil. "I have a couple of things to take care of first." He furrowed his brow and she nodded ever so slightly.

"Protection is very important," she said.

"It's the most important thing on my mind," he said. With that, he finished his Guinness in two large quaffs and sat the glass on the bar. A grizzled old man sitting near him straightened up.

"An Aussie, are ye?" he asked in a high-pitched voice which didn't seem to match his appearance.

"What makes you think that?" asked Vigil.

"The foam ring in yer glass," answered the old Scotsman. "An American will leave seven rings when he drinks Guinness. An Irishman will leave only three. An Aussie nearly always leaves one."

"What about a Scotsman?" asked Vigil smiling.

"We don't leave any," he replied. Then he laughed so hard, he began to wheeze.

"That's not always true Rabbie," said Leslie. "Drink up and leave the gent alone."

"Aam nae botherin' nobody. Thes braw chiel an' me ur jist havin' a pleasant conversation." Vigil couldn't tell if it was his brogue or if his words were slurring. He decided it was probably a bit of both.

"It's okay," he said. "I have some business to be about anyway. Enjoy your evening Rabbie." He looked at Leslie and added, "I plan to return soon. Keep my seat warm."

"You keep yer own seat warm, ya cheeky monkey." Leslie seemed to relax a little, even though Vigil was about to leave her on her own. He smiled at her and paid his tab. The two men had heightened her intuition, but Leslie seemed to know that Vigil could handle the situation. He nodded and left the pub.

The night air had an unpleasant chill to it; almost as if it was transmitting some horrible deed that had taken place or was about to. He breathed it in and the inside of his nose almost seemed to frost. When Vigil was alone in the street, he pulled his P99 Walther from its compartment and attached the silencer with a sharp click. The only target he knew the whereabouts of was still in the pub; but his intuition had been screaming to him that he needed to leave before he was recognized. His best option was to conceal himself outside the pub and wait for Adriel to leave or for Zuriel to return.

Next to the pub was a low stone wall that separated the alley from a long gated drive. The spiked wrought iron gate wasn't locked, but the hinges were in need of oil. The gate protested loudly when Vigil slowly opened it with a resounding screech. He considered leaving it open once he was inside, but knew that might alert someone to his presence. Bracing himself, he closed the gate quickly. The screech was much less obvious, but the gate clanged when it latched. *I used to be better than this*, thought Vigil. *Must be the Guinness...or the afternoon sex.*

Vigil knelt behind the stone wall, keeping watch through the bars of the iron gates. There were no windows on the north wall of the pub, so he would have to watch the entrance closely. Patrons came and went for an hour. Vigil extended his legs in front of him one at a time to ward off cramps. To make matters worse, it started to rain in a heavy mist. The falling precipitation looked like static in the streetlights and his breath became visible. He heard a flapping sound and saw a familiar figure exit the pub. Adriel hadn't realized it was raining and was hastily donning his overcoat.

The streets were nearly devoid of traffic as well as pedestrians. A warm cozy home or pub was just the ticket in this weather. Vigil would like to have been warm and cozy in either one. He jumped the stone wall rather than risk the noise from the squeaky gate and followed Adriel from almost a block away. Twice he lost sight of him in the mist that seemed to be turning into fog. He wondered if *Plunder* and *Pillage* had a car and if the other one was in it. Vigil thought it might have been possible that they both had a car and Adriel had just parked very far away. After three blocks, it became apparent that he hadn't. Since they were obscured by the weather, he considered using Jillian's FN with its viridian green laser sight; but in the mist and fog, its beam would look like a light sabre. That would probably alert Adriel, so he chose not to use it. Instead, he quickened his pace to close the gap between the two of them.

After five blocks, Adriel turned west and was out of sight for a full thirty seconds while Vigil caught up. He crouched low as he rounded the corner. The precaution probably saved him a world of hurt. A tactical throwing knife sailed over his head so close, he felt the wind from it. The knife made a cracking sound as it made contact with the window of a car parked across the street. Then the night air was filled with the whooping sound of a car alarm. Adriel turned to run, but Vigil was right on top of him. He jumped on Adriel's back, forcing him to the ground and the two men slid for at least three feet. Adriel would probably have sustained a much more severe case of *road rash* on his face if the pavement had not been so slick from the rain.

"Look," said Adriel angrily as he struggled to turn over. "...I don't know who you are or what you want, but this is not going to work out well for you!"

"I *do* know who you are," said Vigil. "...and I was about to say the same thing to you. You just stay like that on the ground for right now. How does it feel to be the one in the submissive position for a change?"

"Who are you, you son of a bitch?" Adriel spat as he talked because he was frothing at the mouth.

"Does it really matter? Knowing that won't make this any easier for you." Vigil was trying to keep calm and menacing. If he let his absolute disgust for this excuse of a human rise up, he would totally lose it.

"Make what easier?" Steam was rising from Adriel's forehead.

"Let's just say, I plan to *resolve* a couple of issues tonight," Vigil said absently. "Enough talk for now." Adriel was prepared to ask more questions when Vigil grabbed him by the hair and slammed his head into the sidewalk several times. He stopped breathing, but Vigil knew that wouldn't last. He grabbed him by the collar of his overcoat and dragged him back in the direction of the pub, avoiding the street lights when possible. It wasn't easy, and Vigil had to duck into more than one alley or doorway; but he finally made it back to the pub. His car was parked just a few doors down. It had another parking citation under the wiper. *The law must really be out to get me here*, he thought.

Adriel was placed securely in the *boot* of the BMW.

143

Vigil devised an ingenious series of zip ties to keep his prisoner immobile. The ties were made of metal instead of plastic, so trying to remove them would cause more harm than good. He wadded up a dirty oil rag and placed it in Adriel's mouth. Then he kept it there by affixing a zip tie around his head like a gag. Another tie was affixed around his throat like a choker. The two were joined together in the back and linked with a few more to Adriel's bound wrists. If he struggled, even a little, the ties would cut into his flesh and possibly sever arteries. More ties were linked together to bind his elbows, thighs and ankles. They too were linked to his wrists in a hogtieing configuration. Vigil wasn't taking any chances...except one.

The logical action to take would have been to *resolve* Adriel right then and there, but Vigil had other plans for him. The suffering this man and his brother had inflicted in the world could not be balanced by simple elimination. There was a reason that this country would be the site of their final confrontation and Vigil was going to take full advantage of it. Adriel had started breathing again, so Vigil hit him in the head with a brass hammer he had purchased at an Edinburg hardware store. He hadn't needed it at the time, but he saw it in a bin and just had to have it. Adriel ceased breathing again for the time being. Vigil closed the boot, looked around to see if there were any witnesses and then walked back to the pub.

Leslie breathed an audible sigh of relief when Vigil came through the door. Her intuition had been working overtime and she found herself imagining all of the most horrible possibilities. She practically cried when Vigil ordered another pint of Guinness, but she managed to maintain her composure for her other customers.

"One down, one to go," he said softly. Even though Leslie didn't know the situation, she sensed what he meant. They both looked over at the table the brothers had occupied.

Vigil had hoped Adriel would lead him to Zuriel, but the attack had changed that strategy.

"I have some business to attend to," he said. "I may not be able to stay the night as we planned."

"I can't explain why," said Leslie. "...but I don't feel safe. I was hoping you would stay with me. The pub is open until midnight and then I have to clean up here before my walk home."

"I can stay around until then," Vigil assured her. "Then I can take you home in my car."

"I am not afraid of a little wet weather," she said. "I am a Scot ye know."

"It's not the weather," said Vigil. "I have an errand to run."

"After midnight? Seriously? What kind of errand would you have in the middle of the night?" A few of the pub patrons began to huff and grumble with impatience while their conversation went on.

"We will talk about it later," said Vigil. The crowd was making him uneasy. "Another pint if you please." Leslie pulled a dark pint from the tap and handed it to Vigil. There was concern in her eyes, laced with worry. Vigil gave her another reassuring look. Half of his problem was solved. The other half could wait for a bit. Taking down the second target was going to be easy compared to facing the two brothers together.

Vigil sat down in a recently vacated stool at the end of the bar. His seat in the corner had been occupied and the new tenants did not look as though they would be leaving any time soon. The subdued roar of the crowd was actually soothing to him. The atmosphere in pubs seemed to be something that transcended centuries and borders. Whether he was in

Thirteenth Century France sitting next to a man who smelled of elderberries, or the Seventeenth Century American Colonies drinking stout ale with a man who would one day become one of the Founding Fathers; the atmosphere was always one of subtle belonging.

That may have been one reason Vigil liked pubs. They were like the best relationships he had been in. The warm feelings were there and he felt secure; but everybody minded their own business for the most part. That was a perfect arrangement for Vigil, when he could find it. He looked over at Leslie. She hadn't wasted any time getting intimate with him. Vigil had known that type of woman from time to time and he always felt their loss the deepest when they grew old and passed away. Of course, he could always disappear and never know what happened to them; but that was just as difficult to deal with. Still, he couldn't bring himself to disconnect from relationships altogether. Maybe that was what his brothers did. It may have been one of the reasons they chose their psychopathic ways. Vigil wanted to keep Leslie safe and that was his weakness.

"Time gentlemen…and ladies," Leslie announced. Midnight had come sooner than Vigil had expected. Time flies when one is subduing and restraining a target…that reminded him that he needed to go check on his *guest*. He finished the last of his pint and settled up his bill.

"I'm going to move my car closer to the entrance," Vigil said.

"I'd very much like to go with you on your errand," said Leslie. "I want to make sure you're not meeting up with some little tart ye met tonight."

"Your intuition would tell you if I did. That is not the case," said Vigil. "Besides, no tart could hold a candle to you."

"I know," said Leslie. "You are just a little hard to read

146

right now and it worries me. I feel there is something dangerous you aren't telling me."

"I'll go get the car. We'll talk about it on the way home." Vigil touched her hand and left behind a group who seemed to be singing a school song or something. Their accents were so thick and they were so off-key, he couldn't tell what it might be. His prisoner was just coming around when he got back to his car. Adriel had been bleeding from the eyes because of the sheer rage he was projecting and it had begun to clot. It gave him a fearsome look...like a *berserker* of centuries past.

"I suppose it would be fruitless to ask you to be quiet for the next hour or so, right?" Adriel struggled in his bonds, causing deeper cuts in his face and throat. Vigil tightened the loosened bonds and Adriel gurgled a stifled scream. His eyes blazed with hatred and he was already plotting horrible forms of retribution for his captor. Vigil was sure Adriel wasn't pleading to die; but if all went as planned, he would be by tomorrow.

"I will give you a little time to think about it," said Vigil. Then he struck Adriel in the temple with the brass hammer. The light went out of his eyes as quickly as turning off a light switch. Vigil closed the boot and made sure he didn't have any of Adriel's blood on him anywhere. He parked in front of the pub and waited for Leslie. The lights of the pub went out and she came out immediately after. Noticing the parking citations on the windscreen, she began to laugh.

"You must have made an impression on Nigel," she said getting in.

"Nigel?" asked Vigil.

"One of our local constables," said Leslie. "He and I dated a few times. He thought it was more than something physical. I enjoyed it, but he was just someone to pass the time

147

with. He doesn't usually issue parking tickets. You must have made him very jealous."

"It's not the first one I got today," said Vigil. "He must really hate me."

"Well," said Leslie. "I wouldn't go breaking any serious laws. It probably wouldn't go well for you; if you know what I mean."

"I will try to be careful," said Vigil. He wondered what Leslie would say about the body that lay bleeding in the boot of his BMW.

Vigil's mental map failed him on the way back to Leslie's duplex. He hadn't navigated it at night and he wasn't in his car during the day. Plus, it had been quite an emotional evening. Leslie helped him find it and he would be ready for the next time...if there was a next time. He pulled next to the curb in front of the duplex and Leslie leaned over and placed her hand on the inside of his thigh.

"Are your errands really so important that they can't wait?" She kissed him under his left ear and he shivered uncontrollably.

"I really need to attend to this," said Vigil. "Besides, there's no place to park."

"What do you call this?" asked Leslie.

"I didn't think I could park on this street," said Vigil.

"That's only on a couple of days a month for the street sweeper," said Leslie. Vigil didn't really want to make the long trip he was planning. With another application of the brass hammer, Adriel should be incapacitated until morning. Anyway, it wouldn't do for him to get pulled over because of erratic driving due to sleep deprivation. In reality, he didn't want to pass up a night with Leslie, considering the mood she was in and that it might be his last night with her.

"I guess it can wait until tomorrow then. You go on in. I just need to take care of something in the boot."

"Don't take too long," said Leslie. There was something almost supernaturally sensual about her. After she was inside, Vigil made two sound blows with his hammer, grabbed his bag from the back seat and headed inside. He used his key fob to set the car alarm. Its reassuring *whoop whoop* echoed down the quiet street.

"Damned right, whoop whoop," he said. Breakfast wouldn't be awkward, but it would be interesting.

Chapter Fourteen: Exposed

Adriel wasn't dead for long. None of those who shared his unique ability died from wounds they received unless they were inflicted in just the right way. Each of their cells contained perfect blueprints for repairing themselves, even their brain cells. Memories were also backed up in countless redundant organic files. That way they didn't find themselves lost in a world unfamiliar to them when they recovered from their wounds. While their brains or bodies were mortally damaged, the children of Lazarus entered a form of self-induced coma while their cells repaired themselves. Unlike comas that mortals might experience, the children of Lazarus could dream during theirs. Oh and how they did dream.

* * *

Adriel stood at the bow of the Viking long ship and peered out at the misty horizon. The light wind blew sea spray across his face but he didn't seem to care. His eye was on the prize that awaited his raiding party on the other side of the North Sea. It wasn't the treasures housed in the monasteries he sought. He was longing to look into the faces of new victims as he extinguished their life forces.

Zuriel sat on a long bench behind him tending to his favorite weapon. It was a sword similar to a Roman spatha, except it had a longer cross-guard. The pommel, tang and cross-guard were all crafted out of one piece of metal. The tang was wrapped in an unusual color of tanned leather. It was an unusual color because it was fashioned from human skin. The sword's wooden sheath was covered in human skin as well. Zuriel remembered the hours he had spent torturing the

151

victim whose skin adorned his sword. She did not give her skin up willingly and he did not wait until she was dead to secure it. The girl's name was Solveig and she could have been no more than fifteen. While fifteen might have been an acceptable age for intercourse during that century, what he did to her wouldn't be acceptable at any age or any time period...ever. Zuriel didn't care. She could have been a hundred for all he cared. His rage and lust were for her suffering and her blood. Taking her skin was just a bonus. He actually thought she should have felt honored. He remembered her soft cries and sorrowful tears as she exhaled her last breath.

Zuriel had left her staked out naked in the deep woods for the fowl and wild animals to feast upon. No amount of pleading by her family could get him to reveal where he had left her body. Their anguish was as pleasing to him as deflowering and torturing their daughter had been. He let her family live for just that reason. They believed that without a proper burial, Solveig would rise from the dead and haunt their village as a malevolent spirit. He gripped the skin covering on the sheath and felt an erotic tremor go through his body. Zuriel had promised himself that in this new world to which they were headed, he would make his clothes from the skins of his victims. He kept that gruesome promise.

Adriel's passion was much more covert; one would never know that he ever got excited by looking at him. When snuffing out a life, he would close his eyes and experience a sweet rapture that he would never have been able to put into words. Then he would take the person's gold, silver or precious possessions as compensation for ending their meaningless lives. If they owned nothing of value, he took their children and sold them to other raiders. The levels of debauchery that those animals stooped to were too horrible to record. Adriel knew full well what terrible short lives those children were going to experience and knowing that gave him as much deviant pleasure as slaughtering people did.

* * *

Vigil and Leslie had a quiet night of passion. Neither felt that it was necessary to be quite as robust as they had been in the afternoon. Vigil was tired from tracking and capturing Adriel. Leslie was exhausted from her job and from the emotional stress she could only sort of explain. Their gentle lovemaking was more of a release valve for both of them. Afterward, they lay basking in each other's embrace while listening to the heavy rain on the roof.

"I got mental images," said Leslie. For a moment, Vigil didn't know what she was talking about. "Those men at the pub; they were horrible people, weren't they?"

"Yes, they are," said Vigil. "...some of the worst on the planet."

"Is that why you do what you do?" she asked.

"I am pretty sure I never told you what I do," said Vigil.

"You didn't have to," said Leslie. "Part of my job is to read people. I have a gift. Remember?"

"I guess you do," said Vigil. "What kind of images did you get from those men?"

"The most horrible images possible," she said. "I can't get them out of my mind."

"Would it help to talk about it?" asked Vigil.

"Maybe," she said. "...if I can bring myself to do it."

"Well, you can tell me anything," said Vigil. "This is a *judgment free zone*." Leslie kissed him softly and then braced herself before speaking again.

"When I looked at those men...and heard them

speak…" Leslie shuddered. "I saw monsters…literal monsters. Black-hearted they were…and bloodthirsty. I saw images of skin being stripped away and human flesh being consumed! I have never beheld such images in my life. It was as if evil was passed down from generation to generation in a way that isn't possible."

"They have been busy," said Vigil. "…and you are right about their being evil. There is not a shred of good in them."

"So what will you do?" she asked.

"I will do what I was trained to do," said Vigil. "…I will do what I think I was born to do." Leslie knew what he meant, but she thought better than to say it out loud. Instead, his words gave her a deep sense of security and she kissed him again before drifting off to sleep. Vigil remained awake for a few more minutes and listened to the falling rain. Beneath the pattern of raindrops, he could barely make out a rhythmic thumping. His first thought was that Adriel had regained consciousness and was struggling to escape. Getting out of a warm bed and going out into the rainy night was among the last things he wanted to do. Just as he was about to get up, the thumping became louder. Vigil placed his hand against the wall and felt the vibration in time with the thumping. *Hazel's fiancé must be here for a visit*, he thought. *Good for you Hazel.* The combination of sounds and subtle vibrations lulled him to sleep as he felt the most rested he had been in months.

Leslie slept so quietly that Vigil had to check to make sure she was next to him. Then he checked to make sure she was breathing. He had experienced some horrible things in his past and always needed to be prepared for the worst. Leaning in close, he could barely make out her breath. It was as soft as a kitten's purring. Vigil kissed her on the forehead and she stirred slightly. Her eyes opened just enough to indicate her half-conscious state. She kissed him with *morning breath* that would have put most men off. Vigil hardly noticed. Many hygienic concepts such as mouthwash and deodorant were relatively recent developments of the last century. If he was to be honest, her breath made him just a little nostalgic. She drifted back off to sleep and he pulled her close to him.

Vigil wasn't quite sure how to handle his present predicament. He couldn't leave Adriel tied up in the boot of his car forever; but he didn't want to leave Leslie unprotected while he dealt with the matter. Zuriel was still nowhere to be seen and was undoubtedly looking for his brother by this time. Vigil could be completely honest with Leslie and that might be the best route to take. She possessed uncanny intuition, so lying to her would probably be futile anyway. He could just disappear into the night as he often did. That idea dissolved like morning mist when he felt her fingers lightly trace his abdominal muscles and then begin to move farther south. Vigil closed his eyes and prepared to receive a morning treat.

"Best be finishing him off quickly there luv," said Hazel. "We'll be having *bangers and mash* this morning and it will be ready soon." She lingered longer at the door than was necessary and Vigil wondered how long she had been there. He also wondered if she was going to stay for the whole performance. Hazel grinned widely as she turned to leave. "Me mum will be having breakfast with us this morning," she said from down the hall. "No need to get dressed on her account though." She cackled slightly as she left.

"Good morning," said Leslie sleepily. She kissed Vigil passionately and whispered, "I best be about it then. I don't want to disappoint me mum."

"I am not sure that is a good idea," said Vigil. "She could come back at any..." A serious amount of blood left his brain and he was powerless to continue his sentence. At that

155

moment, it wouldn't have mattered to him if Leslie's entire family was watching them from stadium seats. Vigil may have been nearly immortal, but he was human...and he was a man. His mind was only operating at the brain stem level at the moment and he gave no thought to the individual who was probably agonizing in the boot of his BMW. The fog suddenly cleared from his mind as he fought to remember what day of the week it was. It would not do for his car to be towed in because of street cleaning.

He jumped out of bed, startling Leslie and ran to the front door to check the street. Vigil breathed a sigh of relief when he saw the curb lined with other cars. It was then that he noticed the woman standing in front of the semi-detached. Her eyes were wide, but not shocked. She stood admiring Vigil's naked physique, especially his level of arousal which had not quite subsided.

"Mornin' *Bishop*," she said chuckling. Vigil moved behind the door, smiled awkwardly and waved. *I guess I will be flashing this whole town before I leave*, he thought. Living in societies that didn't wear clothes was a lot different than being the only one naked in a crowd. By the time he returned to the bedroom, his mood had faded and he began to get dressed.

"Is everything alright luv?" asked Leslie. "I thought maybe I had scared you off."

"Everything is fine," said Vigil. "I was just worried about my car."

"You Americans and your automobiles," she said. "I will never understand your obsession with them."

"I should warn you," he said. "One of your neighbors got quite an eyeful just now. I hope she isn't going to cause a problem for you."

"You're not the first one of my gentleman guests to exit my home with his kit off," said Leslie. "I threw a couple of them out the door myself. Lying bastards, they were. Besides, you probably gave her a little excitement in her life. It's pretty dull around here."

Leslie dressed quickly and kissed Vigil passionately before leading him next door for breakfast with the family. He stopped for a moment to make sure all of his weapons were secure and fully functional. They were almost to the door to the other half of the semi-detached when he suddenly said, "You go on in. I have to check something in my car."

"Again with the car," said Leslie. "As I said, you Americans…okay, be quick about it. We shouldn't keep mum waiting. She will want to know all about last night." Vigil's mouth dropped open.

"You really need to learn to tell when I am putting you on," laughed Leslie.

"You shouldn't be so good at telling lies," said Vigil.

"That's what makes me popular at my job," said Leslie.

Vigil waited until the door closed behind Leslie before popping open the boot of his car. Adriel's eyes were bloodshot and his head was obscenely swollen. He was most likely experiencing a brain hemorrhage and the pain was excruciating. Unfortunately, it probably wouldn't kill him unless his metabolism had changed. At least it had kept him quiet. Vigil decided to forego another blow to Adriel's temple. Unlike his prisoner, he wasn't a monster. He closed the boot and looked around cautiously to make sure he hadn't been observed; then he went into the house.

Hazel's home was quirky in a way that Vigil liked. Items like the salt lamp, crystals, assorted talismans, candles and dragon figurines made him feel as though he was in the presence of a medieval sorceress. A gentle scent of incense drifted through the air. His mind almost drifted back to the Dark Ages. Then someone called from the kitchen.

"Are ye just gonna stay out there? Would ye like us to bring ye a plate?" Hazel was being her usual facetious self.

"I'm on my way," answered Vigil.

"There ye are at last," she said. "I'd like to introduce ye to me mum, Jackie."

"Oh, we've met," said Jackie. Her smile bordered on salacious. "He was taking the *Bishop* out for some morning air I believe just a wee bit ago."

"Oh?" Hazel's eyes widened. "Gettin' familiar with me mum are ye?"

"I...am very sorry," stammered Vigil.

"Oh, my dear. No need to be sorry," said Jackie. "You made my day. My week even."

"Would ye be more comfortable if we all had breakfast in the nude?" asked Hazel. Her eyes glowed with mischief.

"Mum! That's enough," said Leslie. "You're making Vigil uncomfortable. Besides, I'm not ready to share him...yet."

"Alrighty dear," said Hazel. "...just havin' a bit of fun. I am a little disappointed in ye though. I thought I taught ye the importance of sharin'."

"Mum!"

"I'm sorry," said Hazel laughing. "Here, sit down and have something to eat."

Vigil had not known how interesting breakfast was going to be; and it was a little more uncomfortable than he had expected. He hadn't expected to be the only male at the table. Hazel's guest must have left before dawn. Vigil decided to be discrete and not say anything about the noises he had heard the night before. Jackie looked at him as if she was undressing him with her eyes. She probably was, and she had a lot of information to work with. Leslie placed her hand on his thigh under the table and he had a literal knee-jerk reaction. He hit the underside of the table with his knee and nearly upset the tea service.

"Sorry," she said. "You can relax now. I think we are done." Vigil smiled. He could handle people trying to kill him. He could also handle executing his targets and doing *wet work*. This was a whole new experience for him. If he was being honest with himself, he really didn't hate it.

The bangers and mash were delicious and the conversation got less awkward by the end of the meal. Vigil had business to attend to and needed to talk to Leslie alone. Hazel hated for them to rush off, but Jackie suspected that *business* was just a code word for having sex. It wasn't…this time.

It may have seemed that Vigil was being more casual than he should be for someone who had abducted someone, tortured them and was keeping them captive in the boot of his car; but this wasn't the first time he had done it. It was his job and he did it well. Sure, he got a lot of satisfaction from it sometimes. Sometimes he didn't. Sometimes, there would never be enough retribution for the crimes his brothers had committed. Vigil was torn between leaving Lochgelly without a word, or taking Leslie into his confidence. He had been honest with a few people before and he had a pretty good instinct about who he could confide in. Leslie was someone he trusted, but he couldn't really say why. It might be the fact that he didn't want to leave her unprotected. Getting *acquainted* with her family hadn't helped.

159

They went back to Leslie's semi-detached and she took it as a cue to get undressed. Vigil stopped her, even though he would have loved to continue with her idea.

"We need to talk," said Vigil.

"Oh no," Leslie replied. "I was afraid this would happen. You're pregnant, aren't you?" She coped with her nervousness by using humor.

"I want to take you into my confidence and I need for you to remain calm," said Vigil. Leslie got serious and feared he was about to say something terrible. She wasn't worried he would tell her that he was a criminal or even that he was married. She was afraid he would tell her some fantastic lie and expect her to believe it. Above most things, Leslie hated being lied to. It was the worst form of disrespect.

"Let's start with an easy confession," said Vigil. "First, I am older than I look."

"That doesn't sound all that serious," Leslie said. "You just have good genes."

"You have no idea," said Vigil. "Second, I do work for the government."

"I suspected," she said. "Which government?"

"The U.S. government...at the moment," he said. "The work I do is sanctioned, but is the type of work you won't see in the news or online."

"I have had blokes use lines like that who were trying to get into my knickers," she said. "...but since you've already been there and done that, I can't imagine that you would make anything up. Are you going to have to kill me now?"

"I would never," said Vigil. He knew she was joking, but still didn't even like to hear the words coming out of her mouth. "I trust you. That is why I am telling you."

160

"Do you have a card or a badge or something?" she asked. "I trust you too, but I would just like to see it. This is kind of exciting."

"I don't work for the type of agency that gives out identification," he said. "I am more like an independent contractor…with the emphasis on independent."

"It's a good thing I have amazing intuition," said Leslie. "It would be really easy to doubt you otherwise."

"I do have some specialized equipment," he said.

"I'll say you do," said Leslie. She smiled and raised an eyebrow.

"Don't get me off track," said Vigil. "This isn't easy."

"You were going to say *hard enough*, weren't you?"

"Now stop it," said Vigil. He was having a difficult time not laughing. This was almost as bad as proposing marriage. "Okay, here is the last thing. I have a body in the boot of my car." The color drained from Leslie's face. Her mind was adrift in a whirlpool of emotions. If Vigil was telling her the truth, she couldn't fathom how she hadn't picked up on it sooner. If he was lying, she wasn't getting that vibe either.

"I don't expect you to believe me," said Vigil. "That's why I am going to show you." The whirlpool suddenly stopped spinning and her mind filled with a white light. This was a totally new experience for her.

"Come on," he said. "…but prepare yourself. This is going to be pretty sick." Leslie followed Vigil out of the house and to the back of his car. He opened the boot just a crack and Leslie was struck with an awful odor she wasn't familiar with. She concluded that it was what dried blood smelled like when mixed with vomit and urine. She was right on the money and the resale value of the BMW had probably dropped significantly. Vigil opened the boot the rest of the way and Leslie's eyes looked upon a sight as horrific as the smell.

Adriel's swelling had gone down some, but not much from the last time Vigil had seen him. His face had healed around the metal zip ties and fresh cuts had appeared around his mouth. Adriel's bloodshot eyes were masked in dried blood and they were looking directly at Leslie. The shock to her senses was too much for her stomach and she threw up her bangers and mash on the curb. It was a good thing the street cleaner would come by the next day. She began to dry heave and Vigil helped her back into the house after closing the boot.

Vigil placed a cold compress on her head and helped her relax.

"Why...why would you do something like that?" she asked.

"He is a bad man," said Vigil. "...a very bad man. He has done things so horrible that I dare not tell you about them. Just know...there is no punishment I can dish out that he doesn't deserve."

"You didn't tell me he was still alive," said Leslie. "You said you had a body in the boot."

"I am not sure you are ready for that part of the story," said Vigil.

"There's more?"

"I'm afraid so," he said. "Quite a bit. I can tell you about it, but I really need to get on the road. I have a lot to do today. I was wondering if you would go with me."

"To do what?" asked Leslie. Her tone was a bit accusatory.

"I need to dispose of the body," said Vigil. "I can explain everything on the way."

"You want me to be an accessory to murder? I'm not going to do that!"

"It is government sanctioned," said Vigil. "Your hands will be clean...figuratively anyway." Leslie was silent for a few moments.

"I can't tell if you are lying," said Leslie. "I usually can, but you are a mystery. My instincts tell me you are telling the truth, but this is just too incredible. I'll admit, something about you has always seemed a bit off. I should refuse, just for my own safety."

"It's for your safety that I want you to go," said Vigil softly. He told her of the events the night before and that the man in the boot of his car was one of the men who had troubled her in the pub."

"He didn't look the same," she said. "...but, to be fair, I didn't get a good look at him last night."

"His brother is still here in town somewhere," said Vigil. "If he knows we have made a connection, he will come after you to get to me."

"What about me mum," said Leslie. "...is she going to be alright?"

"There's no reason to think he should make any connection to her," answered Vigil. He hoped he was right. Adriel and Zuriel were vicious, but they were not known for doing their homework on victims. Still, the sooner they could leave town, the better.

"Okay," said Leslie. "I will go with you. I trust you, but that's not why. There are just too many questions I want answered. I want to know everything."

"I will tell you everything," said Vigil. "...but you will need to have an open mind. A *very* open mind."

163

Chapter Fifteen: Bogged Down

A major problem with existing for more than a thousand years is processing the vast quantity of accumulated knowledge and memories. The average person would be overwhelmed by the staggering number of traumatic events that Vigil had experienced in his lifetime. His siblings and many of their offspring experienced the same thing and they all dealt with it in the same way. Memories and information were compartmentalized in their brains in an efficient and enviable filing process that theoretical physicists would kill for. It was as if each period in their lives was a life all in itself; a *past life*, if you will. It wouldn't do for Vigil to be constantly haunted by the tragedies and losses he had experienced over the centuries. Maybe his siblings were. Maybe that was why they lost all sense of compassion for humanity.

If Vigil had not been capable of keeping his memories in check, he would have destroyed Adriel at his earliest convenience. Plagues, accidents and congenital problems had taken many people he loved from him. Those things, he could deal with. They were facts of life and he had no control over them. It was the atrocities committed by his own brothers that filled him with rage. They were some of the worst offenders in the history of the world. After committing some of the worst acts mankind had ever known, they managed to fake their deaths and start fresh in a different part of the world.

Vigil had *resolved* many individuals in the past. He preferred to do it without witnesses if possible. This was why it was important to keep his personal life separate from his professional life. However, sometimes the two crossed paths and conflict was unavoidable. It might have been avoidable this time, but there was something different about Leslie.

* * *

The last time Vigil travelled to the Southern Uplands in Scotland, the road was little more than a game trail. The sky was a blanket of dark winter clouds that threatened to snow at any moment. He had a thick beard back then. It was the color of rust and was additionally tinted by the blood of his enemies. He rode a large draught horse which would one day be an ancestor of a Clydesdale. It pulled a *travois* bearing a lifeless body wrapped in an animal skin. Blood had seeped through the buckskin around the face creating a hideous stain resembling a death mask. Their destination was an isolated peat bog to the northwest. The region was cold and seemed to have perpetual cloud cover. Some of the rocky hills were nearly impassible if one did not know where they were going. Vigil knew exactly where he wanted to go.

Some of the narrow passages through the hills were very steep. Even the horse wasn't sure of his footing. More than once, the leather ties that bound the body came loose and it rolled off of the travois. Vigil hadn't noticed right away and had to go back some distance to retrieve it. The corpse seemed heavier than it should have been, but maybe he was just tired.

The conflict he had just come from had been going on for months. Calling it a conflict was a bit of a misnomer. Vigil had been battling warriors of several nationalities who had invaded the land from different directions; each for their own reasons. They were not a collective, nor did they have a common goal. They were just trying to occupy the same region for their own gain.

The body on the travois was different. It was one of Vigil's kin. Vigil didn't know he existed, but his traits were

166

unmistakable. It wasn't just his physical appearance; it was something about his countenance. Vigil could tell this man had lived so long that he had no respect for human life. He had no use for love or caring because in his mind, he was going to live forever. The lives of others meant nothing to him. People were inferior. They were obstacles...they were insects to be crushed beneath his thumb.

His name was Staak. Vigil didn't know the origin of the name or much about the man himself; but he had seen the carnage Staak had left in his wake. His main targets had been babies and children. He saw humans as weak, so he saw their children as something less than parasites. Staak brought terror and torment to every village he passed through. Often, hunting parties were formed to capture and put an end to him; but they were to no avail. Staak was too smart, too strong and too immortal to vanquish. Each time they tried, he returned their ferocity on them tenfold.

Vigil caught up with Staak right after one of his rampages. He managed to subdue him while Staak was still drained from the carnage he had inflicted in battle. Vigil had focused on his quarry and ignored the dead and dying all around him. If he had allowed himself to be distracted, it might have given Staak the edge he needed to escape or to turn the tables on him. Instead, Vigil was able to temporarily slay Staak and bind him in a rawhide shroud fitted with iron bands before he could revive. He then wet the rawhide so it would contract around his body as it dried, reinforcing the bonds. Several times, Staak had awakened and yelled curses and obscenities at Vigil. Each time, Vigil halted his horse, dismounted and calmly smashed Staak in the side of the head with a blacksmith's hammer. The last time he did it, Staak had suddenly turned his head. Vigil knew he had probably taken out all of his prisoner's front teeth. He couldn't tell because of the shroud over his face. A second blow had the desired effect of squelching his protests.

Vigil was tired when he finally reached the blanket bog he was looking for. It was remote and desolate. The vegetation around it looked petrified and what few trees there were had died long ago. A layer of fog gave the setting a surreal quality which was both intriguing and unsettling. Vigil set about to accomplish his task and leave as quickly as possible. He didn't want to remain in that loathsome place any longer than he had to.

* * *

If Leslie had been like most other women, she would have been certain she wouldn't be returning from the journey. But then, most other women wouldn't have gone along with Vigil in the first place. Leslie's phenomenal intuition had served her well in the past and continued to do so. The longer she was around Vigil, the more she trusted him; so she sat patiently in the passenger seat and waited for his explanation.

Vigil went over things in his mind for a long time. He was giving himself a headache because of the mental conflicts he had going on. It wasn't that he didn't want to tell Leslie the truth. It was that the truth was so fantastic, he was sure she would think it was a lie. Not just any lie mind you; a lie insulting to her intelligence. After they had been on the road for nearly an hour, he took a deep breath and a hard swallow.

"Please don't be angry with me for what I am about to tell you," he said. "...and know right up front that I am not crazy."

"I'll be the judge of that," said Leslie. "...but I'm waiting."

"I told you I was older than I look," he continued. "Well...almost two thousand years older." Leslie's expression was hard to read. Somehow it was comprised of amusement, doubt, disappointment and bewilderment all at the same time. She wanted to be angry, believing she was being played as a fool; however, her instincts told her that Vigil was telling the truth, or at least what he believed to be true.

"I can show you evidence," he said. "...but we are a bit pressed for time and demonstrations tend to hurt quite a bit. I will show you when we get to our destination...I promise."

"What is our destination?" she asked.

"We are headed for a location I know of," he said. "It's remote and secluded; one of the worst places on the planet."

"Oooo...just what every girl wants to hear when she's out for a drive." Leslie's casual attitude helped Vigil relax a bit and his headache abated. "So...tell me more about your life," she continued. "You must have a few adventures you can tell me about with two thousand years of living under your belt."

"Not quite two thousand," said Vigil.

"Seriously? You are going to tell me you are sensitive about your age?" Leslie folded her arms and huffed. There was an awkward silent moment and then they both burst out laughing. Vigil relaxed and realized he had been just a bit defensive about how old he was. It made him feel better. It meant he was human and not one of the monsters he hunted.

"You are right," he said. "I guess it is kind of silly. I also guess I am kind of nervous."

"What have you got to be nervous about?" she asked.

"I am afraid you aren't going to believe me," Vigil said. "It's important that you do. It worries me if I tell you some of my history, you will not believe it and never believe me again."

"I am trusting you on faith at the moment," responded Leslie. "I will take what you say the way I would treat a legend. It might be true. It might be exaggerated. If it's a good story, I don't mind if it isn't one hundred percent factual."

Vigil wasn't quite sure how to take that and he didn't know how to continue. There was so much he could tell her and it all ranged from incredibly boring to unbelievably fantastic. He planned to start off with something in between, but Leslie interrupted him.

"Have you met anyone historically famous?" she asked. The question took Vigil off guard. Answering that question would lean more in the direction of the fantastic. Vigil wasn't used to relating those accounts and he wasn't sure how authentic he would sound.

"I guess I should start at the beginning," he replied.

"Always a good idea," said Leslie.

"You have probably heard of my father."

"Really? Your father is famous?" Leslie seemed genuinely excited.

"Pretty much," said Vigil. "He lived in a town called Bethany. His sisters Mary and Martha lived there too."

"Are you talking about Lazarus?" asked Leslie. "...from the Bible?" Her multiple emotion expression was back.

"I guess you've heard of him," said Vigil.

"Yes," said Leslie. "I've been to Sunday school once or twice. They never said anything about him having children."

"Not everything gets recorded," he said. "It was a time of Roman occupation and a lot of things got shuffled around. Lazarus had a lot of kids and they scattered to the four corners of the earth. I was born on a small Greek island in the year 116

170

by the Julian Calendar. I was born on *Leap Day*, so technically I am only four hundred and seventy-five years old."

"Well," said Leslie. "If you are lying to me, you are certainly committed to the part."

"When you hear the rest, you will know that I am telling the truth or certifiably insane," Vigil replied. "Maybe a little bit of both."

"Maybe a lot of both," said Leslie. "Pray, continue."

"I left the island when I was about twenty-two in human years. My father wanted me to stay because he trusted me. He, like you, had good instincts about people and he knew I was less likely to stray from the right path the way my brothers had. I had seen how a couple of my brothers had behaved on the island and their attitudes about humans with normal lifespans. Since I was only in my early twenties, I could relate to the humans, but also to my brothers. My own mortal wounds had healed miraculously, unlike the other inhabitants of the island.

"Word came from the outside world of others who I knew to be my siblings. Some had committed unspeakable acts for no reason other than bloodlust and rage. I felt compelled to find them and reason with them if I could. My father knew it would do no good, but I was young, inexperienced and determined. I sailed to the mainland on a merchant vessel and arrived in Athens about the time of the death of Emperor Hadrian in Baiae. His death was a shame because I had heard so many good things about him and would have liked to have met him. I even worried one of my brothers had caused his death; but it was suspected that his heart failed him.

"I travelled to Rome where I found two of my brothers heavily involved in gladiatorial combat. Gladiators in Rome were not always as they are depicted in the movies. Even noblemen would compete sometimes and gladiators were treated like sports legends. They very seldom fought to the death because they were worth so much as entertainers. One of my brothers, Vanaerus fought to the death in spite of the wishes of the crowds...and the senators. When he was banned from the arena, he took vengeance on those who banned him. Then he simply changed his appearance and returned to the arena as a new combatant. I guess I should mention that we can change our appearance at will if we need to."

"My goodness," said Leslie. "*That* could be interesting...especially in bed."

"I'm being serious here," said Vigil.

"Oh...and I'm not?" Leslie raised one eyebrow. Vigil smiled and said, "Well...maybe we can explore that later. Be thinking about what kind of change you want me to make; but remember, it takes a lot out of me to do it. So you might have to do most of the work."

"Just my luck," said Leslie. "Still...I'm game. Just don't judge me."

"Well you just piqued my curiosity," he said. "I am not sure I will be ready for that."

"Oh, don't worry luv," she said. "I will make it worth the effort. Now, go on with your fantastic story."

"I waited for the gladiatorial games to be over and followed Vanaerus back to where he was staying. It surprised me that it was the Temple of Bellona. Bellona used to be a goddess of war in Rome. That made sense for a gladiator. Near there was a nondescript dwelling that was really a brothel. That was where I confronted Vanaerus. He was lying on a bed being, uh...tended to by four naked concubines"

"Concubines?" asked Leslie skeptically.

"Well...prostitutes," Vigil answered. "I was trying to be polite."

"I am not shocked by prostitutes," said Leslie. "I've even entertained the thought..."

"You've what?" Vigil swerved on the road and Leslie burst out laughing.

"You are so easy," she giggled. "Two thousand years old and you are that gullible?"

"You said you were a good liar," he said. "I guess you are."

"Who said I'm lying?" She burst out laughing again.

"Anyway...the conversation with Vanaerus was uncomfortable on many levels," continued Vigil. "...but while his actions were less than commendable, they were not really criminal. He had no intention of changing his ways. As far as I know, he never did until gladiatorial contests were banned."

"So who was one of the famous people you knew," said Leslie. "I've never heard of a gladiator name Vanaerus. Wait, he wasn't Spartacus, was he?"

"No...not at all. Spartacus was from a period long before I was born. I guess I got distracted by my own memories. Let me think of any of the notables I knew."

"When did we leave the main road?" asked Leslie. "This landscape is so bleak. I don't believe I have ever been around here before."

"It is going to get bleaker before we get to our destination," said Vigil. "It will make this look like a paradise by comparison." Leslie looked out at the scenery and sighed softly.

"Okay...famous people," said Vigil, trying to lighten

the mood. "Uh…have you ever heard of Vlad Tepes?"

"Vlad Tepes? Vlad the Impaler? The Prince of Darkness? You knew Dracula?"

"I am pretty sure we were related," said Vigil. "After a few hundred years, it's a little easy to lose track." He shared the story of the village of Zothmara in the Carpathians. He almost got to the interesting part when a horrible thumping came from the boot of the vehicle. Vigil cursed under his breath and looked for a place to pull over. He got out and after a few exchanged expletives from the back of the car and a couple of sharp thuds, they were back on track. The road became nearly nonexistent but Vigil's extraordinary sense of direction guided him to his destination.

It was just past midafternoon when Vigil halted the car. It had gone as far as it could go without sinking into the soil. The region hadn't changed at all from the last time Vigil had been there; and that had been centuries ago. The sky was overcast and as dark as late dusk, yet the sun wouldn't go down for a few hours. He retrieved the lifeless body from the boot of the car and began dragging it through the damp terrain. He did so without a word and Leslie wasn't sure he wanted her to follow. She looked around at the forsaken landscape and decided she didn't want to be left alone there. She was glad she had worn sensible shoes. Heels would have sunk into the ground and been impossible. She would have found herself walking barefoot in who knows what.

Leslie was surprised that the surrounding area smelled only a little. Peat bogs produce very little oxygen, so there is only a small amount of decay evident. That didn't make the walk any less uncomfortable. It was just one less assault on the senses. Vigil seemed to be effortlessly dragging the body to what she suspected would be its final resting place. If she had let it, her mind would have torn itself apart. Emotions conflicted within her like arguing family members at a holiday dinner. Instead, she placed all of her emotions in a closet inside her head and observed the events taking place as an objective observer.

After ascending a small rise, a flat area about the size of a cricket field came into view that appeared to be completely devoid of vegetation. Had Leslie been alone, she might have continued to walk forward on the lifeless piece of ground. Vigil walked cautiously to the edge and knelt down. As he did, sunlight out of nowhere shimmered across the surface of the bog and then was gone. Leslie could have walked straight into the bog without knowing it. It wouldn't have been very deep, but she would have smelled to high heaven on their return trip to Lochgelly. Vigil seemed to be kneeling next to a couple of branches sticking up from the bog or its bank. It was hard to tell in the light. Closer inspection revealed that one of the branches looked like a fist carved out of wood. The smaller one looked like the hilt of a sword.

"Do you want to tell me about this," asked Leslie. "...or is this one of those things I'd be better off not knowin'?"

"There's no point in keeping secrets from you now," said Vigil. "The gentleman in the bog was called Staak. I am not sure if he had any other names. Trust me when I tell you he was a terrible person and got, or is getting, what he deserves. I won't go into some of the horrible things he did. They are the types of things one never forgets."

"So this is his fist? That's a real person?" Leslie stepped back without thinking.

"Yes it is," Vigil answered. "This bog did a good job of mummifying him. I am not sure he is actually dead though. I've been fooled before. I plunged a sword into his chest for good measure and it still seems to be intact."

"So this is what you have planned for...our guest

here?" asked Leslie.

"Absolutely," said Vigil. "...and he deserves a lot worse, believe me."

"I think you are right," said Leslie. "I got that feeling the first time I saw him."

"I really love and admire your intuition."

"You are too sweet," said Leslie. "So can we get on with this? This place is horrible now. I can't imagine what it's like after dark."

"What? I thought we would camp here," said Vigil. "I was gonna make s'mores." The bog suppressed his attempt at humor the way it suppressed the exchange of oxygen and carbon dioxide.

"I know you think you are funny..." Leslie replied. The rest of her sentence caught in her throat when Vigil jammed the sharp end of the tire iron into Adriel's eye. Then he stirred it around vigorously to scramble his brain. It was pretty unceremonious, but Vigil didn't think Adriel deserved ceremony. His victims usually didn't receive any. Leslie couldn't breathe. She had never seen anything like that before and definitely nothing close to that being committed by someone she had just slept with. It was a side of Vigil she didn't know existed. It didn't worry her, but she would look at him differently from this point on.

Vigil slid the now permanently lifeless body into the bog. A layer of peat moss formed over the surface, erasing any evidence it had ever been disturbed. An uncharacteristic wind blew across the bog and Leslie thought she heard the slightest hint of music being carried aloft on the air currents. It might have simply been the wind howling through the dead branches of long dead trees, but she could have sworn it was the sound of bagpipes; specifically, the Black Watch. More than likely,

176

the disturbed bog had raised up a mixture of decay into the air that was acting as a hallucinogen. This was what she was going to tell herself anyway. Vigil remained silent as he tried to recall as many of Adriel's victims as he could. It was his way of honoring them and putting them to rest in his own mind. It only helped a little, but at least it was something.

"Okay," said Vigil. "Fair is fair. I said I would prove my claim. I need you to kill me now."

"You need me to what?" Leslie's eyes widened.

"Don't worry," said Vigil. "I won't stay dead. Here. Just shoot me in the chest." He reached out with his automatic pistol.

"You are out of your mind," said Leslie. She refused to take his gun.

"I will only be dead for an hour or so," he assured her.

"Okay," she said. "Let's think this through. If you are lying and I kill you, I will be stuck getting back by myself. I am not sure I know the way. If you are telling the truth, I am still stuck out here by myself for over an hour. I don't want either of those."

"Well, I am not sure what I can do then," said Vigil.

"Look," said Leslie. "If you are lying, this whole day has been an elaborate ruse. I can't imagine anyone would go to this much trouble. After all, I don't have a lot of money and we have already slept together. So what reason would you have to lie to me? I am willing to accept your word on faith for the time being. Can we just get out of here?"

"Absolutely," said Vigil

Much of the ride home was in silence. Small talk was difficult to accomplish after what had been witnessed. Leslie stared out the passenger window and watched the landscape grow darker, but less bleak, if that was possible. By the time they reached the outskirts of civilization, it was completely dark with small pinpricks of light on the horizon. Leslie imagined the origins of those lights being the houses of happy families oblivious to the horrors of the world. In her mind, the dwellers were having a late supper or making sure the little ones had brushed their teeth before scurrying off to bed. Sinister shadows seemed to blot out the lights. Vigil broke the long silence.

"Have you thought anymore about how you want me to change my appearance?"

"I was wondering," said Leslie. "Do you think you could become that American sportsperson, Michael Jordan?"

"I don't do celebrities," said Vigil.

"Too bad," said Leslie. "I've always wanted to do a celebrity."

"You have a wicked streak," said Vigil. "I like it. I might be able to get close."

"No," said Leslie. "I want the real thing or nothing. So I suppose Conan O'Brien is out of the question?"

"Wow…Michael Jordan to Conan O'Brien! That's quite a range."

"I like variety," she said. "What can I say?"

"I will see what I can do," said Vigil. With the tension broken, their conversation returned to normal, except it was a bit more sensual. So much so that neither of them noticed that a car had been following them for the past fifteen miles.

Chapter Sixteen: Circles of Light

There were pinpricks of light everywhere. Some were moving; some were fixed points in the night sky. There was no moon and the darkness was as thick as smoke from a coal fire. Some of the pinpricks of light blinked on and off like the illumination of fireflies in a field. As Vigil moved in the direction of the intermittent blinking, he became aware of an arrangement of monoliths. He had known they existed in the area, but had just never seen this arrangement before. Vigil had seen Stonehenge and the Ring of Brodgar, but this one was unexpected. There was no way of knowing how many such configurations existed in Britannia at that time. It would be several more centuries before many more would be discovered and their commercial value exploited by the tourist industry.

Vigil slowed his pace and crouched low to the ground. A chilly wind muffled what he thought sounded like a ritualistic droning coming from the arrangement of stones. The wind whistled through the stones and the lights flickered. Shapes moved behind the line of monoliths and proved to be robed figures. Each carried a clay lantern suspended from a length of coarse rope. The amber glow from the lanterns cast unworldly shadows on the roughly erected stones. The weather was always cold that far north, but the shapes gave Vigil an even deeper chill. He had little to fear, so it must have been because of something elemental in his nature that froze his bones.

Woven within the fabric of the droning, Vigil could make out faint moans sounding like those of a young girl or a very small child. He reached one of the larger stones and knelt behind it.   In the center of the ellipse was a wooden construction made of tree branches and more coarse rope. He suspected it was a sacrificial altar, or possibly a funeral pyre. Possibly, it was both. In the irregular light, Vigil could make out the forms of a young girl who could not have been older than fourteen, two much younger children, and an infant. The young children whimpered in a way which seemed to indicate they had been mildly drugged. The older girl cried openly with expressions of fear mixed with rage. The baby lay silent and motionless. Vigil found that to be the most disconcerting.

The group in robes had stopped moving and stood in a circle around the altar. They continued to chant in a language Vigil did not recognize or understand; and he knew many languages. The dim light revealed that most of the robes were dyed the color of dark red wine. Only one of the group wore a different color. He was probably the high priest. His robe was tan with dark wine-colored trim. Not an attractive tan, mind you. It was the color of an infected wound. As he took a bundle of herbs from the sleeve of his robe and lit the end with his lantern, the wind seemed to obediently die down as he did. He smudged the altar with the smoke from the herbs.

Vigil thought the smudging was probably to prepare the altar and the children for a sacrifice. The smoke from the herbs reached Vigil's nostrils and he almost audibly gagged.   The herb being used certainly wasn't sage and they were definitely not using cedar. The smell was hideously acrid and made Vigil's eyes water. He didn't know what was about to take place, but the horrible scent told him it was not going to be honorable. He reached beneath his jerkin and pulled out a double-edged bladed weapon. Some would call it a dagger; some, a short sword. Truth be told, it was something in between. The children on the altar began to choke because of the vile stench coming from the smudging. Even the infant began to cough within its swaddling clothes. Knowing that the baby was still alive strengthened Vigil's resolve.

The robed high priest only saw the flash of the blade a fraction of a second before it plunged into his throat. He wasn't even able to cry out before he was on the ground clutching his neck. He tried to stem the fountain of blood spewing from the open wound, but to no avail. A robed figure closest to him stood frozen by the sight. All of the figures must have taken some hallucinogen before the rite. Vigil could only imagine how they perceived the things that were happening. He swung his double-edged weapon toward the robed figure, but he was slightly out of range. Instead, the blade hit the clay lantern, shattering it. Flammable oil drenched the robe and ignited. It took the robed figure a moment to realize he was engulfed in flames. He ran screaming into the night, igniting dried grass and brush as he did. Eventually, he fell into a heap and formed his own personal funeral pyre.

Several other robed figures moved toward Vigil. He could have taken them one at a time, but a more efficient solution had presented itself. With one swift arc, he shattered all of their lanterns and they all went up in flames. Two actually tried to attack Vigil while they were on fire. He dispatched them pretty easily. The rest ran away in all directions, starting their own brush fires and funeral pyres along the way. Only four robed figures remained and they smashed their clay lanterns against the wooden altar in unison, igniting the dry branches and then they fled into the night like the cowards they were. Vigil reached through the flames without hesitation and rescued the infant. Then he cut the bonds of the other children and roughly pulled them from the altar before it was completely engulfed in flames.

The light from the fire lit up the area within the arrangement of the ancient stones. The young girl held the baby in her arms to quiet and calm it; even though it seemed unaffected by the ordeal. The two younger children, a boy and a girl, held each other for security. Vigil returned to the place where the figure in the tan robe had fallen. A large pool of blood was in his stead, with a trail of blood leading away into the night. Vigil knew it would be useless to follow the trail. It would disappear soon enough, just the way the high priest had. He went back to the children to comfort them and take them back to their village. Several centuries later, he would be in the same region...being followed by an unknown subject.

* * *

"Where are you?" asked Leslie. "You are scaring me just a little. Are you paying attention to the road?"

"Sorry," said Vigil absently. "I just had a little flashback to something that happened around here a long time ago."

"How long ago?" asked Leslie.

"About three hundred years or so," Vigil answered. "I never know for sure what triggers these memories. Maybe I am a little OCD."

"Do you want to talk about it? Maybe it might help." Leslie placed her hand on Vigil's leg.

"I am not sure it will," he said. "...but I guess I don't mind." Vigil was concerned about the headlights that were still visible in his rearview mirror. The vehicle behind them wasn't getting any closer, but it wasn't going anywhere either.

"I was searching for one of my brothers in the region," he continued. "There was word that a group of druids had arrived who had revived some of the old beliefs involving human sacrifice. Traditionally, the sacrifice involved convicted criminals and the Romans had been in favor of that. Those sacrifices killed two birds with one stone, if you'll pardon the pun. They performed executions while appeasing the gods in one form or another. However, when criminals

182

were in short supply, innocents would suffice. Virgins, children and infants were burned on altars or in effigies to insure a plentiful harvest for the coming year.

"The sacrifices were to be performed during sacred times of the year; the Summer Solstice or Autumnal Equinox and the like. I had heard about sacrifices being performed with uncommon frequency and innocents were being used, even when criminals were available. It was obvious the sacrifices were being carried out for the sole purpose of satisfying someone's perverted bloodlust.

"Unfortunately, there was no regular pattern or dates to follow that would lead me to their ritual sites. I wandered aimlessly through the landscape and talked to locals, hoping to run across some clue as to where I could find them. It was completely by accident that I stumbled upon them during a cold windy night; or so I thought. It wasn't really by accident. On some occasions, members of my family are mentally drawn to each other. If the druids had been only humans, I might never have found them."

"So you are drawn to your siblings? All the time?" asked Leslie.

"Not all the time," said Vigil. "I can't say why it works sometimes and not others. I suppose it's a good thing, or they would find me or know when I was coming after them. My brother who was leading the druid assembly didn't see me coming, but he also managed to survive my attack. He trailed blood into the darkness, but disappeared into the night. At least the sacrifices stopped; in that area anyway."

"Did they manage to kill the victims?" asked Leslie.

"No," said Vigil. "I got to them in time. The older girl suffered a couple of minor burns, but nothing serious...all things being considered. The baby's swaddling clothes were scorched, but she was unharmed." Vigil told Leslie of the

183

druids who had burned to death and the return of the children to their village.

"I still have a hard time believing people could be so evil," she said.

"They are not all evil," said Vigil. "Sometimes they are just weak-willed. They follow leaders blindly because they are susceptible to their words and promises. When you tell people what they want to hear, the weaker ones don't question the motives. They just follow blindly.

"I guess the gods really did get their sacrifice that night though, in the form of the burned druid acolytes. The year that followed did have unusually plentiful crops."

"Now you are just putting me on," said Leslie. She slapped Vigil's thigh hard with the hand that had been resting on it. The car swerved into the opposing lane for a moment before Vigil corrected its course.

"Oh...I am so sorry," exclaimed Leslie. "I didn't mean to hit you so hard."

"It's alright," said Vigil. "I just thought you were initiating foreplay."

"You are so bad," said Leslie. "Wait until I get you alone."

"That may be a problem," said Vigil. He was suddenly serious. "Our mysterious tail has decided to close the gap between us."

The headlights in the rearview mirror were unmistakable. Vigil had noted their ultraviolet blue tint when they were in the distance. He knew that kind of headlight was only standard on high-end luxury vehicles. The desolate area they were driving through wasn't home to very many well-to-do families or individuals. The hair on his arms stood up the way it usually did when he was in the presence of a member of his own genetic disposition. He had a strong intuition that Zuriel was in the car that was following them. A dark realization fell over him. In Vigil's mind, he could see Zuriel rescuing his brother from the murky bog and imagined the two of them in hot pursuit.

Vigil didn't panic; he never panicked. He forced his mind to consider the facts. If Zuriel had been in the vicinity of the bog, Vigil would have felt his presence, or at very least seen some sign of him. The area had been too remote and was devoid of hiding places. It was much more likely that Vigil picked up a tail in the last hour or so. The driver could still be Zuriel, but he probably had no way of knowing where their brother had been taken. If it was Zuriel, he would probably be fuming. It wasn't that this brother cared a great deal for anyone but himself; he just couldn't stand the thought of anyone getting the better of him. Zuriel had no respect for anyone, but no one had better disrespect him. Such is the mindset of a sociopath.

Vigil worked through the problem systematically. There was nowhere to make four right turns in the countryside. Besides, he didn't really need confirmation that they were being followed. He suspected a sudden case of *road rage* had inspired his pursuer to close the gap between their cars. At one point, Vigil thought the pursuing vehicle was flashing its lights at him. Closer observation showed the illusion to be caused by potholes in the road or by running over debris. Still, the tail was relentless. He kept a consistent distance of four car lengths between them...no more, no less. Vigil half expected a projectile to shatter his rear window at any moment. That wasn't Zuriel's style though, if the driver was indeed Zuriel. No, Zuriel much preferred face-to-face confrontations so he could glean the looks of fear and dread from his victims. He would shoot a foe in the back if the situation called for it, but not if revenge was his objective.

Leslie pretended to touch up her makeup using the vanity mirror. Really, she was watching the car behind them with much trepidation. She remained calm though. Her years of working in the pub had taught her how to keep her cool in tense situations. She kept a cautious eye on Vigil and prepared to act if he showed any sign of heightened urgency. He remained perfectly calm as if they were out for a leisurely drive in the country. That was why Leslie was caught off guard when she was suddenly thrust against the door like a child in a spinning carnival ride.

Vigil shifted into a lower gear and applied the hand brake and accelerator at the same time while turning the steering wheel sharply. The two outer wheels left the ground for a fraction of a second. Leslie had only a second to realize they were now going in the exact opposite direction of the way they had been headed. The headlights she had observed in the mirror moments before were now blinding her and they were headed for them straight on. At the last possible nanosecond, Vigil cut the car to the right and passed his pursuer within a paper-thin margin. As he did, he fired a volley of bullets through the other driver's window, shattering it. Leslie barely had time to notice the blood-spattered windows before they were a good fifteen car lengths away. With the intensity of the moment, she still had time to wonder how Vigil had lowered his own window and procured his weapon while executing a move which stunt drivers would have envied.

Vigil made a wide, slow arc and returned to their original heading. Leslie had to force herself to breathe because for a moment, she had forgotten how. They slowly drove past the wreck...smoking and steaming in a ditch just off the road. Leslie managed to find some words and string them together in a coherent sentence.

"How...when did you...what if...?" Okay, not completely coherent; but Vigil grasped the meaning.

"How did I know who was in the car? I had a feeling, a strong feeling," he said. "I knew for a long time, but more so when he got closer. As for *what if I had been wrong?* I never have been; but we can stop and check if you like. He might even still be alive." Leslie shook her head. She was glad Vigil grasped her meaning.

Vigil really wanted to stop and check. Even though he had used his specially designed bullets, he could never be sure of how effective they might be. Some of his siblings possessed denser cell structures, in addition to rapid regeneration. Penetrating their skulls was like penetrating plate metal. It was possible, but it took a concentrated effort. He didn't want to take the chance with Leslie's life. She was at risk just being along. Vigil didn't want to expose her to any more danger than he had to. If he had been successful, he would find out. If not, there would be another day. He wanted to get Leslie home and back to her normal life. Leslie knew her life would never be normal again. She would look at every stranger differently from now on.

It was in the wee small hours of the morning when Vigil pulled up in front of Leslie's semi-detached. Nothing seemed out of place and Vigil breathed a silent sigh of relief. Even with all of the abilities his siblings possessed, they couldn't be two places at once. Stress and excitement finally took its toll on Leslie. She had fallen asleep with her head bowed. A wet spot of drool had formed on her blouse. Vigil thought it might be best to simply wake her and drop her off, but the last twenty-four hours had taken its toll on him too. Her bed was calling him for more than one reason, but he took a moment to send in a report text with his phone. He heard thunder crack in the distance and soft flashes of lightning glow and fade in the west. He thought he should get her in before it started to storm. Going around to the passenger side door, he was surprised to see her looking up at him. She had the wide-eyed look of someone who wasn't quite sure they were really awake. Vigil smiled and opened her door.

"We're home sweetness," he said. It was as much cheer as he could muster.

"That...that stuff really happened, didn't it?" Leslie's voice was a little raspy.

"Yes," said Vigil. "...but it's over now."

"I am not sure it will ever be over," said Leslie. "...and I'm not sure I will ever sleep again."

"I'll take that bet," said Vigil. "Let's get you to bed."

"Do, let's..." agreed Leslie. "You really know how to sweet-talk a lass."

"I didn't mean...okay, maybe I did mean that," said Vigil. "...but I think we need some rest first."

"Not even a quickie? It might help me sleep," she said.

"Well...okay. Just to help you sleep though," said Vigil smiling.

"Cheeky devil, you are," said Leslie.

It was indeed a quickie; and they both slept soundly until midafternoon. Hazel slipped in to check on her daughter and left without waking them. Vigil dreamed of a storm; no doubt because of the actual thunderstorm taking place outside. He dreamed of men in dark coats standing in the street in front of the semi-detached. They wore hats, and the collars of their coats were turned up. The rain poured off their brims, obscuring their faces. Only their eyes seemed to be visible. They were glowing orange embers embedded in a setting of black. An image formed in front of them. As it materialized,

Vigil could see that it was Leslie. Her long hair hung down and stuck to her shoulders as the rain poured straight down. She seemed oblivious to the threats that were behind her. Looking at her, one might think she was the leader of the faceless group of threats. Probably in an effort to put the thought from his mind, Vigil started awake. Hazel was standing in the doorway of the bedroom smiling.

"I've made you something to eat," she said softly. "Would you like to get up now or would you rather wait until you've taken down your *pup tent*."

"Now who's the cheeky devil?" Vigil contemplated his aroused condition. "I think I'm too hungry to wait," he said. With that, he got out of bed and Hazel was at a loss for words, which didn't happen to her too often.

"Remember to breathe mum," said Leslie. "We can't have you passing out." Hazel let out the breath she had unconsciously been holding in.

"Are you sure you don't want to share him dear?" she asked. "I promise not to break him."

"Maybe when I am done with him," said Leslie. That joke hit Vigil a little harder than it probably should have. The dream he had just had was unclear on its symbolism; if it had any to begin with.

"For now, be off to your own chambers. I and my gentleman caller have some unfinished business to attend to." Leslie reached out for Vigil's hand and pulled him back into bed.

"I could wait just outside the door," said Hazel. "As a lady-in-waitin' as it were. You might need some assistance."

"I am pretty sure I can handle things from here," replied Leslie. "Be off now!"

Hazel feigned a huff of disgust and disappointment. She had only been bluffing, but she liked to watch her daughter's reaction and the reactions of her gentlemen. She let herself out and Leslie made good on her statement. Finishing their business took over an hour and Hazel had to reheat their afternoon meal.

Vigil took Leslie to work and took up his guardian post in the corner of the pub. He wanted to make sure none of the patrons were a threat and he wanted to keep an eye out for Zuriel. He had hoped to be finished with his business by this time, but that didn't look like it was going to happen any time soon. He hadn't heard back from his intelligence contacts about the bullet-riddled vehicle or the status of the driver. No news in this case was not good news. He might be waiting for nothing, but he couldn't take the chance.

The regular patrons shuffled in over the next couple of hours. No one stood out as a threat and Vigil prepared to leave. He wanted to investigate the town a bit more to make sure it was completely secure. As he reached the door, the brass bell mounted to its frame announced another patron. It was not a regular. This was someone new and someone Vigil knew very well.

"Disciple?" Vigil uttered. The man in the door smiled.

"No screen names, please. How have you been, Vigil?"

Vigil wasn't used to being surprised. He stammered, "I thought you were dead."

Chapter Seventeen: No Second Chances

Even the sun had no time to glint off of the polished projectile as it exited the barrel of the custom-designed sniper rifle. The copper jacketed boat-tail bullet created percussion ripples that disturbed the still air as it began its journey to its target. It travelled the distance of eight football fields in just under a second. A second is an eternity to a sniper's bullet. There are no second chances; everything has to be perfect.

Emil Traste sat on a metal park bench at midday and appeared to be feeding breadcrumbs to the pigeons. To an observant passerby, he seemed to be talking to himself. In reality, he was passing information along to a contact who was sitting on the bench behind him and to his right. Traste continued to converse even after the projectile entered his skull just above his left eye. It transected his frontal lobe and passed through his temporal lobe, causing everything to slow down in his mind. The bullet decimated his occipital lobe and made a hasty exit through the back of his head. So as not to waste its effort, the projectile came to rest in the upper thorax of Emil Traste's contact.

At the exact moment the projectile entered Emil Traste's brain, an identical one penetrated his skull on the other side...mirroring the original wound. The bullets actually passed each other as they transected both sides of his brain and made identical exit wounds. The only collateral damage the second projectile did was to a brightly colored balloon held by a small child. That bullet lodged in the trunk of a nearby birch tree and was never found. The child was never in danger in spite of her proximity to the target. The sniper was just that good. However, the balloon was just in the wrong place at the wrong time.

The sniper packed up his rifle in under ten seconds. He had designed it with several unique features, one of which was the ability to collapse quickly to become small enough to fit into a laptop case. He climbed down from his perch in the tree, straightened his sport coat and walked off toward the heart of the city like a normal junior executive. Elsewhere in the park, a double murder would be reported. So many of the details would be convoluted and the murders would never be solved. That was the way the sniper liked it. He wore anonymity like a well-tailored suit. His name was Mark. His code name was *the Disciple*.

* * *

"Are you going to buy me a pint or are you as cheap as I remember?" Mark had a charming way about him which made an insult seem like a compliment.

"As I recall," said Vigil. "…you owe *me* a pint."

The two men sat in the corner booth and Leslie brought them both a pint. It was uncharacteristic for her to do so, but she wanted a closer look at Mark. She wanted to make sure he wasn't another threat. Besides, he was tall, easy on the eyes and well-tanned in a way that was obviously natural. His dark hair had a slight wave to it and there was evidence he had frosted the tips at one point. Vigil gave her a look that others would have taken as jealousy. Leslie's intuition told her otherwise. Her own expression had softened; Vigil had not been aware of how stressed she had been until it did. She must have been grateful he had an ally for a change instead of someone who was trying to kill them both.

After Leslie went back to the bar, Vigil leaned in and spoke in low tones.

"You aren't part of the cleanup team, are you?" he asked. "That would be like using a scalpel to slice bread."

"No," said Mark. "I was in the area for another reason. I joined the team just out of curiosity. You did a number on that vehicle by the way. They never found the driver though. You must be slipping in your old age."

"Well, we can't all be like you," said Vigil. "You never miss a shot, from what I hear."

"I can't afford to," said Mark. "Speaking of shots...what's say we do a few."

"Are you crazy?" asked Vigil. "We are working; and we are in Scotland...of course we are going to do shots!" As if on cue, Leslie brought them two cocktail glasses with two fingers of eighteen-year-old Glenfiddich whiskey.

"How does she do that?" asked Mark.

"I think she reads minds," said Vigil.

"Uh oh...you should have warned me sooner," said Mark.

"Yes, he should have," said Leslie. "...and you should be ashamed of yourself, thinking such things...and thank you. They are nice, aren't they?"

Mark had a sudden rush of conflicting emotions. The apparent reading of his mind made him uncomfortably vulnerable and turned-on at the same time. He tried to stem the flow of thoughts pouring out of his mind, but found that to be impossible. He blushed, but it nearly went unnoticed because of his deep tan. Leslie noticed though, and the corner of her mouth turned up with a smile that could only be described as diabolical. Mark sought to quickly change the subject but couldn't come up with anything. Vigil perceived his discomfort and came to his rescue.

"So...no sign of the driver?" he asked.

"Driver? Oh, yeah...driver. No. Just a lot of blood. I mean a LOT of blood." Mark took a sip of scotch and savored its rich flavor. "There was no way a person could survive that much blood loss. Was there anyone else in the car?"

"Not that I saw," said Vigil. "...but I was a little busy at the time."

"Well, someone must have dragged him off. There was a trail of blood leading out a few yards and then it stopped. I figured someone must have picked them up there. That's the only explanation I can come up with."

"Something will turn up," said Vigil. "It usually does." He took a sip of his own whiskey and savored it as well. His own intuition had been on target. He knew there was no one else in the car. The driver had been one of his *own kind* and had healed enough to slink away into the night. That meant he was still out there. It might take him a while to fully recover, but he would be back. Vigil began to regret making any physical or emotional connections in this town. He hated putting innocent people in danger. It was a necessary risk though if he was going to remain human. If he couldn't connect with people, there was no point in living such a long life. Vigil's compassion ran deep.

Leslie returned to her bartending duties and there was an awkward pause in their conversation. Vigil looked out the window at the approaching dusk. Whoever the driver of the car was, probably wouldn't make an appearance this evening. It still felt like he should fear sundown because a bloodsucking monster might arise from the dead. He shook off a sudden chill.

"Can you talk about your latest mission?" he asked absently.

"Not under any circumstances," said Mark. "...so, of course I have to. What's the point of doing all this exciting spy stuff if I can't tell anybody?"

"Well of course," said Vigil. "...but just the facts. No unnecessary details."

"Program analyst...let's call him Archie, was meeting with his contact...let's call him Jughead. It was in a park in Baltimore."

"Wait a minute," said Vigil. "Archie and Jughead? Those are the best codenames you could think of?"

"Hey...I don't make the names up," said Mark.

"You just totally made them up," said Vigil.

"Are you going to let me continue with my story?"

"Pray, continue," said Vigil, shaking his head.

"Anyway...Archie was meeting with his contact in the park." Mark took another sip of scotch. "He was selling classified material to a foreign power by way of a *cyber dead drop*."

"If they were using a cyber dead drop, why did they need to meet?" asked Vigil.

"Because Archie was clever," said Mark. "He knew that even the most sophisticated encryption can be hacked; but if he delivered a backdoor key code in person, there would be no digital trail. It was a risky move and didn't pan out too well for him in the end."

"It never ceases to amaze me how you are able to fire so many shots so quickly and take out more than one target in the blink of an eye," said Vigil.

"It's all in the wrist," said Mark wryly. "Maybe I will show you my secret someday...but not today. Today, we

195

drink. Today we make our ancestors proud."

"I am not sure my ancestors were such big drinkers," said Vigil.

"Then you can make *my* ancestors proud," said Mark. "Drink up. The next round is on you."

"I think the last round was on me," said Vigil.

"I'm not drunk enough for you to pull that on me," said Mark. "...but the night is still young. I am pretty sure I bought this round."

"Actually, I bought the round," said Leslie. She had returned from the bar with two more glasses of scotch. "You two will have to fight over who pays for these."

"Vigil my boy, I think she is trying to get us drunk," said Mark. "Do you think she plans to take advantage of us?"

"God I hope so," said Vigil. He smiled at Leslie and she gave him a seductive wink.

"Am I going to have to separate you two?" she asked. Her tone was equally seductive.

"Only if you are not into group activities," said Mark. His tone was also pretty seductive.

"I will let you know," said Leslie. "It has been a long day and I might not be able to concentrate on more than one *thing* at a time."

"Where did you find her, mate? She is definitely a keeper." Mark touched her hand and she gripped his. She looked deep into his eyes and said, "I am a keeper. The problem is, no one can hold on long enough to keep me."

"That sounds like a challenge," said Mark.

"It's a challenge you won't be able to accept," said

Vigil. "You know you love your job too much to stay in one place for too long."

"That is true," said Mark. "Sorry, love. I guess it's not meant to be."

"It's alright," said Leslie. "I'm not quite ready to settle down myself. Now that Vigil has mentioned it though, what kind of work do you do?" Mark was about to use the old *if I told you I'd have to kill you* line, but thought better of it. Instead, he said, "I am a troubleshooter. I eliminate problems before they get out of hand."

"So basically, you do what he does," said Leslie. Vigil lowered his eyes as Mark looked at him with a mix of judgment and surprise.

"Yes...I guess I do," said Mark. "It's really not supposed to be public knowledge though."

"All secrets are safe with me," said Leslie. "You should hear what some of these blokes tell me when they are deep into their cups. Some things I can never unhear. I am probably scarred for life." She laughed louder than usual. It was uncharacteristic for her. She always tried to maintain a professional but reserved demeanor. Vigil laughed, but it concerned him.

"Well," said Mark. "If Vigil vouches for you, then you are okay by me. Keep me abreast of your decision about the group thing. Depending on your verdict, I might have to make other plans."

"I see what you did there," Vigil said. "Abreast? Really? Could you be any more obvious?"

"What? That's one of my more subtle moves," said Mark. He touched Leslie's hand again. "Did it work?" Leslie looked deeply into his eyes.

"I am getting turned on just thinking...about...it. Wait..." Leslie's eyes rolled back in her head and she panted heavily while firmly placing both hands on the table to brace herself. After a moment, she resumed her professional posture.

"Sorry," she said. "I had a lovely time. You were the best. Call me." She laughed all the way back to the bar muttering, "Guys are so easy."

Vigil tried his best not to burst out laughing. His best was not good enough. Mark tried to be angry, but Leslie was just too funny and too attractive. He began to laugh as well. Then they both downed their glasses of scotch and soaked in the flavor of the quaint pub. Outside, a thin layer of fog turned the streetlamps into silver puffs of light. The yellow glow from the windows of the pub was the color of melted butter.

* * *

Somewhere, miles away, Zuriel writhed in anguish in the hayloft of a barn. The isolated farmhouse in the middle of nowhere had been his only haven of refuge. His wounds had opened again and he appeared to be bleeding out on the bails of straw that comprised his makeshift cot. Over the years, his healing factor had started to take longer. It worried him like it would anyone. He was sure that he was immortal, but the way his clotting factor was acting made him realize that he might have an expiration date after all.

The bleeding finally stopped and he drifted in and out of consciousness. Zuriel was hungry, but too weak to move at the moment. In the morning, he would probably need to visit the family in the farmhouse. Of course he would murder them; but only after a good meal and a fair amount of torture. He hoped the man of the house was about his size and had at least a modicum of fashion sense. He needed clothes that were not bloodstained and bullet riddled. Style didn't really matter of course. He would take whatever he could get. He lost

198

consciousness again. This time, he slept until midmorning.

*   *   *

The Wyoming Territory was the first United States territory to grant women the right to vote in 1869. It also led the way for women to serve on juries and eventually to be elected to public office. Zuriel went by the title "Z" in those days, but most misunderstood him and called him "Zeke". He didn't care much for people in general, but he had a special animosity toward women. No one knew why. No one ever got to know him long enough to find out why.

The town of Laramie was a lawless and corrupt community. It was a perfect place for Zuriel to blend in. He actually enjoyed the fact that the brothers running the town were even more vicious and morally bankrupt than he was. He didn't own land or anything of real value, so they didn't have any reason to extort anything from him. In a couple of cases, he inadvertently helped their cause by visiting the homesteads of a few settlers and making their lives living nightmares.

The wife of one settler name named Eliza Anne Hammond caught his attention one cloudy afternoon. She was alone at the ranch that she and her husband were trying to maintain. Her husband Abel Hammond had gone to town to purchase simple provisions and a few building materials.

Eliza Anne was a blonde beauty with milky skin and eyes the color of blue topaz. She was almost too beautiful for this hostile environment. Zuriel thought she was far too beautiful...even to exist. He was perched high on a rise when he saw her. She was sure she was alone and was unobserved, so she was taking the opportunity to bathe. She had filled a large metal wash basin with water from the pump and stripped to the waist. Her plain linen petticoat skirt was tattered and patched, so it mattered little when she knelt in the dirt to wash herself. Zuriel was as stealthy as a cat and moved to a hiding place behind her. Horses in the corral snorted, but paid him little attention. Eliza Anne felt a sudden cold chill and looked over her shoulder. She kept looking for a moment or two, but Zuriel remained hidden.

Because the sky was overcast, Eliza Anne did not see a shadow of the monster that slipped up behind her. As he wrapped his arm around her throat, her first reaction was to cover up for the sake of modesty. A moment later, she realized she should fear for her life and modesty was no longer a priority. Zuriel's grip was not life-threatening but was intimidating. She struggled to free herself and he gripped tighter. He took a moment to run his free hand over her bare breasts....not so much because he was aroused by them, but because he knew he was violating her vows to her husband. So tight was his hold on her neck that she couldn't even open her mouth. The idea she had of biting Zuriel's arm was completely out of the question.

Zuriel took out his hunting knife and held the blade in front of her eyes. They widened with fear and followed the blade down as he lowered it to her stomach. Barely touching the blade to her skin, Zuriel made a long arcing cut just below her navel. The cut was so shallow that he had completed it before Eliza Anne felt the sting from it. Tendrils of blood seeped out from the wound and ran down her belly, converting her torso into a macabre bloody smile. The longest tendrils stained the waist of her petticoat.

That first wound was like a mother's gentle kiss on the forehead compared to the wounds Zuriel inflicted on her over the next three hours. Eliza Anne endured them all, crying out as little as possible. She didn't want to give her attacker the satisfaction. She cried out only two times; and both of those times were when she thought she heard the approach of her husband's horse. Each time, she had been mistaken. She had hoped Abel would have seen how she was being tortured and violated and rain vengeance down on her attacker. However, her hope was never realized. After three hours, her life finally drained from the precise incisions Zuriel had made. He was an expert at extending torture to the last possible moment. When Eliza Anne breathed her final breath, her eyes were wide with despair. Dried tears mixed with the dried blood that trickled down her cheeks.

Zuriel was never satisfied with just taking a life. He needed to torment the living as well. He wished Eliza Anne had had children. He would have tortured them in front of her. As it was, he would have to be content with leaving her husband a *surprise* for when he returned home. Zuriel took his hunting knife and savagely slashed Eliza's petticoat off of her. Then he did the same thing to her undergarments until she lay naked in the light of day. The sun came out and glistened off the fresh streams of blood issuing from Eliza's wounds. The sight was hideous, but Zuriel found it exhilarating. After admiring his work for a few moments, he went inside the humble dwelling the couple had built with their own hands and loaded up all of their provisions. Then he sat down and had a meal. Afterwards, he waited for the husband to return. He really wanted to see his reaction, but would never get that satisfaction.

About the time Zuriel was inflicting mortal wounds into Eliza Anne Hammond, Abel Hammond was being gunned down in the street in front of the *Bucket of Blood* saloon. He had refused to hand over the deed to his property and was goaded into a gunfight that he could not possibly win. In the battle, he was gut shot and didn't die immediately. Instead, he lay in the street, agonizing in pain as bar patrons stepped over him to get inside. In the end, he died about the same time as Eliza Anne.

Zuriel waited around the ranch, but eventually got bored. He set fire to the cabin and the barn. When he finally left, he decided not to head back to town. Instead, he headed east and took the Hammond's horses with him. He planned to meet up with his brother anyway and had had enough of the west. People in the west were just too easy to kill for his liking.

Chapter Eighteen: Rivers of Blood

Zuriel took pleasure in brutally murdering the innocent family, but that was only an added bonus. He really only needed some food and a few items of clothing. The farmer had come to the barn before the sun had peeked up over the horizon and Zuriel had pounced on him like a jaguar on a peccary. The farmer didn't squeal the way the wild pig would have. Instead, he fought valiantly, but to no avail. Zuriel used a broken farm implement of some kind he found in the loft to slay the farmer. Its rusty blade made a jagged cut along the side of the farmer's throat and sliced his flannel shirt across his chest. The brave farmer had grabbed the blade and gripped it tightly as blood ran down his arms from between his fingers. Zuriel had nearly severed two of the farmer's fingers when he pulled the blade back before plunging it deep into his liver. He could have plunged it into his heart, but that would have been too quick for his liking. He wanted to watch the farmer bleed out. The rich black ooze that issued forth from the mortal wound was immensely gratifying. The farmer agonized with intense pain and the knowledge that his wife would soon be facing a similar fate. His helplessness had been more than he could stand and he longed for death. Yet he withstood the agony for a full twenty-two minutes before his life force finally left his body.

As horrific as the farmer's death was, it paled in comparison to the fate that his wife had in store for her. Zuriel subdued her and bound her to a kitchen chair so he could take his time with her. Because their farm was so isolated, her screams of torment and terror would go unheeded. It would actually be several days before they were even missed and anyone would come to investigate. Her screams did manage to get on Zuriel's nerves however; so he gagged her with a dirty dishrag and secured it in her mouth with her bra.

The farmer's wife was named Aggie. It was short for Agatha...a name she hated. Her husband's name had been Beathan; but the few friends he had, called him *Bean*. He had not been very fond of the name Beathan either. It was more the shame that they would be forever labeled with those names chiseled in marble above their graves. That was the last thing on Aggie's mind at the moment. At the moment, she sat bound hand and foot to a chair in her own kitchen. Zuriel had ruthlessly shredded her clothing off of her after securing her bindings. While she wasn't an attractive woman by Hollywood or Fifth Avenue standards, she had a wholesome sincere quality which made her attractive in an understated way. Zuriel didn't care. He would have stripped her naked whether she was a beauty queen or an overweight bearded lady in the circus. It was simply a matter of making women vulnerable that he lusted after. Aggie's clothes hung in tatters behind her and nervous sweat made her skin glisten. She was shaking so badly that her large breasts appeared to be vibrating. Zuriel thought it was terribly amusing.

"You should relax and enjoy this," he said. "It's not like you have too many other choices. People never seem to change though. I have been around over a thousand years and killed thousands of people. Yet none of them choose to enjoy the exquisite rush of sensations during the last few moments of their lives. One would think they would savor every last second; but no, they just cry and plead as if it will make a difference." He removed Aggie's gag so he could have a two-way conversation.

"Yer an animal," she said immediately. She hated the way her voice quavered when she spoke. She really wanted to appear strong. The last thing she wanted to do was give this monster any form of satisfaction.

"We are all animals," said Zuriel. "I just happen to be at the very tip top of the food chain. Literally. I have actually eaten people."

"That doesn't surprise me," said Aggie. What did surprise her was the sudden wave of courage that washed over her. "Do you plan to eat me? I hope so...and I hope you choke on me."

"Let's not get ahead of ourselves," said Zuriel. "I might just want a snack to hold me over though. Is there anything here you might suggest?"

"How 'bout you take a big bite out of my arse!" Aggie's voice broke on the last syllable. Again, she wished she could be stronger, but tears flowed from her eyes.

"I said a snack," said Zuriel. "Your arse could feed a whole banquet hall." Aggie's fear turned into a burning hatred.

"Yer a wicked son of a bitch," she screamed. Aggie usually never cursed...not even in front of her husband. Her eyes kept darting to the door in the vain hope that he would come in and rescue her. Zuriel noticed the first time she did it, but kept quiet. After the third time, he decided the time was right.

"I want to ask you a question," he said. "I don't usually wear hats, but I rather fancy this one. What do you think?" From his back pocket, Zuriel produced Bean's tartan cap. The colors were so bold they were almost embarrassing. Bean had loved it so much when Aggie gave it to him that he said he was going to be buried in it. Aggie's heart sank and her hopes faded upon seeing it. There was a small blood spatter on the left side and she knew the small stain would be the last she would ever see of her beloved husband. Her hopes, fears and anger abated. They all turned to despair and resignation to her fate. She bowed her head and mentally crossed herself. It had been years since she had been to confession, but the circumstance seemed to call for some kind of Holy Sacrament. She prayed that her circumstances would be taken into consideration when she was judged in the afterlife.

In the barn, Bean's lifeless eyes stared up at the wooden beams and supports. The large pool of black blood and bile under him had seeped through the cracks of the rough wooden floor. Low cries came from the farmhouse and soon escalated into screams of pain and terror. If Bean's spirit remained, it was helpless to aid his tortured wife. She screamed longer than one would think humanly possible; but only the cows in the field heard the sounds. They looked up briefly from the grass and hay they were eating; then returned to it as if nothing of interest was happening. Maybe it took hours for her to die or maybe it just seemed like hours. To Aggie, it seemed like an eternity.

When the screaming finally stopped, Zuriel thought the silence in the house was deafening. The pool of blood under Aggie was so large, Zuriel could no longer step around it. Between the slashes and being drenched with her own blood, Aggie no longer looked naked. Instead, she looked as though she was clothed in a crimson satin gown that shimmered in the light. Zuriel admired his work as he hungrily devoured a bowl of stew he found in the refrigerator. It had probably been saved there for Bean's lunch.

After finishing his meal, Zuriel searched the house for whatever he could find. Bean had only one suit and it would never fit him. Zuriel settled for a dress shirt and a pair of workpants which were slightly too short. He laid them out on the bed, stripped down and took a long hot shower. The hot water from the bright brass fixtures cascaded over his body, cleansing him of the evidence of his brutality. Rivers of diluted blood washed down the drain of the antique clawfoot bathtub. The scarlet streams of water mesmerized Zuriel. His mind drifted off to a place he hadn't thought of for a long time.

* * *

While the Holy Office of the Inquisition was conducting trials to purge the population of Europe of impure thoughts and undesirables, Zuriel and his brother Adriel were conducting their own personal Inquisitions. They were skilled forgers and had presented many churches in the outlying areas with documents so authentic that they would have fooled the very monarchs who were supposed to have written them.

Ferdinand II of Aragon and Isabella I of Castile established the Spanish Inquisition as a way to replace the *Medieval Inquisition* that was under Papal control. Zuriel and Adriel were zealous believers in bending the will of the people to serve the needs of a few. In the beginning, their methods were effective because they were so severe. After a disproportionate amount of burnings at the stake, the local churches began to question those methods. Zuriel and Adriel would then move on to other small villages and begin again; but not before massacring the priests and acolytes who had questioned their motives.

Adriel loved his work, but he also liked to watch Zuriel in the performance of his *duties*. He sometimes allowed females charged with heresy to go free after their trial; but not before Zuriel planted his *Holy Seed* within them. Zuriel loved the play on words and it continued to amuse him for many decades. Adriel would still play his part and mutilated the women in a way that would still allow them to deliver and care for the children they bore. After all, those children were Adriel's nieces and nephews; but mostly he just liked to mutilate women.

Zuriel cared only for his brother. The relationship they

shared was more than just that of siblings. They shared DNA to be sure, but they also shared identical beliefs. They shared a common goal of eradicating inferior life forms on the planet. The feelings he had for his brother were the closest thing Zuriel could feel to spiritual love. In Portugal, he nearly went insane when one of the accused rose up, wrested a poleax from a guard and split Adriel's skull. Zuriel was sure Adriel would not survive. He flayed the accused alive, had his wounds dressed until he healed and then flayed him again. Zuriel repeated the process three times. Many thought it was a miracle that the man survived. After Adriel recovered, they realized it was a curse. Instead of flaying the accused again, he was drawn and quartered as slowly as possible. Rather than using draft horses, Zuriel ordered slow oxen to be used. The oxen were then fitted with iron weights on their fetlocks to impede their progress, making the execution slow and agonizing. When the accused man's joints finally dislocated, he was confessing to killing Christ himself. As the tendons stretched out and eventually snapped, a few of the guards standing by projectile vomited because of the sight and sound, as well as the resulting stench. The blood ran down the gutters in scarlet streams for over an hour. Adriel was satisfied by his brother's *get well* gift to him. It also served as a crowning achievement for their Inquisitions and they moved on overnight; but not before relieving the local church of its gold and other offerings.

* * *

The water turned cold on Zuriel's back. He hardly noticed. However, he did notice the hard lump in his throat. He missed Adriel. If he only could find him, he knew he might be able to bring him back. Wherever Vigil had taken him had been remote and impossible to find. He planned to torture Vigil to the edge of his immortality. Zuriel would find out where his brother was or he would make Vigil's life an eternal

Hell in ways he could only dream of.

He dressed in Bean's ill-fitting clothes and hated every aspect of them. *Apparently, the lady of the house has never heard of fabric softener*, he thought. Zuriel was used to the finest materials and tailored clothing. He would be properly attired soon enough, but he needed to get back to civilization. He considered setting the farmhouse on fire. That was his usual way of dealing with victims, but instead, he left them to bloat and decompose. Smiling, he thought about the reaction of whoever would discover them. He hoped it was some close relative. It didn't matter if it wasn't. In his mind, it already was.

Zuriel cut across several fields until he reached a country road. He didn't want to be associated with the farmhouse or its deceased residents for the time being. That would ruin the surprise for whoever discovered them. A lorry that was heading in the opposite direction of where he wanted to go gave him a lift. Zuriel thought it might look less suspicious if he went back to Lochgelly from a different direction anyway. He had a lot of experience with alibis.

About the time Zuriel was torturing Aggie, Vigil was waking up next to Leslie. She was still sleeping, so he gently kissed her on the cheek. Her sheets were always crisp and clean, as though she had a maid. He suspected that Hazel changed them for her each day. Hazel was a treasure and he seriously considered settling down in this part of the world. That would never be possible though for so many reasons.

Leslie stirred and coiled her way into Vigil's arms. He held her for a long time. He admired her strength, but felt a strong inclination to protect her. That would never be possible, but was something he greatly desired. Vigil could protect her from many things, but not from time itself. Time was the culprit that had robbed him of so many loves over the centuries. No matter how many relationships he lost, it never got any easier.

"Where's me mum?" Leslie asked softly. "She's usually on to me about coming to breakfast. It's a wonder I don't weigh thirty stones."

"I'm sure she'll be along," said Vigil. "I think she goes out of her way to see me naked."

"Well, who wouldn't …and while we're on the subject, can we pick up where we left off last night?"

"I would love to," said Vigil. "…but I really need to meet up with someone this morning. It's work related."

"Mark? I am really disappointed you didn't invite him to join us," said Leslie. "He was quite entertaining. I am sure he had a lot to offer."

"Are you trying to make me jealous?"

"Not at all," she said. "You just seemed a little tired and I thought he could help you with…how is it you Americans put it…a tag team."

"You are asking for a spanking," said Vigil.

"You mean you finally got the hint?" said Leslie. "Great! Just my luck! You're getting ready to leave!"

"I will return soon," he said. "Then you will get what's coming to you."

"I'd better. You might want to prepare yourself for something special as well." Leslie's smile was cryptic and intriguing. Vigil had no idea what she was talking about; and he was usually pretty good at figuring things like that out. He kissed her for a long time and then dressed as she watched. He kissed her again and headed for the door. As he opened it, she embraced him from behind and he lost his balance. Leslie lost hers as well and they both found themselves on the stoop in front of her front door. The door eased shut behind her and she felt a surge of electricity go through her body when she realized it had just locked. She was completely naked and stood behind Vigil on her stoop in the broad light of day. As it happened, it seemed as though everyone who lived in the neighborhood was out for a walk that day. They all stopped to take in the sight and wait to see what was going to transpire. Leslie was mortified, but she wasn't going to give the neighbors the satisfaction of letting them know it. She circled around Vigil, stood on her toes and gave him a long passionate kiss. Her bare behind was as white as polished marble. She turned and waved at the passersby before walking boldly to her mother's half of the semi-detached. She stood there naked and cold, waiting for her mother to answer her door. The weather was brisk and the wait felt like an eternity. Vigil was immensely amused, but he was sure he would hear about it when he returned. He thought it might not be a good idea to let Leslie know that he could have picked the lock.

Vigil was meeting with Mark one last time before he headed back to D.C. There were a few details about the events of the previous day he needed to know. The wrecked car had been searched, but there was little to lead to the identity of the driver. Whoever he was, he was skilled at keeping hid identity a secret. The very fact that there was nothing to go on led Vigil to suspect the driver was Zuriel...that and the sick feeling of intuition that rumbled in his stomach. He didn't like the feeling, but it was useful to him. It was like an early warning system forcing him to keep his guard up. Zuriel would be coming for him, but he planned to be ready.

Zuriel wouldn't be coming for him just yet. He would be going to Edinburgh for a suit of clothes and a few other specialized items. Vigil wasn't the only one with contacts all over the world. Zuriel had also designed a few specialized weapons of his own. His designs were less immediately lethal and much more diabolical. He would find out where Adriel was if it was the last thing he ever did.

Chapter Nineteen: All Things Must End

Vigil had attended Mark's funeral, if one could call it that. It barely qualified as a *celebration of life*. A few of Mark's colleagues covertly entered the *Olde Handley's Pub* in Newport, Rhode Island over a period of two hours. None of them sat together or even spoke to one another. Each ordered a shot of Irish whiskey and placed it in front of them. They waited until the prearranged time, placed the shot to their lips, said a silent toast and downed it. That was the extent of the celebration. Each left the pub at the same intervals as they had arrived. No one in the pub suspected a thing. Vigil was the last one to leave.

A successful assassin never brings attention to himself, even in death. No one would ever attend an actual funeral of an assassin. That would put too many potential targets in one place at one time. Instead, a simple personalized remembrance was arranged through clandestine means. Mark's funeral had an Irish theme because of his heritage. It was the way he would have wanted it. Vigil always wondered what his own remembrance would be like. He was even more private than his fellow agents and wasn't sure what kind of theme they might choose for him.

Mark's death had been a shock to the agency because he had always been so cautious. When he was on assignment, he always chose the highest vantage point with the clearest view of his target, without fail. This practice became his signature, but he would have preferred to remain fully anonymous. His signature also proved to be his undoing in the end. The assignment didn't allow for both of his conditions to be met and the cleanest shot to his target was not from the highest vantage point. Trees blocked the view from there, so it was necessary for him to choose a perch two stories lower than he liked. It had still been a good perch...just not ideal.

Mark remained motionless for five hours waiting for his target to arrive. When she finally did, Mark took only eleven seconds to seal her fate. His specialized projectile hit its target as usual; but just as it did, a second shot echoed between the buildings. No one saw the muzzle flash on top of the highest vantage point, but two stories down brain matter spattered on the rooftop like a melon dropped from a great height.

Mark's final assignment had been a successful one, but it had cost him his life. Mark's body was a perfect DNA match, which was a good thing. Its head had been nearly obliterated and the face therefore, unrecognizable. A cleanup team was quickly dispatched and after the required protocols, the body was cremated and the ashes dispersed. There was nothing left to prove that Mark had ever existed.

* * *

Vigil sat across from the *dead man* at a cafe on the other side of town. They sat smiling for a long time before either spoke.

"Okay," said Vigil. "How did you do it?"

"Do what?" asked Mark coyly. "...oh, you mean the dying thing. I'm not sure I should let you in on all my secrets."

"Well, I'm not threatening you or anything..." said Vigil. "...but if I start digging around to find out, you may end up getting some unwanted attention."

"Funny how you make *not threatening me* sound like a threat," Mark said. "Well, it's not much of a secret anyway. Not in our circles, at least. How familiar are you with 3-D Printing?"

"I've used it before," Vigil answered. "I've fabricated some pretty useful weapons a couple of times."

"Did you know they can fabricate things using DNA?"

"I read a little about it a short time ago," he said. "They hope to fabricate human organs from a person's own DNA someday. They say that is years off though."

"It may not be as far off as they think," said Mark. "For my purposes, the technology works just fine."

"I am not quite sure what you're getting at," said Vigil.

"Using my DNA, they were able to print a nearly perfect replica of my entire body. Is that wild or what?"

"I still may be missing your point."

"They, and by *they* I mean some lab tech friends of mine, printed a body that I used as a decoy." Mark was almost giddy. Evidently, he had been dying to tell someone about it. "I found out there was a mole in the organization and he had been contracted to eliminate me. It's one of the hazards of being very good at one's job, I guess. I leaked just enough information about my target to allow the mole to know where I was going to be.

"I then set up my decoy in the best spot possible. It was too perfect an opportunity for the mole to resist. He took the highest vantage point and blew my printed body's head off. It was pretty gruesome. I, in the meantime, had taken up a position in a parking garage a block away so I could complete my assignment. It was a perfectly executed diversion, if you'll pardon the pun."

"I will pardon it this time," said Vigil. "...but don't make too many more of them."

"Sorry," said Mark. "Anyway, I had set up surveillance equipment all around my decoy so I could make a positive ID of the shooter. I wasn't too surprised to find out he was one of our own. What did surprise me was that the bastard had the nerve to show up at my funeral."

"Say what?"

"I know, right? Some nerve."

"No…I mean, you went to your own funeral?" asked Vigil.

"Well, I didn't actually attend," said Mark. "That would be in bad taste. I just wanted to see who showed up. I was glad to see you there."

"I don't know how to respond to that," said Vigil. "You're welcome?"

"Well anyway, I was concealed on the roof of a building just half a block from O'Handley's. My original thought was to blow the mole's brains out as he came out of the bar; but a better idea came to mind. He had parked his car about a half a block away and there was a perfect spot right before he would reach it. It was perfect because there was a plain blank brick wall at a narrow point in the sidewalk.

"When he reached the spot, I fired. The projectile hit the wall right next to the mole's face. It exploded and released a puff of vapor that the mole inhaled before he could react. He must have known what it was, because he ran as fast as he could to his car. The nice thing about cars being all computerized these days is the fact that they are so easy to hack. The mole was desperate to get to an antidote for the poison he had just inhaled. He had, at best, twenty minutes before it would be too late. Sure, I could have made it so he died instantly, but where's the fun in that?"

"You used a Foxglove derivative, I presume?" inferred Vigil.

"No...that's too *old school*," countered Mark. "There are a lot of designer toxins on the market these days. Get with the 21st Century old man."

"Okay, enough with the insults," said Vigil. "Get on with your story."

"The mole knew there was a clinic that had what he needed located about eleven miles away," continued Mark. "He knew he could make it if he broke all the speed limit laws and didn't get delayed somehow. That was where my hacking skills came into play. I didn't disable his car. That would have been too easy also. Instead, I simply adjusted his fuel intake so his maximum speed was thirty-eight miles an hour.

"It must have felt like he was crawling as the clock ticked down and his time ran out. I programmed his car to return to normal after seventeen minutes. It was just about then that the toxin caused his heart to stop. His car sped up and he blew right through an intersection and right into the path of a semi-trailer truck. Some call it overkill. I call it a job well done."

"Well, it's not like you planned the semi," said Vigil.

"No," Mark said. "It was more of a happy accident; happy for me anyway."

"Well, it got the job done," said Vigil. "I hope I never show up on your radar."

"If you did," said Mark, "...I would contract that work out. I don't want on your bad side either. From what I have seen, you are a bit of an overkill artist yourself."

"Sometimes I have to be," said Vigil. "I hate the thought of leaving a job half done."

"Like your altercation with the driver of the car following you?"

"Yes," said Vigil. "...and thanks for bringing that up."

"Hey, I'm not judging," said Mark. "With the way his car was peppered with bullets and the amount of blood spilled, I would have thought the job would have been done as well. The guy must have been immortal." Mark chuckled at his quip, but Vigil didn't even smile. He knew how close Mark had hit upon the truth.

"I need to get out there and look for him," said Vigil. "...but I wouldn't even know where to start."

"The cleanup crew searched the immediate area," said Mark. "...about a half mile diameter. They found nothing and figured the un-sub got a ride or somebody removed his body. That was the only explanation they could come up with."

"I suspect it won't matter anyway," said Vigil. "If it's who I think it is, he will be coming back here as soon as he is healed. He has a score to settle with me."

"I figured you had a history with the guy," Mark replied. "That car was too shot up for a simple case of *road rage.*"

"I don't get road rage," said Vigil. "Life's too short...for most people." Mark wasn't sure what Vigil meant by the last part, but he let it pass.

"Well," he said. "Good luck on your search. I am heading back to the states in a few hours...you know, unless you and your girlfriend need help with anything. I saw the way she was looking at me."

"She looks at everybody that way," said Vigil. "You're nothing special."

"Let's let her be the judge," said Mark.

"What time does your plane leave? Soon I hope." Vigil had a way of making a joke almost seem like a veiled threat.

"I am supposed to be on the red eye at 4:00 a.m.," said Mark.

"Have a safe trip," said Vigil. "I will meet up again with you soon. I might have an assignment for you."

"Try to give me a little advance warning," said Mark. "My calendar gets pretty full sometimes."

"Will do," said Vigil. Mark paid both of their checks, shook hands with Vigil and then pulled him in for a brotherly hug. "Keep me in mind if you need any help with Leslie," he said grinning.

"Get out of here, you bum," Vigil huffed. "I am not good at sharing." Mark winked at him and was gone. Vigil stood at the door for a moment. He usually had things planned ahead by at least two or three steps. This time, Zuriel had to make the next move. Vigil hated that.

*   *   *

In Edinburgh, Zuriel had acquired new attire in brown tweed. He had excellent sartorial taste, but managed to remain unexceptional...even unmemorable. That was the way he wanted it. He made his way to a sparsely populated part of town to an old radio repair shop. In its own way, it was much like Zuriel's clothes. It was unexceptional as well and the shop only stood out because it was still in business. Few people have radios repaired in their current *disposable* lifestyles. Everyone wants the latest technology with the most bells and whistles. The shop managed to stay in business despite the march of progress.

Customers who happened upon the store felt as though they were stepping back in time. Seasoned wood floors were clean and polished, and creaked when walked upon. They matched the rich wood of the long counter at the right of the door. Vintage radios populated one end of the counter and an antique cash register sat majestically at the other end. The man behind the counter was just as one would expect to find as a proprietor of such an elegant shop. His hair was white and his hairline was fashionably receding. He had a full mustache that matched the color of his hair and he wore round wire-rimmed glasses. He wore a white dress shirt under a black vest. A gold watch chain arched from one vest pocket to the other and he had a black garter on each sleeve.

Zuriel admired his style as he walked up to the counter. The owner's shirt was classic and possibly antique. The cuffs were folded back and elegant cufflinks held them closed. The bowtie he wore was not just for fashion. It served the original purpose for a bowtie by securing the collar of his shirt.

"It's been some time, eh Neville? You are still going by that name, right?"

"I've no reason to change it," he said. "...unless you are here to give me one."

"Not this time," said Zuriel. "I just need a custom item."

"How soon do you need it? I prefer advance notice on custom items. It isn't always easy to get the components right away. Things aren't as simple these days as they used to be." Neville seemed more than a little disturbed at Zuriel.

"I realize it is an imposition," he said. "...but I will make it worth the effort. I am in a bit of a pinch for time here."

"I will see what I can do," said Neville. "Can I still reach you in the usual way?"

"The usual way...but a different pass code," answered Zuriel. He handed Neville an average-looking grocery receipt. On it were fourteen separate purchase items and their prices. Within the ordinary list of numbers and items was an embedded code if one knew what to look for. Neville did. He smiled and nodded in confirmation.

"I expect to hear from you soon," said Zuriel. His tone was cordial enough, but with an underlying threat embedded in it as well. Neville nodded again, but this time he didn't smile. Zuriel wasn't smiling either as he left the shop. He navigated his way back to the 21st Century and returned to where he was staying. It was a simple but well-appointed apartment in an average part of town. The current occupant resided decomposing in the hall closet, packaged in a pair of odor-proof garbage bags. Zuriel was sure she wouldn't be missed for a while. Her only visitor was the lady upstairs who checked in on her from time to time; and she was currently decomposing in her own closet.

Zuriel thought about the irony of going to an antiquated clock repair shop to obtain the latest in technological advances. All advances are built on the foundations of the past he supposed. His business deals had taught him that. Sometimes his dealings were legitimate; often times they were not. Occasionally, he just outright stole ideas of others. Some of the best ones came from one man in particular.

* * *

Zuriel had called him *Nick*. To his knowledge, he was the only person who did. He met him towards the end of the 19th Century when he was working in Pittsburg on an Alternating Current system to power streetcars. The system that Nick designed wasn't suitable for streetcars, but Zuriel saw brilliance in this man. He also saw that the man had the innocence and gullibility of a child that Zuriel took full advantage of. He borrowed his ideas and contracted them to be constructed by individuals under his control. That was the same year a lunatic terrorized London's East End by murdering and mutilating prostitutes.

Zuriel and Nick eventually parted ways and didn't meet up again for almost sixty years. Nick thought Zuriel looked just the same as he remembered. He was sure he must be hallucinating. It was in the middle of the Second World War; Zuriel was stateside to take advantage of the ladies and the absence of able-bodied men.

It was January of 1943, Zuriel tracked Nick to a room at the New Yorker Hotel. He surprised him in his room on the thirty-third floor and Nick treated him as if they had only parted on the previous day. Since Nick was somewhat disoriented, he showed Zuriel pages of diagrams of projects he was working on. Zuriel couldn't believe his luck. Some of the designs were decades ahead of anything in use at the time. Nick had kept many secrets because of their potential to be used for nefarious purposes. Zuriel had everything he needed from Nick and told his old friend that he looked tired. He suggested he take a nap. Nick was tired and took the suggestion to lie down on the bed. Zuriel convinced him that he was a physician and could ease any problems he was having.

According to a coroner's report, Nick died during the night of a coronary thrombosis. Perhaps he did; but in that day and age, a coronary thrombosis could be faked with a simple injection. The F.B.I. even investigated the death because it was war time and because Nick was originally from Croatia. The report stated that they found nothing suspicious. Zuriel made off with everything that might have been of use to the wartime effort.

Some of what the F.B.I. did find was also left out of reports. A few of Nick's designs were for aircraft that operated in an entirely different method than conventional aircraft. Four years later, a test craft crashed somewhere in New Mexico. All of the craft wreckage was recovered and it was dismissed as a weather balloon. Zuriel didn't realize what he had passed up in that hotel room. Then again, it was never about the money or the fame for Zuriel. Only one thing excited him. It was something he never tired of, and there were endless ways he could enjoy his diversion.

Chapter Twenty: Arc Angel

Vigil had been lost before, both figuratively and literally. Being lost literally was a lot easier. He knew that no matter how lost he was, that he would eventually find his way to someplace familiar. Figuratively was far worse. There was no way of knowing if he would ever find his destination because he wasn't sure of where he wanted to be.

He really cared for Leslie, but he wished he didn't. It would be much easier to leave her behind and let her go on with her life. His job had always prevented him from getting close to anyone; and that acted as a safety net for him. It he couldn't get close, he couldn't get hurt. Vigil knew it would probably hurt Leslie if he left, but he also knew her life was in danger the longer he stayed. *If I leave...*, he thought. In the past, it had always been *WHEN I leave*. She must have really got to him. His head ached from indecision. The problem might be partially alleviated if he could *resolve* Zuriel. Maybe his feelings were attached to his mission. Maybe once the problem was solved, his emotional state would return to normal. At the moment, his only option was to stay put in Lochgelly and use himself as bait for Zuriel. Unfortunately, that meant using Leslie as bait as well.

Vigil wandered around the quiet streets of Lochgelly. Compared to the other places and time periods he had visited, the town was unexceptional; but Vigil had grown fond of it and took in everything. Unlike many of his brothers, Vigil was glad to be alive and cherished every moment. He stood outside an Indian restaurant and took in the aroma of the curry, mixed with those of coconut, cinnamon and cloves. The blend of spices was unfamiliar to him, but it smelled delicious. It took him back to one of the many times he had visited India. The experiences there had been both positive and negative, as in most places. In spite of his skills in the art of warfare, Vigil hated taking lives.

He walked aimlessly down the narrow streets and happened upon a small pub, that at first he took for the office of a CPA. Perhaps that had been what the previous tenant was. Vigil stepped inside the unassuming entrance and stood in a short hallway until his eyes adjusted to the dim lighting. A public bulletin board mounted to one wall advertised everything from lost pets to bail bonds services. Tabs with phone numbers extended from the bottom of the home-printed postings. More tabs were removed from the bail bonds' posts than any of the others. That probably said a lot about the neighborhood. Stepping through the door at the end of the hallway, Vigil was surprised to see the pub was much bigger on the inside than it appeared from its exterior. It also seemed to be richly appointed, though that might have been a trick of the subdued lighting.

The main concentration of illumination was directly over the bar, but not on the pub patrons. It gave the impression of the barman performing on a small off-Broadway stage to an appreciative, but silent audience. Since it was a little past two in the afternoon, the audience only consisted of one rumpled man at the end of the bar and two men engaged in a less-than-spirited game of darts. The man at the bar looked as though he might actually live on his bar stool. Almost as if to prove Vigil's impression wrong, the man rose from his bar stool and made his way to the *public convenience*. Vigil smiled, approached the bar and ordered a pull of Guinness. After receiving his pint, he located a spot in a dark corner booth and seated himself there. The dark rich wood of the seat was as hard as a puritan church pew...and he knew exactly what those felt like. He sipped his pint and pondered his options in dealing with Zuriel.

Vigil thought about giving up his life's mission and settling down with Leslie. He was almost ready to give up one of his lives for her, in a matter of speaking. He wasn't sure he was ready to watch her wither and die like a flower in a window box at the approach of winter. This was one of the curses he lived with. Living an unnaturally long life has its advantages, to be sure; but life is about balance whether one wants it to be or not. Leslie's whole life might seem little more than a flicker to Vigil. That didn't matter. He lived life for the moment; and if all he had was a moment with her, it would have to be enough.

A few pub patrons entered unnoticed and began to populate the empty seats as it got later in the afternoon. Regulars, who came in to play darts or shoot pool, gravitated to their usual spots. Others just came in to have a pint and watch sports on the large television screen that Vigil hadn't noticed when he entered the pub. He finished another pint and realized he had lost count of how many he had imbibed. His bladder however didn't lose track and he found it necessary to visit the public convenience himself. He had almost waited too long when he found he needed thirty pence to gain entry. The upside of using a pay toilet in Great Britain was that they were usually pretty clean. This one was no exception.

Vigil didn't realize how badly he had needed to go. An involuntary shiver went through his body as he relieved himself at the urinal. He suspected it was how a person with a high fever might feel going, though he had never had a high fever himself. One of his advantages, he supposed. Vigil had just finished his business and made sure everything was zipped up when he felt a new sensation. It was a sensation he was familiar with, and his guard immediately went up; but not soon enough. Another shiver ran though his body; only this time it was electrical. Vigil felt as though he had been submerged in a sea of static and pain. His head pulsated with intense pain like that of ten migraines. He could feel his teeth grinding to the point of being irreparably damaged as darkness engulfed him, but the pain didn't diminish. He was sure he lost consciousness, but that didn't provide him with any relief as it had in the past. His only thought was, *perhaps this is Hell.*

* * *

Lazarus once told Vigil that early Jewish doctrines did not have a concept for Hell. He had said they believed they should concentrate on the here and now. He told him that doing what was right should be its own reward and one should not behave out of fear of punishment or promise of a reward. Lazarus believed God was loving and forgiving. His God was a god of endless second chances. Vigil came to believe that there might be a Hell, but it was a place where the soul is purified and made ready to enter *Olam Habah*, meaning the *Afterlife* or *The World to Come.*

Vigil was at peace with his belief. This made it easier for him to know that he would meet up with his brothers again and they would be like they were when they were children...innocent and devoid of malice. The teachings of his father gave him hope. However, his hope didn't stop Vigil from worrying about the torments that might await them, or even the ones he himself might have to experience. He knew that actions speak louder than words, but he wasn't sure if they spoke louder than intentions. He surmised that was why people were not supposed to judge. One shouldn't judge until one has all the facts; and one can't know all the facts until they have passed through the veil of death.

Vigil had dreamed of the realm of the dead, a place some called *Abaddon.* It was also called a place of destruction. He was sure it was a place where the dead went to begin spiritual reconstruction. Destruction was necessary before reconstruction could commence. But destruction, no matter how necessary, was painful. In Abaddon though, the pain seemed just, and therefore tolerable. Vigil awoke many times feeling his skin was on fire, though it was probably his own cellular regeneration. It was much like *growing pains* for the children of Lazarus.

Other times, he would dream of *Tzalmavet* or *Gehenna*. One was the *Shadow of Death*; the other, the *Lake of Fire*. Vigil's childhood dreams had been like a modern-day horror movie. His worst dreams involved being engulfed in fire and being beaten on the back with a thick wooden bat. He didn't think it was possible to feel two different forms of pain simultaneously, but apparently it was for him. Sometimes, he was well aware that he was dreaming, but couldn't make himself wake up. The pain would just grow more intense and the beatings would become more rapid. He thought he had outgrown those dreams. He might have been wrong.

* * *

Vigil felt another sharp blow across his kidneys and his skin burned with unquenchable fire. He found himself gnashing his teeth while he dwelt in *outer darkness*. There was an acrid smell that reminded him of the stench of the dead; it mixed with something unidentifiable, yet familiar. There was an underlying vibration that was only interrupted by irregular blows to his back. Vigil's head was filled with so much pain, he was sure he could see it in a solid form. It was like a lace made of mist in a void of blackness.

In an instant, the vibration stopped with a final jolt to Vigil's spine. His entire body and head ached, as though every nerve ending was raw and irritated. He couldn't believe that death felt this way; but then, he had no absolute frame of reference about death. Over the centuries, he had been present when others recounted their visits to Hell after near-death experiences. Most seemed to be describing conditions they had

229

heard about and therefore expected to see. Others related details that were a little hard to discount. Either the individuals had incredible imaginations, or they had really been there. As far as Vigil was concerned, the jury was still deliberating.

Vigil became aware of a high-pitched sound that didn't really exist. The noise seemed to be the sound of silence increasing in frequency until it reached an ultrasonic level. It was probably his brain healing itself and trying to return to normal, but that didn't make the experience any less painful. This was almost pleasant compared to the torment he had experienced only a few moments before. He breathed a small sigh of relief and realized he was actually breathing. That gave him a glimmer of hope and he prepared himself for an inevitable confrontation. He just wasn't sure with whom.

A beam of light stabbed his retinas and pain traced lines along his neural pathways. Vigil's brain felt trapped in an electrified metal netting. His teeth gnashed and tried to grind themselves to powder as visions of Hell presented themselves again. He was pretty sure actual Hell couldn't be as bad as the pain he was experiencing.

"I have the best toys," said Zuriel. "I ought to send Nick a thank you note…you know, if he hadn't been dead for seventy-five years. But then, I was the one to make the improvements."

The beam of light went dark and Vigil thought he was experiencing the sweet release of death. Then he felt the back of his head smash against the metal bumper of the lorry as Zuriel pulled him from the rear door. Through squinted eyes, Vigil could see it was night, that it was clear and that there was an incredibly starry sky. He could also see that he was bound with surgical wire saw blades…the kind used to amputate limbs. Zuriel dragged him up a slight incline to a place Vigil was familiar with. It was the arrangement of stones that was the site of the druid sacrifice he had interrupted long ago. It would be too much of a coincidence that Zuriel would have picked this location at random.

"So you were the druid in charge of the sacrifice," said Vigil. "I really wasn't sure until just now."

"I went to a lot of trouble to obtain those victims," said Zuriel. "...and I had spent months conditioning those acolytes. You couldn't just leave things alone, could you?"

"We all have our jobs to do, I guess. What's on the schedule for this evening?" Vigil was trying to unclench his teeth and sound nonchalant as he spoke. He hoped his voice sounded calm and confident.

"I am glad you asked," said Zuriel. "I have another toy I want to show you."

He dragged Vigil into the arrangement of stones and with some effort, lifted him onto a makeshift altar made from bags of fertilizer. Vigil recognized the smell as the one he could not identify in the lorry.

"Sorry for the crude altar," said Zuriel. "I had to use what I had available. It should burn pretty well though, don't you think?"

"It's perfect," said Vigil. "...and when I think about you, I think of fertilizer."

"Awww...you think about me? You are so sweet." Zuriel began to drive posts into the ground in a circle around Vigil.

"Now...understand, if I had acolytes," he began. "...they would be holding these." Zuriel held up metallic devices about the size of cell phones; twelve in all. He placed them on top of the posts and positioned them just so.

"What few people know," he said. "...is that these

231

stones have a unique resonance. They amplify sound and energy waves in ways that are undreamed of."

Vigil struggled against his bonds, but only succeeded in opening wounds in his arms and spilling blood on the crude altar.

"Thank you," said Zuriel. "Your blood will help sanctify the altar. Now…where was I? Oh, yes…I don't know what the ancients knew about this place or these stones, but they work really well with Nick's particle beam transmitters. The beams can be bounced off the stones at just the right angle and intensify when they do. Other forms of energy just tend to diminish. Awesome, huh?"

"I am riveted," said Vigil. "Please, go on."

"You are not very good at sarcasm," said Zuriel. "Well…no matter. I used only one of these beam emitters to take you out at the pub and keep you under control in the lorry. Oh, and sorry about the bumpy ride here. There are no good roads to get to this location. That's because it is so remote."

"What exactly did that thing do to me?" asked Vigil.

"This is extremely interesting," said Zuriel. "It causes cells to explode from the inside. It turns them inside out, as it were. If yours did not instantly regenerate, you would have been dead in less than a second. To tell you the truth, I am quite anxious to see what all twelve of them at one time are going to do. This should be quite a revelation for both of us"

"Aren't you afraid it will kill me too fast?" asked Vigil. He regretted saying it the moment the words left his mouth, but he had to admit that his own curiosity was piqued.

"Well, you know…in the past I have worked with some of the great scientists and thinkers of the world…" said Zuriel.

"Now how would I know that?" Vigil asked.

"It's a figure of speech," said Zuriel. "...anyway, I have studied with Da Vinci, Newton, Fermi...many others. They all taught me about incremental levels of experimentation. I plan to activate each particle beam transmitter one by one, over a period of hours if necessary. I will find out where you left Adriel, believe me."

"That's all? I thought you wanted to know something important." Vigil's laugh was a bit too taunting and Zuriel touched the screen on the device in his hand. A familiar bolt of pain shot through Vigil's system. It was similar to electricity, but not like it at all. His body went rigid and the surgical wire cut into his flesh, spilling more blood. After a moment, Zuriel touched the screen again and the pain ceased.

"Do you want to make any more remarks smartass?" he shouted. Zuriel was trying to stay calm and maintain his *evil villain* persona; but Vigil apparently knew just which buttons to push.

"I am not sure you really want to know," he said after the pain subsided. "I am sure there is very little left of him by now." Vigil couldn't seem to help himself. Zuriel touched the screen again and Vigil reacted as before. This time, the pain went on for what seemed like hours. In reality, it was only eleven seconds.

"To tell you the truth," said Zuriel. "I really didn't expect you to tell me right away. That would have been too easy and would have diminished the importance of my experiments. I'll tell you what...let's try two particle beam transmissions this time..." He touched a second icon on his screen and Vigil was plunged into a literal rainbow of pain. The sights were so beautiful, yet monstrous at the same time. In spite of his intense agony, he could not bear to look away. His senses were heightened to a point he had not thought possible. He tasted many metals in his mouth. They were probably the elements that made up his physical body. Other tastes took their places: proteins, salt compounds, acids…all of the things that are probably listed on the nutritional labels on food packaging.

"Are we ready to talk yet?" asked Zuriel as he touched the screen again. "I have a lot of things I want to know; and the night is young."

Vigil threw up and it wasn't a pretty sight. He tried turning his head to the side but only succeeded in plastering the side of his face with what must have been his most recent meal. He had no idea how long ago he had eaten, but it was the last thing on his mind at the moment. Only two of the particle beam emitters had been activated and he was already considering confessing his sins to Zuriel. The only thing holding him back was the thought of unleashing the two brothers back into the world. It might happen on its own, but he was determined not to be a party to it.

"What else are you going to want to know?" asked Vigil. His stomach acids were sour in his mouth and he felt the urge to vomit again. He managed to suppress it and even smiled. Zuriel was fuming, but struggled to regain his composure. He thought of making a crude comment about throwing up, but decided to take the higher road.

"I want to know what you are experiencing while the emitters are on you," he said. "Mortals don't survive long enough to give me any details. I want to use the report as a selling point when I sell these to hostile governments."

"Well, there's an incentive for me to talk if I ever heard one," said Vigil. "I know…let's change places and then you can see for yourself." Zuriel moved his finger close to the third icon on his screen. He let his finger hover over it for a moment. It wasn't really a threat; he just wasn't sure how much more Vigil could take. If he died before he could tell him where Adriel was, Zuriel might never find him. When he considered it might also be possible that Leslie might know the location, he touched the icon anyway.

Vigil's body contorted in a level of pain that no man on earth had ever experienced. He convulsed so badly, the surgical wire shredded his skin and muscle tissue. Wave after wave of pain seared his brain and their frequency increased until they were an emanation of torment and color. The colors that had been a rainbow blended together like paints spilled on a sidewalk, until the only discernable color was a dull brownish purple. It was as if Vigil was being consumed by a sentient tumor. He readied himself to die. Darkness closed in on him and he knew death had arrived.

The Afterlife was nothing like Vigil had expected. He thought it would be full of light and color...or darkness...or flames. Instead, it was gray...a gray swirling fog. The closest thing he had to sentience was the slightest awareness of consciousness. He was disembodied and simply quasi-existed. It wasn't good, nor was it bad. It simply was. If this was death, he could live with it. That thought made him laugh and the laugh made him choke. He coughed up blood and instantly returned to the land of the living.

"Welcome back."

Vigil wasn't sure he actually heard a voice. It may have been his own mind speaking to him. He kept his eyes closed and breathed an exasperated sigh.

Chapter Twenty-One: Hell Fire

Vigil's eyes didn't want to focus. Objects were little more than blurry images with outlines like broken glass. Something was illuminating the area, but he couldn't tell what the light source was. He had no idea how long he had been out this time. Zuriel was standing next to one of the larger monoliths in the arrangement of stones. His visage was distorted by the intense cellular disruption Vigil had suffered. Zuriel's face looked as if it was malformed in some grotesque fashion. His eyes appeared sunken to the point of only being empty sockets and his mouth seemed frozen in a toothless smile. Vigil tried to open his eyes wider, but it hurt too much. There was not a part of his body that didn't pulsate with pain.

He wanted to move, but couldn't. He wanted to die, but also couldn't. Vigil was trapped in a tormented limbo from which he could not escape. Still, Zuriel simply stared at him with an unrelenting mocking grin. The thought of finally losing his life had seemed like a remote possibility for centuries. Now it might possibly be happening. In his profession, he knew that it would probably be an enemy that would do him in and Vigil could accept that. He just didn't want the enemy to be Zuriel. He was one of those tremendously obnoxious winners that Vigil couldn't stand. He would rather just die and get it over with.

He isn't moving, thought Vigil. *He should be over here next to me gloating or something.* He knew Zuriel had a level of inhuman patience that mortals couldn't begin to comprehend. His patience had allowed him to commit

237

unspeakable crimes in the past and prolong tortures to unbelievable durations. One could only imagine the madness that must have overtaken the minds of his victims. Vigil could do more than imagine. His own sanity was very near its breaking point.

As Vigil's eyes began to focus, Zuriel's countenance grew more grotesque. He finally began to move in Vigil's direction in a comical slow-motion manner. He moved in front of a light source Vigil hadn't noticed before and his eyes glowed like fiery embers. He seemed to dissolve in the night, leaving Vigil to stare at the same bright light that people who have had Near Death Experiences say they see. Glowing pulsating rings seemed to emanate from it forming a tunnel of illumination. Vigil felt at peace enough to let the light absorb him and take him wherever he was destined to go. He was breathing out what he thought was his last breath when a shadow blocked the light.

"Take it easy buddy," said Mark. "Getting you out of this wire is going to be tricky."

* * *

Mark's intention of taking the redeye back to the states was derailed when his target was eliminated by a Special Ops team during a raid on a warehouse. Low-yield tactical nuclear weapons had been recovered; and those who were going to sell the weapons had been eliminated. One of them was an arms dealer named Yamarez. It was the only name he went by. The Disciple had been charged with taking him out, but the Special Ops team got there first. Mark didn't mind being shut out in this case. The leader of the Special Ops team was an old friend of his; and in his business, friends were hard to keep.

Richard Hughes (Dick to his friends) was a former decorated Federal Marshal who had been recruited by the Special Ops Division seven years earlier. His skillset made him too valuable an asset to just allow to retire. Dick didn't mind at all. Special Ops offered him access to training and equipment he couldn't use as a Federal Marshal. Dick was a tall man and built like a linebacker; but he moved like a cheetah under cover of darkness. Surgical extractions and terminations with extreme prejudice were his specialties, and his team was hand-selected for just those purposes.

If you met him in a bar, he was the friendliest man one would ever hope to get to know. He enjoyed people and he enjoyed life. Maybe that was why he took his work so seriously when it came to eliminating those who would take life on a massive scale. Mark had to make a mental note to buy the first round the next time he and Dick were in town at the same time. He really didn't need to make the mental note. Dick wouldn't forget. He had a way of reminding people it was their turn to buy, and make it feel like he was doing them a favor by doing so.

Mark was glad the assignment was concluded without him. He actually wanted to spend a little more time in Lochgelly. The little town had grown on him a bit and he thought if he didn't have a chance with Leslie, she might be able to introduce him to someone. Maybe she had a sister. He was only a couple of hours away when he got the message about the assignment cancellation. He turned his rental around and checked his GPS; then he punched in a passcode. The screen changed to a satellite map of Lochgelly and a small red reticle softly flashed over a location. Mark smiled and shook his head. "Rookie mistake Vigil," he muttered.

The reticle was indicating Vigil's location by way of the tracking device Mark had placed on his jacket as they left the pub. The hug Mark had given him seemed innocent enough, so Vigil had no reason to suspect he was being tracked. Mark had no concrete reason to track him. Truth be told, Mark really didn't know why he placed the tracker there.

Part of the reason was that he was curious about Vigil, but mostly he just had a gnawing feeling that something was terribly wrong. From what he could tell from the GPS, his intuition had been wrong. Nothing seemed to be amiss at that moment; but one can only tell so much from a small circle on a GPS screen.

Mark was forty-one kilometers from Lochgelly when the reticle on the screen began to move rapidly down a narrow street and headed toward the edge of town. It picked up even more speed as it reached the outskirts of the city and moved into the sparsely populated countryside. Mark thought something didn't look right and changed his course to intercept Vigil. He wanted to reach him but still maintain a discrete distance just in case he was in pursuit of someone. There was no direct route to get there, so it was two hours before he was within range of his target. By then, the GPS indicated that Vigil had left the main road and must have been on some kind of service road not on the map.

Mark drove along the last main road, trying to find where the vehicle pulled off and began crossing the tough terrain. Finally, he pulled to the side of the road and sent a text message. It wasn't to Vigil, or to headquarters. He texted someone he worked with on a regular basis. Someone he trusted with his life.

Going to the boot of his car, Mark removed one of the cases he had stored there. The case was the size of a briefcase, but much thicker. It was constructed of a reinforced steel alloy and had a futuristic look to it. Inside was a specially constructed drone with so many features that even Mark didn't know them all. He put a Bluetooth headset on and launched the drone into the overcast sky. Then he returned to his vehicle, established a link with the person he had texted, and waited for directions. Within two minutes, a voice in the headset directed Mark to the most efficient route across the terrain to intercept Vigil without being spotted...or ripping the undercarriage out of his rental. It was dark before he actually had a visual sighting of the other vehicle using night vision glasses. He was only a little surprised to see it was a lorry and not Vigil's car. He had known something had to be wrong.

Mark approached the arrangement of stones in his usual stealth mode. Using enhanced optics on his night vision glasses, he could see Vigil bound with wire on top of a stack of bags of some kind. A figure wearing a hoodie stood near him, and a circle of electronic devices were mounted on posts and aimed in Vigil's direction. Mark tried to amplify his directional microphone, but something seemed to be interfering with the signal. Yet he had no problem maintaining the connection with the drone and the person operating it. He suspected it had something to do with the electronic devices mounted on the posts or the harmonics from the arrangement of stones...maybe both. Really, he didn't need to know what the hooded figure was saying to know he needed to eliminate him as a threat.

The hooded figure touched a screen on a device in his hand and Vigil convulsed in pain. Capillaries burst in his face and Mark was sure he could see an eerie glow envelop his body. There was more conversation and then the hooded figure touched the screen again. Vigil's reaction was worse than before and Mark had no idea how he was surviving the intense torture. There was a slight crackle in the Bluetooth earpiece and a voice softly asked, "How much longer do you want this to go on?" Mark didn't speak. He touched a small button on the side of the earpiece twice. When he was in the field, conversation was kept to a minimum. The button produced a tone. Two tones meant an affirmative response and also signaled to begin a thirty-second countdown.

Mark had already unpacked and assembled his custom sniper rifle. The shot was going to be tricky because of the odd angles of the stones; but he was a professional and unmatched as a sniper...with perhaps one exception. As the seconds counted down, Mark slowed his breathing and calmed his thoughts. He entered a Zen state so that he, the rifle, the bullet and the target all became as one. At the exact thirty-second point, he squeezed the trigger and a projectile issued forth from the end of the noise suppressor mounted to the barrel of his rifle. In Mark's Zen state, he could see the glistening copper-jacketed bullet leave the barrel and fly swiftly to its destination. He could envision the bullet trail and the shockwave ripples as it continued along its path. The first stop for the projectile was one of the irregular stones. It impacted leaving a considerable divot, changed direction and ran parallel to the surface of the stone. Ricochets act differently than one might expect. A spinning projectile tends to run parallel to whatever surface it strikes.

As the velocity of the bullet decreased, its ricochet pattern became more predictable, at least to Mark. The projectile's second stop was the tallest monolith at the head of the arrangement of stones. It struck with less intensity and changed trajectory predictably. The bullet entered the back of the hooded figure's head at a mere 1450 feet per second...about that of a 44 Magnum. When the projectile exited the hooded figure's face, it took his right eye and socket with it. At the exact same moment, another projectile took out his left eye in the same fashion. He stood for an unbelievably long period of time before lurching forward with his arms outstretched. It was as if he were trying to feel his way around in the darkness. Mark had never seen someone that was so mortally wounded behave in such a manner.

The hooded figure moved in front of one of the lights mounted on top of the electronic devices. The light showed through the openings in his head and looked as though he had glowing embers for eyes. It was really a sight to behold and

Mark took it all in. He was sure he would never see anything like it again.

"Did you see that?" asked the voice in his headset. "That was amazing."

"It truly was," said Mark. "...and nice bank shot. I may have to step up my game the next time we shoot pool."

"Only if you let me use the drone."

"Not a chance," said Mark. "Thanks for the assist, as usual."

"Not a problem bro. Always happy to help. I don't even need to get paid this time."

"I never said you were getting paid," said Mark.

"I know. Just pulling your chain. Can you finish up here okay? I have some other things I need to attend to."

"I've got this," said Mark. "...and again, thanks." He knew the voice at the other end had nodded his affirmation. He knew him as well as he knew himself. They had shared a womb together many years before. The man on the other end was Mark's twin brother Michael...also known as *Archangel*. They often worked in tandem when an assassination needed to be absolutely insured. Michael's specialty was of a cyber nature. He could fire a projectile from a drone with deadly accuracy and be half the world away when he did it. That made him invaluable to the agency and to his brother when need be.

* * *

Mark struggled a lot with the saw blade bonds, but Vigil was too out of it to notice. The pain of the incisions they were making was nothing compared to the pain he had suffered from within. When he couldn't loose the bonds without doing what he thought would be irreparable damage, Mark took the drone back to his vehicle and brought back a tactical knife with a titanium sawback. The knife usually made short work of cutting through galvanized steel fences, so he thought it might work in this situation. The bonds were a bit tougher than the fencing he was used to, but Mark had Vigil free in a few minutes.

It was still close to three quarters of an hour before Vigil was able to speak coherently. By then, his serious wounds had healed and the capillary damage to his face had completely gone away.

"I am pretty sure there is something about yourself that you are not telling me," said Mark.

"There are a lot of things I don't tell you," said Vigil.

"Come on," said Mark. "We just saved your life."

"We? Sounds like you have a few things you haven't told *me*," said Vigil.

"Well, we work for the government," said Mark. "I guess that's a given; but this wound healing thing you have…I think you should share that."

"I really wish I could," said Vigil. "It's something I was born with. I don't let people know…well…because if it got back to the agency, I would probably be locked away and tested for the rest of my life. You know how governments are…especially when there are potential military applications involved."

"I guess you're right," said Mark. "Say…what about a blood transfusion?"

"It's been tried," said Vigil. "…doesn't work. I guess it's a DNA thing."

"Oh, well…it was worth asking, I suppose," said Mark. "I guess I will just have to live with being strikingly handsome."

"You are that," said Vigil. "I often feel like striking you because you are so handsome."

"I would take offense if it wasn't so damned true," said Mark. They were just about back to the main road when Vigil bolted upright so violently, his seatbelt locked. "What about Zuriel?" he shouted.

"Zuriel? Was that the guy's name?"

"We have to go back!" exclaimed Vigil.

"I don't think so," said Mark smiling. "He's in the boot of my car. That location was a bit too remote for a quick clean-up, so I brought him along. Besides, I don't really want to fill out any reports on this one. Whatever those devices were are going to be pretty valuable to us...I mean, me."

"I would prefer it if you just destroyed those things once and for all," said Vigil.

"Are you sure? You really don't know how many more there are out there. Somebody had to construct them and so somebody out there has the designs." Vigil couldn't argue, but he didn't want to think about a weapon like that on the market.

"...besides," Mark said. "I plan to use them in my line of work."

"I hope I don't wind up on *your* target list," said Vigil. He tried to sound like he was joking, but Mark knew he was serious.

"I don't think that will be a problem," he said.

Vigil settled in and was in deep thought by the time they returned to Lochgelly. Burying Zuriel in a desolate area would just be prolonging the inevitable. If he took him to the bog where he had left Adriel, it might be leading Zuriel to the very location he was trying to get to in the first place.

Mark's intuition must have been in overdrive because he came up with the solution to the problem without either of the men saying a word.

"I made some arrangements to meet a man near here," he said. "I will owe him a favor and if need be, you can settle it for me if I am not available."

"I am not sure what you are talking about," said Vigil.

"Our friend in the boot," said Mark. "We are going to permanently resolve this issue once and for all."

They circled around the edge of town until they pulled up in front of a simple but elegant building. A short stout man in a dark suit directed them to pull around to the back. He went into the building and met them in the back with a long stainless-steel cart with a folded white sheet. Mark got out and lifted the eyeless body onto the cart. The short stout man looked curiously at the face. It wasn't the missing eyes that puzzled him. As a mortician, he had seen all manner of injuries and mutilations in his lifetime. What was puzzling to him was that the wounds appeared to be healing. Two large scabs were recessed into the sockets and looked fresh to some degree; even pulsating. He simply shook his head and covered the body with the sheet.

"This way gentlemen," he said, as he pulled the cart into the double doors at the back of the building. After everyone was inside, he looked around to make sure no one had seen them. Then he secured the doors and proceeded with the business at hand.

"We have coffins available if you like," said Mr. Connary. His name was not on the sign outside, so Vigil figured he must be a partner or employee of the funeral home. "Of course, I will have to charge you for that," he said.

"I don't think we will be needing a coffin," said Mark. "There won't be a viewing involved."

"Very well," said Mr. Connary. "Most people do not want to be present during the cremation process. Will that be the case here?"

"No," said Vigil. "We will need to see it...and there may be some, uh...unusual aspects to this procedure."

"How so?" asked the mortician.

"Let's just say," said Mark. "...there is a reason for your substantial fee and why you come so highly recommended."

"I understand," he said. "...right this way."

Vigil had to work very hard at reconciling himself to this form of disposal. Even though he didn't practice the faith, he was Jewish by birth...and so was Zuriel. There were strict codes against cremation in the Jewish faith that were only recently being relaxed in some areas. Much of the resistance came in light of the atrocities and cremations committed during the Holocaust. Again, Mark's intuition engaged.

"I am not sure what your opposition is to this kind of disposal, but you are not the one doing this," he said. "I am. In this case, there is no blood on your hands."

"How did you know I have a problem with it?" asked Vigil.

"I am a master at reading facial expressions and body language," answered Mark. "It is a necessary skillset in our line of work. You can wait outside if that would make it easier."

"No...I'll be alright," said Vigil. "I have to do it a few times before."

"Shall we proceed then?" asked Mr. Connary. "Usually, the bodies are nude when they undergo cremation. It's not necessary, but I thought I would ask."

"No," said Mark. "We should get this done as quickly as possible."

"Well," said Mr. Connary. "...the oven is heating. It will take a wee bit of time to reach the required temperature of 750 degrees Celsius. After that, it will take a little over two hours. Are you sure you want to wait in here?"

"Absolutely," said Vigil.

Mark whispered, "I'm a little fuzzy on the Celsius thing. How much is that in American?" Vigil wasn't sure if Mark really didn't know, or if he was just trying to lighten the mood.

"We're not converting money you goof. 750 Celsius is about 1400 degrees...American!" Vigil shook his head and smiled. Mark turned away and smiled also.

"We're ready," said Mr. Connary. "Here. I thought you might want these. They could damage one of the cremation processes."

"What are they?" asked Vigil.

"Personal effects," said Mr. Connary. "Jewelry wreaks havoc with the grinding process. Plus it is a shame to destroy some items." He handed Vigil a stainless steel tray with the items laid out on it. The most striking piece was a large antique pocket watch. It was made of gold and had a simple but elegant face. On the back was an inscription that made Vigil clench his teeth. Etched in the gold back was *Hermann Goering* and below the inscription was *WEIHNACHTEN 1940*. It was thought that Goering gave a watch like this to someone he trusted. Vigil figured Zuriel must have been very close to Goering to receive such a gift; unless he stole it. Both were very real possibilities. Either way, it made it much easier for him to accept his complicity in Zuriel's cremation and the resulting screams that began coming out of the oven.

"Gentlemen," said Mr. Connary calmly. "For the sake of dignity, (and plausible deniability) I must leave you for a few moments. I will return shortly."

"We understand completely," said Mark.

Shortly proved to be almost an hour and it still wasn't long enough. Due to Zuriel's recuperative powers, he was still screaming; though one can only imagine what kind of grotesque visage was uttering the screams. It was a full ninety minutes before the screaming faded into soft cries and then finally a gentle hiss as his body turned to ash. Vigil thought about what it would take to destroy his own body; then drove the thoughts from his head. Mr. Connary returned at the two hour point, but left the body in the oven for another full hour just to be sure. Then he completed the grinding process, making sure Zuriel had finally been *resolved* at last. The ashes were placed in a simple box and he gently, but unceremoniously handed it to Mark.

"I think you will probably want to deal with these," Mark said. "You know, closure and all."

"Thanks Mark," said Vigil. "I'll handle this part."

"Let us know when you want to call in that favor," said Mark. He handed Mr. Connary a card with nothing but an unusual barcode on it. "Take a picture of this with your phone. It will get a message to me no matter where I am in the world. Then I will get back with you…or one of us will."

"Thank you," said Mr. Connary. "Hopefully, I will not need your services any time soon; but it is nice to know they are available. Good day gentlemen."

Mark and Vigil left the way they came in and headed

back to Lochgelly.

"I suggest we go to a pub," said Mark.

"I suggest I find a place to change clothes first," said Vigil. "Mine are kind of shredded."

"And then the pub after, right?"

"Okay...pub after," Vigil agreed. "...and thanks for saving me. That was the closest I have ever been to death. I don't know how you people do it."

"I'm not sure what you mean by *you people*," said Mark. "You mean devilishly attractive people?"

"What else would I mean?" said Vigil. They headed back to town. He was going to have a lot to explain to Leslie.

Chapter Twenty-Two: Disruption

Whatever those cellular disruptors were that Zuriel had used on Vigil, they must have wreaked havoc on his cell phone as well as his memory. He couldn't remember where he had left his car. Mark drove around the streets of Lochgelly and finally found it eleven blocks from the pub where Leslie worked. He had no idea why he had parked so far away, but his brains were pretty scrambled.

Vigil was sure Leslie would be furious with him because he hadn't called. She shouldn't be...considering his line of work; but she probably would be because they were emotionally connected. He didn't usually get so attached to people that it would even bother him, but Leslie was different. She was strong, confident, sexy as hell and accepted him for what he was. She knew his secret, but wasn't overwhelmed or repulsed by it. Finding someone like her was difficult; and it was going to be more difficult to leave her.

"Are you sure Leslie doesn't have a sister?" asked Mark. "Maybe a cousin or something? How about a sexy aunt? Say, is her mom seeing anybody?"

"You sound like you are in high school," said Vigil. "...and yes, her mom is seeing someone, but she might give you a go if you ask nicely."

"I can never tell when you're serious," said Mark. "It doesn't matter though. I really need to be off. I am sure there is another assignment waiting for me when I get back."

"Remember what I said about those devices," said Vigil. "I think they are too dangerous to risk getting into the wrong hands."

"They will be safe with me," Mark assured him. "I have a trusted friend who will look them over. He might be able to tell me who made them." Vigil didn't know that Mark was talking about his twin brother, Michael.

"Just be careful," said Vigil. "Those devices scare the hell out of me; and I can't say that about too many things."

"I'll be careful," said Mark. "*You* be careful." With that, he gave Vigil another one of his signature handshake/embrace combos.

"Did you just place another tracker on my back?" asked Vigil.

"What kind of agent to you take me for? Of course I did."

"I plan to have sex with Leslie soon," said Vigil. "This thing doesn't have a camera or a mic does it?"

"Sadly no," answered Mark. "Would you consider sending me a video? Encrypted of course."

"You'd better get out of here," said Vigil. "...or I won't put in a good word for you with Hazel."

"I'm going. Be safe my friend."

"You as well," said Vigil. "You as well...and thanks, for everything."

Mark tipped his imaginary hat and drove away. Vigil stood watching for a long time. It felt good to have friends for a change. He hadn't realized how long he had distanced himself from people. Seeing Leslie suddenly became very important to him. He touched the unlock button on his key fob, but nothing happened. The disruptors must have shorted it out as well. He manually unlocked the door and started the car.

Soon he was sitting in front of Leslie's semi-detached trying to work up the nerve to go to the door. Facing enemies over the centuries was nothing compared to facing the wrath of an enraged woman of Scottish descent. It took him a full five minutes before he finally got out of the car. He stood at her door and prepared to knock. Even though they had been involved in the most intimate ways possible, he wasn't going to disrespect her by just walking in unannounced. His knock felt much more timid than he wanted it to.

It was a couple of minutes before Leslie finally opened the door. She could have opened it right away but she wanted to properly compose herself first. That turned out to be a waste of time. She embraced Vigil so hard as soon as she saw him that he thought he heard his back pop. Her kiss was so passionate that he lost himself in it. When she finally pulled away, he kept his eyes closed to savor as much of the memory of it as he could. He opened his eyes slowly; but instead of seeing the glowing image of the goddess that he imagined, he was met with a fierce contemptuous stare.

Leslie stood for a moment as if contemplating her next words. Since actions speak louder than words, she struck Vigil on the face so hard that his vision doubled for a moment. He couldn't say that he didn't deserve it. He also couldn't say that he hated it. Any physical contact with Leslie was always a pleasure.

"You couldn't call?" she demanded. "Do you know how worried I was?"

"Actually, I couldn't..." said Vigil softly. "I..."

"I know," yelled Leslie. "...*it was job related*! Is that going to be your excuse for everything from now on?"

"It's a pretty valid excuse," said Vigil. "...at least, this time." He handed her his phone, which was now little more than a shiny coaster with cracks and burn marks. "I would have called if I could."

Leslie noticed for the first time the way his clothes were lacerated.

"Who...what...did this to you?" she asked. Her tone was a mix of anger, concern, compassion and regret. She wished she hadn't hit him, but he loved that she was concerned enough about him to be angry.

"It was Zuriel," he said. "This situation has been permanently... *resolved.*"

"Are you sure?" asked Leslie. She wiped tears from her eyes. "You know how these guys tend to come back."

"I'm sure," said Vigil. "He's in the front seat of my car if you'd care to see."

"You've got a bloody corpse in the front seat of your car? Are ye mental?"

"Well, I do get a psych evaluation every year," said Vigil. "Sometimes the results are inconclusive though." Leslie was not amused. Vigil took her in his arms and kissed her passionately again. "He's in a little container," he said quietly. "...no bigger than a box of porridge. He's gone for good this time."

Leslie breathed out with an involuntary shudder. Her intuition told her it was over, but sometimes the flood of relief washing over one can have just as much effect as the stress.

"There is something we need to do right away then," she said. She grabbed Vigil by the shirt and ripped it open. One of the buttons that hit the floor took a comically long time to stop spinning before coming to a rest. By then, they were already in the bedroom undressing each other. Leslie was much less careful than Vigil because his clothes were already shredded. That meant he was naked long before she was. She helped him with the rest of her clothes and just as they were about the fall into bed, Leslie broke away and ran naked down the hall.

"Where are you going?" asked Vigil. He looked both comical and obscene as he lay there all alone on the bed in his aroused state.

"I am calling off work today," Leslie shouted from the front room. "You deserve my full attention for the rest of the day...and tonight."

When Leslie returned, Vigil was lying there with his groin area covered by the corner of a hand-sewn quilt. It was obvious what he was hiding and it was only slightly less obscene than if he had been lying there exposed. Leslie blushed when she saw him/it...not because she was embarrassed, but because she was trying not to laugh. She knelt down and began to kiss his stomach and then slowly slid her body along his until their lips met. The quilt was pulled away and fell into neat folds on the floor at the foot of the bed. For the rest of the afternoon, they were inseparable; even when Hazel interrupted to remind them that supper was on the table. They hardly acknowledged her and she left. She returned a moment later with two plates of food that she placed on Leslie's kitchen table; then she made a discreet exit.

Long shadows had given way to darkness before Leslie and Vigil came up for air. They ate what Hazel had left in the kitchen like two nudists enjoying dinner at home. The roast beef and potatoes were heated in the microwave to semi-perfection. Vigil was famished because he hadn't eaten since he was abducted. Leslie was famished because she hadn't eaten since Vigil went missing as well.

Vigil thought about telling her of his intention to leave soon, but it just seemed like an awkward time to do it. Leslie knew what he was thinking, but pretended she didn't. If this was going to be their last night together, she wanted it to be perfect. It wasn't, but it was close. It was as perfect as a night can be when both people know they may never see each other again. They held each other for a long time after every erotic romance session. Sometime around one in the morning, Vigil lay awake and stared at the ceiling. Leslie rested in the crook of his arm. Her soft snore still sounded like the gentle purr of a kitten. He hugged her a little tighter and she snuggled in a little deeper.

The thoughts running through his mind were about the loose ends he needed to tie up and those assignments that would present themselves as soon as he returned to the states. He would probably visit Adriel in the bog one last time and put a couple of his special bullets into his head for good measure. It wasn't out of hatred that he would do it; it would be for efficiency. Killing enemy soldiers in wartime was so much easier. At least when you put them down, they didn't get back up. Vigil really didn't like killing mortals...even bad ones. However, sometimes it was necessary and he did it the way he would do any other job he was assigned to. It just felt wrong to take the life of someone who from his perspective, was going to live such a short life to begin with. Vigil's expanded lifespan was both a blessing and a curse.

Leslie would just have to understand and he was pretty sure that she would. Her intuition would tell her how important it was for him to leave. However, it wasn't going to make his departure any easier on her; or him. She would go back to her job and hide her feelings. Vigil figured this was how she got by before he came along. The women in his life always seemed to be like that. Eventually, they would convince themselves that he was no good for them and they were blowing their relationship out of proportion anyway. But it didn't mean that Vigil didn't also suffer for it. Sometimes his heart ached for them long after they passed away. Leslie would probably be one of those.

*   *   *

One cannot live over a thousand years and not become romantically entangled once in a while. Even a few of Vigil's more evil brothers sometimes developed strong bonds with the occasional mortal. Of course, their bonds were more like the type of a bond one develops with a family pet. His brothers would know that the individuals were not going to be around forever, but they enjoyed the time with them anyway. This was not the way Vigil felt about mortals. He savored every moment with them and tried to have relationships as close to normal as possible. The problem was that it tore him up when they finally left him. Death always seems the most difficult to those who are left behind. Elaborate funeral rites were instituted solely for this reason...to give those left behind some illusion of controlling their fate. Fate always won out though.

In the early Eighteenth Century, Vigil earned his passage across the Indian Ocean as a seaman on a merchant ship. The ship carried silks, cloth, spices, jewels and other treasures that made them a target for pirates in the area. One pirate ship in particular was among the most successful at capturing vessels in open water. The captain had an uncanny skill for approaching ships in such a stealthy manner that he was upon them before they could call an alert and ready their cannons. Captain Rahn the Spectre had a reputation as one of the most enigmatic pirates to sail the seas. A few of the ships he encountered were later found nearly intact, but devoid of their treasures; and their entire crews were missing. Other ships were never found at all. One could only imagine the horrible fates those sailors suffered at the hands of Captain Rahn the Spectre.

Captain Rahn was indeed skilled at sailing and warfare. His aim with a pistol was deadly and true; and his proficiency with a sword was unequalled. His most impressive talent however, was his ability to charm the ladies and convince sailors to join his crew. Some said his tongue was made of silver and the words he spoke could convince the most loyal of ship captains to turn everything over to him without a fight. Since the East India companies didn't pay their sailors much, they didn't take a lot of convincing. If Rahn was shorthanded, he would leave conquered ships floating unmanned in the ocean. If he had no vacancies on his ship, he would direct the captains to sail with him to a southern Madagascar port in Antongil Bay.

Vigil readily joined Captain Rahn's crew because he had little reason not to. He could move on if need be sometime in the future. He thought it might be interesting to live a pirate's life for a while. He had experienced nearly everything else the world had to offer at the time. Vigil's one condition was that no sailors were harmed unnecessarily. That didn't appear to be a problem. Captain Rahn the Spectre continued to retain his charm.

Another person with irresistible charm was a girl who poured grog at a pub in the pirate port. She had dark olive skin and her eyes were the color of emeralds. Her name was Cinnamon, and Vigil was attracted to her the first time he ever saw her. Cinnamon found herself equally attracted to Vigil...which was a problem in a port full of rowdy pirates. Many other men hoped to possess her and were not ready for one man to lay claim to her. Vigil had no intentions of controlling Cinnamon in any way. Maybe that was why she found herself so attracted to him. He saw her as a person and not as a possession or a prize to be hoarded.

Vigil was challenged to duels, both with swords and with pistols. He was also ambushed at night on his way back to his quarters on a regular basis. Often, a pirate would be boasting the next day of slitting Vigil's throat, only to have

Vigil would arrive unscathed with a look of amused confusion on his face. The pirate would be branded as a liar and a coward. That usually led to the individual being banished from the port on the next ship out.

The attraction between Vigil and Cinnamon grew stronger as the months passed. During the times he was out to sea, their longing for each other was agony. He wanted to marry her; but he knew if he did, her life would probably be in danger. He could tell that even Captain Rahn was attracted to her. So he contented himself with being with her as much as he could while in port. They would swim in the lagoon under a full moon and make love on the beach. Cinnamon's slender body was as dark as ebony in the subtle lunar light, with a faint glow around her hips and shoulders. Vigil was prepared to give everything up for her...even his pirate life.

His heart ached as he was about to go out to sea for the last time. He was determined to take Cinnamon away from the pirate port and the dangers he had submitted her to, but he would have to make one more mission. This would be his last voyage as a pirate and he would take her far away, perhaps to the New World somewhere. He had amassed enough of a fortune for them to live comfortably for the rest of their lives...well, for the rest of her life anyway. Thinking of their new life together got him through the long sea voyage. It was much longer than usual, probably because Fate was the cruel bastard that it was. Vigil was out to sea for just under a year. As the ship sailed into port, he strained his eyes trying to find Cinnamon on the dock awaiting his return. His heart sank and then began to burn when he didn't see her.

It seemed to take forever to tie up to the dock; Vigil leaped over the railing as soon as it did, and ran toward the village. A small group of women met him at the edge of town. He knew there was something wrong when he saw them. They all stood with their heads bowed, but looked at him as he approached. The women didn't need to say much, for he already knew most of what they wanted to say. He tried to speak without his voice breaking, but that was impossible.

"How?" was all he asked. They didn't answer. Instead, they presented him with his baby daughter. Her skin was only slightly lighter than Cinnamon's, but her infant eyes had just changed from sky blue to deep emerald green. Vigil's mind reeled with conflict. He knew from their expressions that Cinnamon had died giving birth to a baby he didn't even know was on the way. While he was gone, he always feared something might happen to her...that a drunken pirate might go too far and kill her. In the end, it was he who had caused her death.

Vigil didn't know quite what to do. He would take care of his child, but he wasn't sure what kind of life she would have. He didn't know if the baby possessed his regenerative ability, but he knew for certain she was his. Vigil could always tell when he was in the presence of his own family. One of the women in the group was acting as a wet nurse, having lost a child at birth herself. He asked if she could care for the child when he was away. He promised to make sure it would be worth it to her. He also told her that in time, he would take them both to a place they could live without fear of pirates, authorities or reprisals of any kind. Her name was Christelle and she agreed happily. She had become hopelessly attached to the baby she was calling Anja. Vigil liked the name and made it her name officially.

Captain Rahn the Spectre proved to be as much a gentleman as he was a leader of men. He agreed to take Vigil and his newly acquired family to a port up north where they could obtain passage to Europe; but the captain hated to see them go. Vigil had been a hard worker and was handy in a fight. Captain Rahn was sure he would never see Vigil again when he dropped them off at the port in Mombasa. From there, they travelled north to the Nile and to Egypt. Vigil couldn't shake the feeling that someone he knew had been there.

Anja did indeed possess Vigil's regenerative abilities and they travelled together for a number of years. She married a man she met in Spain when she was seventy-one. Of course, the man thought she was only twenty and Vigil kept her secret. They still occasionally crossed paths once in a while over the years and he always kept tabs on her. She looked so much like her mother that it hurt sometimes; but it hurt in a good way.

* * *

When the glowing sunrise illuminated Leslie's bedroom window, she was still nestled in the crook of Vigil's arm. He thought she was still asleep until he felt soft tears fall on his skin. He didn't need to know why she was crying. He would be weeping as well if he allowed himself to.

"Promise me something," she said softly in a raspy voice.

"If I can," said Vigil.

"Promise me you won't come back and see me when I am old. I don't think I could take that."

"You know you will always look the same to me," said Vigil.

"You can say that," said Leslie. "...but I won't believe it. Please, just promise."

"I don't think you realize what that will do to me," he said.

"I don't think you realize what it will do to me if you see me that way." Leslie shuddered as she wept. "It's ideal the way it is right now. If you cannot stay for a while longer, leave me with the perfect memories I have. Can you do that?"

"One thing I have never gotten used to," said Vigil. "…is how I can live for a hundred years with no serious relationships and then be so hopelessly involved over the course of only a few days."

"I guess it is one of the things we have in common," she said. "You can still come visit…just not when I get old." She held Vigil tighter than she ever had and trembled with emotion.

"I will do whatever you want," said Vigil. "Now, since this is our last day…for a while at least, let's do something special. When was the last time you visited Paris?"

"Paris? I have never been to Paris," said Leslie.

"I was thinking of a picnic in the Parisian countryside," said Vigil. "A bottle of wine, a loaf of bread, a rich cheese and your company…a perfect ending."

"If it's an ending, it won't be perfect," said Leslie. "…but it sounds lovely. When can we leave?"

"I need to make a couple of calls," said Vigil. "…then we can be on our way."

* * *

It was as perfect as it could be. Vigil hired a private jet to fly them to Paris and rented the most luxurious car he could find. They drove to a spot overlooking a field of sunflowers like the ones in the Van Gogh painting. They spent the afternoon enjoying wine and bread…and one another's company. That night, they walked along the *Champs-Élysées* and looked at the lights of Paris reflecting on the water. When they kissed, their tears blended on both their faces. There was something symbolic about it. The tears would evaporate eventually or be wiped away. It would be like they never existed in the first place…except for the memory.

Vigil flew back to the United States after making sure Leslie got back home safely. They had said their final goodbyes and he made sure to say goodbye to Hazel. He left them both with a card similar to the one Mark had. It had a barcode on it that one need only take a picture of to send a text message to Vigil, no matter where he was in the world.

The plane ride home seemed to take forever and his stateside apartment seemed much emptier than before. Fortunately, he had an assignment waiting for him when he got back to occupy his mind. A Russian assassin with the codename *Bekka Dark* had surfaced in Prague. Vigil knew the name. He knew Bekka Dark all too well.

Chapter Twenty-Three: Promised Land

Vigil's target, Bekka Dark, had recently been in Scotland on an assignment of her own. Had Vigil not been so preoccupied with other things, he might have been assigned to resolve her while he was there. They just missed each other at the airport; but then, he wasn't looking for her yet and she didn't know she would be his target. Had they seen each other, there might have been some recognition, but not likely. Their history had been brief, but intricate as assignments go. It was physical in the sense that they shared the same bed once. However, that time was purely in the line of duty. Occasionally Vigil's assignments had perks.

Beque Yefimovich Petrovya (Бек Ефимович Петрова) used the code name *Bekka Dark*. She was yet another skilled assassin in the world. Russian-born and fluent in five languages, she could communicate well enough in three more. She hadn't lived in a Soviet orphanage or been sexually assaulted as a child. In fact, she was born to an affluent family with strong political ties. There was no sad backstory to associate with her to suggest why she became a world class assassin. She was at the top of her class in school, and at the age of sixteen, she was recruited by the Committee for State Security. The Russian name for the agency was Komitet Gosudarstvennoy Bezopasnosti (Комитéт госудáрственной безопáсности). The rest of the world knew the organization as the *KGB*. She trained as an assassin and found that vocation much more fulfilling than the life her parents had planned for her in the world of finance.

She was beautiful of course, but she could be

understated when the assignment called for it. It wouldn't do for one of the KGB's top assassins to be noticed because she looked like a supermodel. Her favorite ruse was to pose as a homeless vagrant with a slight mental disability. That persona would sometimes cause her targets to become uncomfortable, but it allowed her to get close to them and even make physical contact without raising suspicion. She often would place a small explosive charge next to one of their vital organs and then move on. The charge was much like a squib used in Hollywood special effects, except much more powerful. The explosive was directional like a Claymore mine, so it could blow a hole in a target's back and not harm a bystander three feet away. The cause of death was usually misdiagnosed as a wound from a sniper round. Meanwhile, Bekka Dark would continue along the street talking to herself; pushing a shopping cart full of aluminum cans and random trash. She would immerse herself so much into the role that she would redeem the cans at a recycling center. Afterwards, what little money she collected from the cans would be dropped into the lap of an actual homeless person.

Bekka Dark's methods of eliminating targets were often less precise and more clinical in nature. She sometimes preferred to take a more psychological approach with a target. On a good day, she could even make her targets take themselves out. She could have been a skilled psychologist if that had been her chosen profession. For some targets, it only took a little nudge to push them over the edge. Other times, she had to *physically* push them over the edge...of a high building. Either way, she got the job done.

Bekka Dark and Vigil had crossed paths a few years before. He was pursuing a high-profile target in Greece; she was pursuing Vigil. She found herself intrigued by him for a reason she couldn't put her finger on. It wasn't because of his looks, even though he was not unattractive. There was just something about him. It was as if he glowed with some invisible aura she was unable to resist.

Vigil had *resolved* the target he had been assigned too and stayed in Greece for another day for a little *R&R*. Bekka positioned herself at the end of the bar in his hotel that night. It was tricky for her because several men (and a couple of women) approached her in the bar for sex. She had to reject them in a way so it didn't look too obvious that she had her sights on Vigil. He might have noticed what she was doing; but he was after all, just a man. He had no more control over his urges than any other male on the planet, no matter how long their lifespans. He found an opportunity to talk to her and she was just as intriguing as she looked. The light amount of perfume she wore was a mixture of cinnamon and spice, with a touch of floral. Vigil hated floral, but this fragrance was exceptional.

They talked for an hour and a half. Both of them related stories of their adventures around the globe. Both of them lied about everything they told the other. It didn't matter. Both of them felt they had succeeded with their goals when they blindly fell through the door of his room while they were locked in a passionate embrace. There was a moment of levity and then back to business as usual as they got up off the floor and picked up where they had left off. They fell onto the bed as they held each other. One of Bekka's stylish heels fell off and she reached down to seductively remove the other one. Vigil kicked off his own shoes rather unceremoniously. He reached over and switched off the lamp so the only light illuminating the room was from the half-closed bathroom door.

Bekka kissed Vigil softly and whispered, "I'll be right back. I have to…take care of something." He watched her as she quietly got out of bed. The room was suddenly shrouded in darkness as she shut the bathroom door behind her. Vigil wasn't sure how presumptuous he ought to be, but chose to err on the side of passion. He quickly removed the rest of his clothes and slipped beneath the crisp sheets of the bed. He rested on one elbow and waited in anticipation of Bekka's return. He didn't have to wait long and he wasn't disappointed.

At that point in time, Vigil didn't know Bekka was an assassin, but he didn't completely trust her either. He didn't completely trust anyone. She stepped into the room wearing a revealing black thong and a matching bra. Both were fashioned in transparent lace that left little if anything to the imagination. She wore a single black garter on her left thigh. It had a small red ribbon on the side that was the only speck of color on her monochromatic ensemble. Thoughts raced through Vigil's mind; thoughts of honeymoons and X-rated movie plots. His mouth suddenly went dry, but the mini-fridge containing bottled water was on the other side of the room. He didn't want to spoil the mood or the presentation by getting up to get a drink; no matter how thirsty he suddenly was.

Bekka stood for a long time letting Vigil admire the view. Then she moved to the bed in what seemed like slow motion. She placed one knee on the corner of the bed and then crawled like a prowling cat up to Vigil's face. He was at her mercy but didn't mind it at all. Her scent was intoxicating and her eyes sparkled. They looked as dark as obsidian in the dim light. Across the room from the bed was a large mirror. The glimpse Vigil caught of Bekka lasted for only a second. From that angle and due to the delicate design of her undergarments, she looked naked...but with a single exception. The black garter she wore held not one, but three stainless steel tactical throwing knifes.

Vigil reacted almost immediately, but his reaction was too slow. Bekka drove the blade of one of the knives into his skull, just behind his left ear. Vigil's eyes blurred as a spray of blood decorated his pillow and the one next to it. He grasped for the knife to use it on his attacker, but she had already removed it and moved out of range. He tried to get to his clothes and draw his pistol; but like an idiot, he had tossed them onto the chair that was across the room. He tried to stem the flow of blood while crawling across the room naked and bleeding. Housekeeping was not going to have an easy time cleaning his room after this.

Meanwhile Bekka Dark, thinking her assignment had been completed, returned to the bathroom and quickly dressed. Her eyes widened when she saw that Vigil was still alive and limply pointing his gun in her direction. She walked over and took it out of his hand. "You must have some kind of constitution," she said. "You should be dead already."

"You...don't know the half of it," said Vigil. Bekka looked down between his legs and softly said, "I wish I could have waited now. I suspect this would have been a night I would not have forgotten."

"I won't forget it," said Vigil. "That's for sure."

"I really do regret this," said Bekka. From her handbag, she pulled out a 9mm Strizh pistol (Russian issue) and placed the silenced barrel between Vigil's eyes. "Maybe we can meet up in the next life," she said, and squeezed the trigger.

* * *

Vigil rubbed the spot between his eyes absently. Their encounter had been years ago, but seeing her name brought back memories as if it had happened last week. Unlike the disdain he felt for his brothers who were still on his unresolved list, Vigil held no animosity for Bekka Dark. She was doing her job and she did it well. It wasn't her fault that he was still alive. She had done her absolute best to send him to the *great beyond*. When he related the story to the few agents he confided in, he said they slept together and let it go at that.

The report he received stated that she was most likely in Israel. A high-priority target was supposed to be there in a couple of days and intelligence reports indicated she had been assigned to eliminate the target. Vigil had friends there, so he could turn the trip into a working vacation of sorts. He might even visit the town of Bethany and get a look at his father's supposed hometown. Then again, it had become such an area of conflict due to tension between religious factions; he might just visit his friends, complete his assignment and come home. He still missed Leslie and he hoped he was able to concentrate. Bekka Dark was a force to be reckoned with and it wouldn't do for Vigil to go in only half prepared.

Spotters throughout the city of Jerusalem created a surveillance network that was second to none in the world. It was said only a fly could get in and out of the net, but only after being fitted with a tracking device. That was usually said by the high-tech specialists who designed the *cyberspotters*, covert reconnaissance drones and satellite surveillance programs; as well as tracking devices. Their area of expertise was not in humor or metaphor, but in spotting targets.

Since the end of World War II, Israel has been a potential *powder keg* waiting for some faction to strike a match. Constant surveillance was necessary to insure some semblance of peace. In the early years, low-level agents collected data and passed it on to the intelligence community through conventional means. With the advent of cyber technology, data collection processes jumped ahead by light years. A single cyber agent seated securely in his cubical could know everything about a subject sitting at a sidewalk café on the other side of the planet.

A subject who had a seventy-one percent probability of being Bekka Dark was detected outside a hotel in the city. The reason for the low probability score was because Bekka Dark was an expert at disguise and at confounding facial recognition software. The very makeup she wore divided her image into fractals and then reassembled them in a way that subtly changed her appearance; all the while looking like conventional makeup. The agency knew of its existence, but had yet to develop a program to counter it. Vigil would have to complete the surveillance in person to make a positive identification. His moral code was that it was better for a hundred guilty people to go free than for one innocent person to die by his hand. The agency didn't agree with his philosophy, but there were a lot of things the agency didn't know. Vigil followed his own rules.

Rather than stay in the city and risk becoming a target himself, Vigil travelled to the town of Rehovot about 50 kilometers to the east of Jerusalem. A couple who he knew well lived there. Lorraine and Lawrence had kept him hidden in their home while he recovered from a very serious chest wound two decades before. During the hour drive to their home, Vigil forced his appearance to change a bit. He wanted to make himself appear older than usual. If he showed up looking the same as he did twenty years ago, there would be too many questions he would have to answer. There had been enough questions to answer when he had miraculously healed from a chest wound that should have been fatal. Lawrence was a physician and a very good one; but even he could not have pulled off that miracle. Vigil tried to convince Lawrence that his medical expertise was responsible for his quick recovery.

Lorraine may have suspected the truth. She had been told stories when she was young...legends about people who couldn't die. People who were ruthless; people who had no regard for human life; people who were not people, but monsters. Vigil could have answered all of her questions when she observed how quickly he healed, but he chose not to at the time. Maybe he would tell her the whole story this time; but only if he thought telling her wouldn't put their lives in danger.

When he met them before, they had two young children. Lorraine and Lawrence didn't know they had put their whole family in danger by taking him in.

Their children, Alon and Hayley, were grown now and had built lives of their own. It mildly surprised him to know that Alon had been working in Glasgow Scotland only an hour or so away from where he had just been. *Small world*, he thought, *and getting smaller with each passing decade.* The work Alon was doing was classified as well and Vigil knew better than to ask about its details. Besides, he had sources that could find out any information he might want if need be.

By the time Vigil arrived at the home of Lawrence and Lorraine, his hair color was sufficiently aged with a distinguished *salt and pepper* quality. His face had new laugh lines around his mouth and eyes, even though Vigil rarely laughed. He thought about Leslie. He never did get a chance to give her that *celebrity* fantasy and wasn't sure whether she was really serious about it or not. He would have to find out. Or, he could just show up with dark skin and surprise her one day. It would depend on her mood the next time he talked to her.

Vigil's appearance must have been exactly what the couple expected because they welcomed him in as an old friend, but that was probably their nature with everyone. The first thing Lawrence did after giving Vigil a hearty embrace was to enquire about his old wound. He was the quintessential physician and felt as though he wasn't doing his job if he didn't do a follow-up on his patients' conditions; even decades later. Lorraine was every bit the hostess one would want her to be. She treated Vigil like family; and considering their collective Hebrew heritage, they may have been related on some distant level.

"See? It didn't even scar," said Vigil, as Lawrence

examined his chest. "That's just how good you are."

"I'm not this good," said Lawrence. Vigil's chest showed no sign of the wound Lawrence had tended; although it did show some scarring from his recent wounds, but those too would disappear in time.

"This is nothing less than miraculous," he said. "You must tell me your secret."

"Good genes," said Vigil. "...and don't sell yourself short. You did a tremendous job. I am lucky you were there when I needed you."

"Alright," said Lawrence. "You don't need to tell me; but flattery will only get you so far." He slapped Vigil on the back as he was rebuttoning his shirt. Lorraine came into the room carrying a tray.

"Oh...did I miss the show? That's not fair." She set the tray down and placed her hands on her hips with a mock pouting expression. "...and after I brought you tea and cake."

"We can do it again if you like," said Vigil.

"No, we can't," Lawrence stated in a matter-of-fact way. "...besides, there is the *doctor/patient confidentiality code* we have to adhere to."

"Really?" said Lorraine. "Just how in depth was this examination?"

"Just never you mind," said Lawrence. "Did I hear you mention tea?"

"Very well," said Lorraine. "You ruin all my fun." She served the tea and sat down.

"So...what have you been up to since the last time we saw you?" Lorraine began. "What has it been...seventeen years?"

"More like nineteen," said Vigil. "...but I stopped counting years. It gets too depressing."

"Age is just a number if you take care of yourself properly," said Lawrence. "...and considering how you have healed, you must be taking very good care of yourself."

"Probably not as well as I should," said Vigil. "...but I get by."

"Is there a special lady in your life?" asked Lorraine.

"Do you mean besides you?" asked Vigil.

"Hey, hey now," said Lawrence. "If you charm her too much, it puts a lot of pressure on me after you are gone." He winked at Vigil and Lorraine huffed slightly.

"There is one," said Vigil. "I only met her a short time ago, but we really seemed to click. I am not sure I will be able to get back to see her any time soon."

"You need to make time if she is that important to you," she advised.

"With my line of work, that may not be as easy as it sounds," said Vigil. "Keeping her safe is my highest priority."

"We never asked you what you do for a living," said Lawrence. "Since you never told us, we thought it best not to ask. But I must ask you now; are we in danger because you are here?"

"Not at all," said Vigil. "I am very careful when it comes to my friends. My assignment is waiting for me in Jerusalem. That's about all I can say about it right now."

"We understand," said Lorraine. "You will stay for dinner, won't you?"

"I wouldn't miss it," said Vigil.

The sun sank into a bank of clouds before disappearing below the horizon. The windows of Lawrence and Lorraine's comfortable flat illuminated with a welcoming glow as the streets grew dark. A few cars were parked along the street, but traffic in the area was light in the evening. A gray van with darkened windows was parked just a few doors down from their flat. Inside, the face of Bekka Dark was illuminated by the light from several display screens. Her intel told her that a high priority target was in the area. She had cyberspotters of her own and the display she was looking at showed the target's face. Even though he looked older than Bekka thought he should, the program said there was an eighty-six percent match. Vigil was, with minimal doubt, her high priority target.

Chapter Twenty-Four: Proper Introductions

Vigil left the home of Lawrence and Lorraine somewhere around one-thirty in the morning. They had insisted he spend the night, but he didn't want to impose. He also didn't want to stay in one place too long. People got hurt when he did that.

"Take care Lawrence," he said as he was leaving. "I will try to get back to see you two again when I can."

"Try to make it sooner than twenty years next time," said Lawrence. "We are not getting any younger you know."

"What? Lorraine hasn't aged a day since the last time I was here," said Vigil.

"I told you to quit that," said Lawrence. "You are going to make her hard to live with."

"You mind your own business," said Lorraine smiling. "Let the man talk. You were saying?"

Vigil leaned over and kissed her on the cheek while Lawrence gave him an obviously fake jealous glance.

"You're next," said Vigil as he leaned in close to Lawrence.

"Oh no," said Lawrence. He shook Vigil's hand vigorously instead. Vigil pulled him in close for a manly hug. Maybe he planted a tracking device on him. Maybe he didn't.

Vigil's empathy for humanity made leaving his friends that much worse. He never knew if it was going to be the last time he would ever see them; and on those occasions when it was, he was always the one who was left behind. Immortality was not without its own set of consequences. He made sure to take in every aspect of his visits so he could relive them when he felt low. Vigil even noted every light in every window and every vehicle parked on the street; although this was also because of his training with the agency. Vans with darkened or no windows were always suspicious...white utility vans especially so. The gray van parked three cars from his own was inconspicuous enough, which made it suspect. He did the cursory check of his rental as he always did and ran a covert electronic sweep of it. Once he was reasonably certain it hadn't been tampered with, he got in to drive to his room at the condo he was renting in Rehovot. Vigil watched in his rearview mirror for headlights as he pulled onto the main road. *If I am being followed, they must be able to see in the dark*, he thought. Of course, with the technology available, that was a distinct possibility; so he was careful to watch for a moment or two after he drove under a streetlight. Nothing appeared to be following him, so he drove on to his condo and went inside.

Even the most cautious agent can slip up. As the lights went on in Vigil's condo, the boot of his rental opened just enough to allow a careful surveillance of the area. Bekka Dark slipped out of the boot and onto the ground like black strap molasses spilling out of a jar. She was so stealthy and silent that she appeared little more than a shadow rolling over the grass in the night. She was dressed entirely in slate gray with the exception of night vision glasses that covered the slit in her ski mask. As she stood next to the stucco wall, she was nothing more than a vague shadowy outline.

Vigil had made his arrangements for the condo in such a way that Bekka Dark wasn't able to know its location ahead of time. If she had followed him in the van, he would have spotted her and driven to a different location. Even if he had checked the boot of his rental, she was clever enough in the art of camouflage that he still wouldn't have spotted her.

Getting into the condo was going to be tricky for Bekka though. Undoubtedly, Vigil had set up surveillance sensors and traps...at least on the first floor. The second floor might offer her a split-second opportunity to effectively eliminate her target, or at least give her some insight as to how he survived the first time.

Bekka climbed up a side of the condo with so little effort, a cat would be jealous. Through the upstairs window, she could see the turned-down bed and a light coming from under the bathroom door. *Prosto, kak mne eto nravitsya*, she thought. (*Just the way I like it.*) *Bystro i prosto.* (*Quick and simple.*) She took out her silenced pistol and placed it against the pane of glass while holding on to the drainpipe with her other hand. She supported herself by placing one foot on the drainpipe bracket and let the other leg dangle. A small amount of perspiration soaked into her ski mask as she held the impossible position for an unreasonable amount of time. *What is he doing in there?* she thought in English. She didn't get the opportunity to answer her own question. A bullet fired from the street pierced the back of her neck and shattered the window as it exited her forehead. She stayed in place for an expanded moment before falling to the ground. Bekka Dark lay prostrate on the ground like the shadow of a crucifix.

"I really didn't want it to end like this," said Vigil, as he prepared to remove her ski mask.

* * *

It is amazing how one person can have so much impact on the world. One would wonder if they knew of the effect they were having or were just an unwitting pawn in the grand scheme of history. A Holy Man had such an impact.

Several attempts had been made on the Holy Man's life

279

due to his influence over the royal family. It was said he had the power to heal, and he gained favor with the court by treating a medical condition of the regent's only son. The boy suffered from hemophilia and would have bled to death had it not been for the miraculous methods of this Holy Man. That alone was enough to allow him access to the royal *inner circle*, but he was also charming, extremely intelligent. There was a level of confidence about him that was undeniable.

In 1914, there was an attempt on his life that by all accounts should have ended him. A peasant woman had managed to get close enough to him to stab him in the abdomen. With an unimaginable amount of stamina, he ran from her; but the peasant woman, fueled by adrenalin and crazed rage, pursued him. Being able to run no more, he turned and struck her in the face as hard as he could. She went down immediately and a crowd gathered around them to assist the Holy Man. He had lost so much blood that he should have died. Yet miraculously, he recovered.

The Holy Man continued to influence the royal family so much so, that a group of nobles determined he was a threat to the empire. They conspired to put an end to him once and for all. Their methods were by no means noble. Instead of making a public statement with his death, they instead chose to cover up their part in it. They invited him to the palace of one of the nobles under false pretenses. Once there, he was welcomed warmly and given some cake laced with poison. The poison seemed to have no effect. He was then given wine with even more poison. This too had no discernable effect. Becoming frustrated, one of the nobles retrieved a revolver and shot the Holy Man in the chest. Convinced they had finally accomplished their bloody deed, they made preparations to cover their tracks. As they prepared to dispose of the body, the Holy Man sprang to life and attacked them once more. It took more than one of the nobles to fight him off and he was finally subdued with two shots from the revolver...one of them directly into his forehead.

The body of the Holy Man was then wrapped in cloth and dropped off a bridge into a river. It was later recovered and unceremoniously taken to a wooded area for a crude cremation. According to some accounts, as the flames leapt up on all sides, the body sat up in the midst of the fire. Maybe it was improper embalming techniques that caused the effect. Maybe it was something else. The Holy Man's name was Grigori: Grigori Yefimovich Rasputin, advisor to the Romanovs. Years later, a young woman claimed to be his descendant, though there was no official record to substantiate it. Her name was Beque Yefimovich Petrovya. The intelligence community knew her as Bekka Dark.

* * *

While Bekka Dark had been scaling the wall of Vigil's condo, Vigil had slipped out of a second story window on the side of the building and crawled down the wall like a spider. He used a remote device to turn lights on inside the condo, giving the impression he was in different rooms. From the street, he used a small caliber sniper rifle and standard issue ammunition to take out his target. When Vigil removed the ski mask and night vision glasses of his victim, he already expected to see the face of Bekka Dark. What he didn't expect to see was that her fatal head wound had begun to heal. Having read her dossier, her condition answered a lot of questions, but raised a few more.

Vigil had wondered how she had managed to survive several attempts on her life. What puzzled him now was her healing ability. He was pretty sure she wasn't related to him; but he couldn't really know for sure. There were other questions he didn't want to answer himself at the moment, especially to the local authorities. He picked her up in his arms and carried her like a bride to his bedchambers; a bride who had been shot in the head. It wasn't nearly as romantic as it sounded.

Vigil used metal zip ties to bind her arms to the bedposts and bound her ankles together. For the moment, he placed duct tape across her mouth, but he would want to talk to her when she recovered. He had been looking forward to a restful sleep that night, but Bekka Dark was, by only a little fault of her own, taking up the whole bed. Vigil knew better than to leave her unattended, so he settled into a chair in the corner and tried to make himself as comfortable as possible. He was certain he wouldn't be able to sleep, but the sunrise coming through the window a few hours later told him he had done otherwise. A muffled groan came from the bed and he knew she would be fully awake soon. Her head would feel like a hundred hangovers inside her skull, but she would be awake. She also wouldn't be happy.

A string of muffled profanities in multiple languages were probably issuing from Bekka Dark's lips behind the adhesive. Vigil waited for them to become less frequent before he considered removing the duct tape. Her eyes were bloodshot and the area around them was horribly bruised because of the bullet wound; but she still managed to pull off looking beautiful.

"I don't want this to hurt," he said. "...so brace yourself. I am going to pull this off fast." He ripped the tape off and she was sure the skin from her lips went with it.

"You shot me in the head and you are worried the tape would hurt? I do not understand American humor," she said.

"Shooting you was business," said Vigil. "There is no reason for me to be inconsiderate. I am sure if the situation was reversed, you would do the same."

"I would not have left you alive," said Bekka.

282

"Well, you kinda did," said Vigil. "That is why we need to talk."

"Are you just going to leave me tied up while we talk, or is this your idea of foreplay?" Bekka smiled weakly from one side of her mouth. The nerves on the other side hadn't properly healed yet.

"Oh, if I was doing foreplay, you would know it," said Vigil. "You should heal some first though. If you *said you had a headache*, I would have to believe it."

"Again, I do not understand your humor," she said. "...or maybe it's that you just aren't funny."

"Fair enough," said Vigil. "Let's be serious then. How do you manage to heal so quickly?"

"How do you?" Bekka countered. "I suspect we have the same reason."

"Do you mean you think we are related somewhere down our bloodlines?" asked Vigil.

"Not necessarily," Bekka said. "Maybe there are just more people who have this condition than you know about. There is already one more than I thought existed. Maybe you just never considered that others might heal in the same way."

Vigil had considered it, but after centuries of pursuing his own kin, he didn't think that was the case. Now he had to re-evaluate his position. Maybe some of those he had resolved had been from bloodlines other than his own. Maybe he didn't need to think every one of the monsters he had put down had been relatives of his. He suddenly felt a little better about himself.

"So tell me about your line," he said.

"This is the interrogation part now? Let me see. How does this go? 'You will get nothing out of me!' Did that sound convincing?"

Vigil wasn't sure if Bekka's sense of humor was returning, but she amused him anyway.

"Look," he said. "I understand about agency secrets. I am not asking about any of those. I suspect you are as curious about me as I am about you. I will tell you about me first. Then, if you think you can trust me, you can tell me about your history. Fair enough?"

Bekka paused for a moment and then nodded in agreement.

"Could you cut me loose first?" she asked.

"Not just yet," said Vigil. "You are after all, the best at what you do. Let's wait a while."

"Can I at least change clothes? These are covered in my blood and...let's just not talk about what else."

"I understand," said Vigil. "I've had those accidents myself in the past. Do you have anything to change into?"

"Back in the van," said Bekka. "...but I suppose you are not willing to leave me long enough to retrieve my bag for me."

"I am afraid you are right," said Vigil. "However, I propose a compromise. How about I let you change into one of my shirts? You can clean up, take care of any other business you need to and then I will secure you to the bed again."

"How can I turn down such an enticing offer? Still, I guess I don't have much of a choice. I agree to your terms." Bekka smiled in a way that was difficult to read. Vigil started snipping the metal bands that bound her wrists...all the while holding his gun on her. Once all her bonds were cut, he watched her walk unsteadily to the bathroom. She tried to shut the door, but he prevented it.

"A little privacy please," said Bekka.

"I think you and I are beyond privacy," said Vigil. "After Greece, there isn't much we don't know about each other."

"I am not sure you want to know *everything*," said Bekka.

"Maybe not," said Vigil. "...but this is protocol. I will try to keep my ears closed though."

"You are such a gentleman," she said sarcastically. She bent over and untied her shoes, which was not a good idea. She barely had time to lift the lid of the toilet before projectile vomiting into the bowl. Head injuries have that effect on people. She wasn't embarrassed by it since it was Vigil's fault for the most part. Granted, she *had* been trying to kill *him*; but like he said, it was just business. Once she was sure the contents of her stomach were emptied, she closed the lid and sat down. She extended her foot toward Vigil.

"Do you mind?" she asked softly. Vigil knew better than to trust her, even in her weakened state. "Don't try anything," he said. He untied her laces and slipped her shoes off. Then he removed her socks without any prompting. He didn't want to see her begin to *dry heave* by having to bend over again. Bekka was right; there were some things he didn't want to know about her...namely, anything to do with her digestive track.

She peeled the tactical jumpsuit off of her shoulders and stepped out of it after she had pulled it to the floor. She had a band strapped around each thigh and was wearing nothing else. The bands held a selection of throwing knives. Bekka Dark gave new meaning to the term *going commando*. She smiled at Vigil almost as if she was embarrassed.

"Oh, sorry," she said. "I forgot I was wearing these."

There was a ripping sound as she pulled the Velcro apart and handed the weapons to him. In spite of the blood in her hair and bruises on her face, he still couldn't help but marvel at her flawless body. *No wonder she is such an effective agent*, he thought. *Who can resist her?*

Bekka spared Vigil any more bodily functions for the time being. Instead, she leaned in, started the shower and waited for the temperature to get to the perfect setting. As she got in, she only pulled the curtain closed half way; partly, because she wanted to establish trust, but mostly because she wanted to be seductive. It was always a good idea to keep her opponents off balance. That was one of her most effective methods. She let the water cascade in scarlet ribbons down her marble white skin as she washed the dried blood from her hair. She winced as she touched the entry wound. It had healed nicely but was still tender to the touch. Her seductive performance wasn't lost on Vigil, but he hid it pretty well. However, he didn't hide it completely. Bekka noticed the bulge in his pants and was reminded of the old joke about *a gun in your pocket*. She began to laugh and Vigil knew what it was about. If the situation had been different, he would have been joining her in the shower; but if the situation had been different, he wouldn't have shot her in the head.

As Bekka Dark dried off, watching her was just as enticing as the shower. Vigil only watched her with his peripheral vision to keep from being completely seduced. Even when he handed her one of his dress shirts to wear, he did it with his head turned slightly to the side. That move was totally contrary to his training, but one has to make adjustments in the field as one sees fit. Once she put the shirt on, she buttoned it up slowly, but left a few buttons at the top undone. Vigil found himself breathing heavily in spite of himself. Then Bekka walked obediently to the bed, lay down and stretched her arms out so he could bind them to the bedposts again. As she did, the shirt rode up and erotically exposed her once more. She pulled the shirt back down with a wiggle and resumed her submissive pose.

"We might be able to forego the bondage for the time being," said Vigil. "…if you can agree to a cease fire for the moment."

"Oh…I was just getting into it," said Bekka. "I was looking forward to feeling your belt against my behind…or, maybe you could just shoot me in the head again. That would be fun."

"I cannot tell how much of this is meant to be funny," said Vigil.

"Trust me," said Bekka. "In my country, I am hilarious. I *kill* back there." She began to laugh at her own joke so hard that Vigil thought she might throw up again.

"I guess it's a translation thing," he said.

"I suppose you are right," said Bekka. "Now, how should we do this?" She got serious so quickly, it made Vigil uneasy.

"As I said, I will tell you about me first. I am taking a big risk trusting you with this information, but for some reason, I feel like I can."

"Under normal circumstances," said Bekka. "You couldn't. I feel like I can trust you too. I can't explain it. Plus, I need some answers."

Vigil spent the next two hours giving Bekka Dark his history that spanned hundreds of years. There were many things he had forgotten about until he started talking about the different time periods. It was as if he were walking down a allegorical hallway with closet doors on each side. Inside each closet was an era or a war or some historic event. He told her of famous people he had known and infamous monsters he had resolved. He didn't expect to surprise her; but when he was finished, there was a look of awe and wonder on her face. That surprised *him*.

"Are you alright?" he asked.

"I don't know," she said. "I am not sure what to think. Are you seriously trying to tell me that you are that old; that you have lived during all those times?"

"I am not sure why it's so unbelievable," said Vigil. "Certainly you must have stories equal to those."

"No," said Bekka. "I don't. I thought we were the same. I thought we both just healed really quickly...that our bodies repaired themselves ridiculously fast."

"So you weren't born hundreds of years ago?" asked Vigil.

"Of course not! I was born in 1973," she said. "I never suspected I might live longer than usual. No one in my family ever has...except maybe..."

"Maybe?" asked Vigil.

"There is a legend about my great grandfather," Bekka said. "It was said he couldn't die no matter how many times they tried to kill him. Some say he is still alive today, but I never believed those stories. Now I have to rethink them. You have heard of Rasputin, right?"

"I have heard of him, but he is one man I can honestly say I have not met," said Vigil. "He has never showed up on my radar, so to speak. I was expecting a whole list of famous people you encountered in your past or could list as having been related to. I guess if you only have one, he's a really good one."

"I guess we may need some time to digest this new

information," stated Bekka. "It has been a difficult night for both of us. Maybe we can get some more sleep, yes?" She raised her arms up over her head exposing herself again.

"You do realize the difficulty here, right?" asked Vigil. "I am pretty sure you wouldn't trust me if our situations were reversed." He sounded as sincere as possible.

"I know," said Bekka. "I don't expect you to trust me. I was serious about the bondage thing...just not the belt. I am not opposed to a little light spanking though."

Vigil's head was spinning. Leslie came to mind again. They never made a commitment to each other, but he felt guilty for being so aroused. Part of what made him feel this way was that Bekka could possibly offer him something Leslie couldn't. She could be a companion for more than a single lifetime. It was a difficult proposition to resist. He might have succeeded in resisting Bekka's charms except that she had already unbuttoned the shirt he had given her and let it fall open.

"This isn't a good idea," he said. "We have to remain professional."

"This is part of what I do...professionally," said Bekka. "I don't just kill people. I also help to establish ties with hostile countries. It's amazing what people will agree to when they are in bed together...both literally and politically."

"I suppose it wouldn't matter if I told you I have a girlfriend," said Vigil.

"From what I can tell," said Bekka. "...you've had a thousand girlfriends."

"Not a thousand," said Vigil. "...not quite a thousand."

"Aren't you just the least bit curious what it would be like to be with someone who is like you, metabolically? I have always had to be so careful. I couldn't get hurt the way my lovers could, at least not physically."

Vigil had never thought about it in this way. He wasn't sure why the time he spent with Leslie had impacted him the way it did. Maybe it was because she was a damsel he had rescued from a dragon. No matter what he felt, he knew it would never be possible for him to be in a committed relationship with her. The fact that she would grow old and die, coupled with the demands of his line of work, would make that impossible. Maybe he was just trying to convince himself to take advantage of the opportunity Bekka was offering to him. In any case, it was working. Besides, he *was* curious. He leaned in and kissed Bekka as passionately as he knew how. She kissed him back in a way he had only dreamed of. If this was an act, she deserved an Oscar.

Bekka rolled Vigil over onto his back and began unbuttoning his shirt. He responded by smacking her hard on her butt cheek. He smacked her harder than he intended, but she softly whispered, "Is that the best you can do?" He reminded himself that he had shot her in the head. There wasn't much he could do to her that she couldn't take. He smacked her harder and her eyes widened with surprise and then half-closed in ecstasy. Much of the remainder of the day was spent with experimentation of pleasure mixed with pain. The French call it *la petite mort*...the little death. The French don't know the half of it.

Chapter Twenty-Five: Pain and Pleasure

Vigil seldom dreamed. When he did, his dreams were so vivid that they were like alternate realities. He had his fill of realities by living so very long. He also had the ability to direct the content and direction of his dreams. The idyllic dreamscapes he could construct would be the envy of any living mortal. Not for Vigil though. His dreamscapes could be so perfect, waking up from them was a depressing disappointment; that was why he rarely dreamed.

This was different. Vigil was working out a problem and he needed resources that were only available on the *back burner* of his unconscious mind. All things being considered, he was probably getting ahead of himself. He hardly knew Bekka Dark...on an emotional level anyway. He considered how tragic it would be to involve himself in an extremely long-term relationship with someone he might not even be able to stand. Sure, she was beautiful, athletic, talented and probably as immortal as he was; but that might not be enough to base a relationship on. It had been a very long time since Vigil even considered being in a *relationship.* He was overthinking a lot of things lately. Leslie must have really done a number on him emotionally. There was a time he would not have given a second thought about relationships. They were complications and therefore, against his mission policy.

One other thing to consider was if Bekka Dark even wanted to be in a relationship. After all, he was a little older than she was, by a millennium or so. Maybe she didn't like older men. Maybe she didn't like Americans, even though technically he wasn't an American. He just worked for them.

She might need time, a lot of time, to appreciate the type of life she was going to be living. Vigil had to come to that very realization himself centuries before. It wasn't until many of his family and friends had grown old and died that he fully realized what life had in store for him. Even then, it took another century for him to be fully aware of the hand Fate had dealt him. Like with most people, his life had its pros and cons.

In his dream state, Vigil played out the various scenarios of a permanent relationship between himself and Bekka. He tried to keep from directing the dream in any particular direction, but he couldn't help making it as idyllic as possible. He dreamt about the two of them jet-setting around the world, working as a team of rogue agents. Their goal would be to make the world a better place for when they brought children into it. Children! That was something else to be considered. Would they have regenerative abilities like their parents? While the odds were in their favor, there was no real way to know for sure. Fate can be, and often is, a bastard.

Vigil, even though he was in full REM sleep, realized he was behaving hormonally. He had not grown up in a time period where high school crushes were a thing; but he was pretty sure that was what he was having at the moment. There was a world of possibilities before him, even if they were only in his mind. All he needed now was for his voice to break and to get an onset of acne. That final thought made him feel disappointed and ashamed of himself. Vigil was a trained assassin and should be immune to such things. He was immune to about anything else. Bekka Dark was a target. He had a job to do, but he knew he was never going to do it. He had methods to end her life, but he wouldn't use them on her. Instead, he would file a report that she had slipped through his fingers in Israel. That was kind of true. They had done quite a few things with their fingers. In any case, he wouldn't kill her.

Maybe it would be best if he just distanced himself from her for a while...both mentally and physically. At least until he could sort things out. Gradually he was beginning to wake up when a new hurdle presented itself.

* * *

The room was not completely dark, but the sun had gone down. There was enough light to make out shapes and objects, but not enough to discern colors. Vigil lay naked on his back. He tried to move his arms, but they were bound to the bedposts in the same way he had bound Bekka Dark. His legs had not been bound together though. Instead, they had each been tied to a leg of the bed. He was spread-eagle and vulnerable. He didn't know Bekka Dark's motives, but he was sure she was responsible for his bondage.

A voice came from a shadow in the corner. It was little more than a whisper and Vigil wasn't sure he even heard it, except in his mind. Goosebumps appeared on his arms and legs as he recognized the timbre of the voice. It wasn't Bekka. It was a man's voice. It spoke more clearly and removed all doubt about his identity.

"You get all the best women," said Ankh. "Honestly, I don't know how you do it. It's not like you are that much to look at. And what are you now...thirteen hundred years old? Fifteen hundred?"

"Where is she, Ankh?" He tried to sound threatening, but his naked vulnerability made it impossible.

"I am afraid I had to dispatch her downstairs," said Ankh. "...and after she was kind enough to bind you up. She must have been preparing a romantic repast for the two of you. Don't worry. It was quick; painless...well, probably painless."

Vigil struggled with the metal restraints, but only succeeded in slashing his wrists a bit. Blood trails ran down his arms and dripped onto the sheets.

"Let's get some light in here," said Ankh. "There, that's better. Oh, my! I guess I interrupted quite a party." Vigil had no choice but to just lay there and pretend he wasn't naked and in a semi-aroused state.

"Let's close these curtains, shall we? By the way, from the looks of this window, I suspect you have lost your security deposit. The wind coming through it is a bit chilly. You'd better be careful; it might cause some *shrinkage*...oops, too late." Vigil pointlessly tried to bring his legs together. In the light, he could see that Bekka had tied them under the bed with a couple of his own neckties.

"You know what surprises me?" Ankh began. "It wasn't like you to let a target live; let alone bring her in and tend to her. You must really have had the hots for that piece of ass. I can't say as I blame you though. Looking at her down in the kitchen, sprawled out all naked and bleeding on the floor, I thought about doing her myself; but I don't do dead women...anymore. And I have an appointment to keep. I have been tracking you since Edinburgh. There are some questions I want answered or you would have been dismembered already."

"I am not going to answer any of your questions," said Vigil. "...so you'd better get started."

"Are you sure?" asked Ankh. "I am sure you know what I am going to dismember first. It's the little things that count, you know."

"You are hilarious," said Vigil. "Knock yourself out. No seriously, knock yourself out."

"Soon," said Ankh. "Oh, wait. You meant for me to really knock myself out. I thought you would have a better comeback than that."

"If you want to give me a few minutes," said Vigil. "I

am sure I can come up with something better. It will probably involve you sucking my..."

"In a few minutes there won't be anything to suck!" Ankh's patience had worn thin and he lost his composure completely. "You know what I want to know. Where can I find Adriel and Zuriel?"

"I didn't know you cared about them any more than I did," said Vigil. "If I had...well, I wouldn't have done anything different. But still...why do you want to know so badly?"

"That's my business," said Ankh, suddenly calm. He composed himself quickly and it took Vigil by surprise. Ankh had a bit of a bipolar thing going on and Vigil wasn't sure how to handle it. He could try to exploit it, but dealing with this kind of disorder was like defusing a bomb; and bound naked to a bed in a room with a maniac is not the most ideal condition under which to do it.

"Adriel is in a bog," said Vigil after a long pause. He had no real reason to keep it a secret. He just didn't want to look like he was giving up information too easily. That would make him look weak. There were hundreds of blanket bogs in Great Britain and Vigil wouldn't even know how to draw him a map. He would have to take Ankh there if he really wanted to find the body.

"A bog? You mummified him in a bog? He's your brother!" Ankh's emotions went round and round on the bipolar roulette wheel and Vigil had no idea which number the ball was going to land on. "What about Zuriel?" Ankh seemed to be back to quietly threatening.

"I would rather not tell you that at the moment," said Vigil. Beads of perspiration appeared on his forehead. Ankh produced a long thin knife that had been concealed under his coat. It was the type of knife used to amputate limbs on the battlefield ages ago. Vigil could tell the knife was at least a hundred years old.

"You know," Ankh continued menacingly. "...there are lots of appendages I could cut off before getting to the main event. The outcome is still going to be the same, but the amount of torment you will experience could be greatly reduced with a little cooperation."

"I am not a stranger to pain," said Vigil. "I've suffered quite a bit of it by your hand, if I recall."

"So be it then," said Ankh. "I may have to get a later flight. Since I will be staying over another night, I might as well visit your friends. Lorraine and Lawrence don't live too far from here do they?"

"I am not sure I would call them friends," said Vigil. He was trying to hide his nervousness. Innocent people were his weakness and Ankh seemed to know that. "I haven't seen them in twenty years. They are hardly close...more like acquaintances." He was sure his bluff wasn't working.

"Well. No matter. I can still use some practice with my vivisection," said Ankh. "I've gotten a little sloppy of late." He examined the long blade of his knife admiringly. "You have no idea how much satisfaction there is to dissecting a person while they are still alive. They are willing to give you anything you want. You should hear the promises they make. They don't realize I am usually torturing them for the pure joy of the torture itself. They can't relate to the kind of monster I am."

Vigil struggled again with his bonds. The metal band around one wrist must have severed a vein because stream of blood ran down his arm and pooled on the sheet next to him.

"Let's not get ahead of ourselves," said Ankh. "There will be plenty of time for bleeding later. By the way, I will probably be borrowing some of your clothes. I am pretty sure these will be covered with your entrails by the time we are finished. I usually just strip down to dismember a body; but considering we are related, that just seems weird."

"This is quite a bit weird already, don't you think? You could at least allow me a little modesty." Vigil's wrist wound had healed already and the dried blood on his arm formed a hideous inkblot test.

"I don't mind," said Ankh. "...I like having you vulnerable and at a disadvantage, so to speak. Of course, you have always been at a disadvantage when it came to me."

"You're older...and a little taller," Vigil said. "That doesn't make you superior."

"In a little while, there won't be any question as to who is superior," said Ankh. "Now, I need those locations. Where are Adriel and Zuriel? You know what? I have been patient long enough!"

Ankh walked over to the end of the bed and placed the long knife blade next to Vigil's shin. With a slow even stroke, he cut a long gash from his ankle to just below his knee. The cut was so precise that Vigil only felt a slight sting in the beginning. When the pain finally hit him, blood was spurting out of the wound like a fountain. Vigil struggled to maintain his composure rather than give Ankh the satisfaction of showing distress.

"I don't expect you to talk right away," said Ankh. "This is just a little warm-up to test the sharpness of my blade. It's a good thing too. The edge is much too sharp. It didn't hurt nearly enough."

"You know we had training about this, right?" Vigil remained calm, but he was sure the beads of sweat on his forehead were as big as cultured pearls. He needed to stall and he needed to exploit one of Ankh's weaknesses. There seemed to be only one available to him at the moment. "Do you know why you should tell me what you need Adriel and Zuriel for?"

"Uh…because I should monologue, like the villains in the movies?" Ankh sneered with contempt. "I suppose I should tell you my *master plan*, so that you can save the world when you miraculously escape my clutches. Is that right?"

"Sort of," said Ankh. He was afraid he was sounding desperate and pathetic. He was pretty much on the money. "I will be the first to admit that I would like to delay what is going to happen; no matter what kind of front I have put on. But I would think you would *want* to tell me your plan. I am going to be dead, so I won't be able to interfere with it; and who else can fully appreciate it? A mortal? I am pretty sure you don't care what they think."

Ankh hated to admit that Vigil was right. He did need someone that was as close to his peer as possible to give him the accolades he felt he deserved. Throughout his life, he never sought approval from anyone, but he was a *God,* and he deserved to be worshipped and feared.

"Since you are my little brother…and I love you *so* much," Ankh began. "…I will tell you what I have in mind." Somehow, Ankh had made his entire sarcastic statement sound sour.

"First, you are right. You won't leave this room alive," he said. "Hell, you won't even leave it in one piece. I will probably be mailing your body parts to the four corners of the world. But don't worry; I will mail your *special bits* to your sweetheart in Scotland. Maybe she will recognize who they used to belong to when she opens the package."

"You are so kind," said Vigil with angry sarcasm. His eyebrows knitted into a single line over his eyes. "Go on. I am on the edge of my seat…so to speak."

"As you wish," said Ankh. He tossed a pillowcase stained with dried blood across Vigil's groin. "If I am going to monologue, I don't what you to be distracted by the future fate of your little buddy."

"Very thoughtful," said Vigil. "Thanks."

"I keep up on most things," began Ankh. "...but even I have my limits; few as they may be. I don't know for instance, if you are aware of the disrupter technology that Zuriel was working on."

"I might have heard a little something about that," said Vigil. "Didn't he steal that from someone?"

"It was only a crude concept when Nikola formulated it," Ankh said defensively. "Zuriel perfected it! Maybe it is more accurate to say that he knows people who perfected it. That does not take away from his vision of how to exploit it."

"Sorry," said Vigil. "I was just repeating what I heard. Please, continue."

"Adriel is much more effective at decoding encrypted systems than anyone I have ever met. It was a natural evolution from simply being a sexual predator I suppose. The knowledge he gained over the decades made him unsurpassed in hacking skills. Do you see where this is going?"

"I am a little fuzzy on what you are trying to say," said Vigil. "...but then, I am a little slow." Ankh breathed and exasperated huff.

"Maybe this is a waste of time," he said. "You aren't going to be able to fully comprehend the magnitude of my plan."

"Give me a chance," said Vigil. "It's not like you are doing anything else at the moment."

"Perhaps you are right. Then pay attention this time!"

Ankh sat down in the chair and crossed his legs. "I have spent the last few decades infiltrating the highest levels of several governments. There are enough international secrets stored in my brain to make the Pentagon and the Kremlin green with envy. Nothing is out of my geopolitical reach."

"I do think I finally see where this is going," said Vigil. "You plan to install those disrupters in the offices of the highest ranking officials of the world."

"Your vision is so limited," said Ankh pompously. "I don't need devices. The devices are already in place. The disrupter program is the key. All I needed was access to each country's communication satellites and telecommunication systems. Every electronic device in the world will be subject to my slightest whim."

"You are going to quite a bit of trouble just to kill people," said Vigil calmly.

"Again, you have no vision!" Ankh was getting impatient. He twirled the long blade in is hand, slit the end of his finger and watched it heal. "Killing is too final! I want subjugation. I want to be worshipped the way I deserve. These mortals go through life believing they are the most superior beings on the planet. It makes me sick. Death is too good for them. What they all need is some good old fashioned oppression, plain and simple!"

"So I guess you are saying you will have more than one setting on your Doomsday program there, right?" Vigil knew he sounded like he was mocking Ankh the moment the words left his lips, and he instantly regretted it. Ankh rose from the chair and stormed over to the bed. Vigil struggled against the metal bonds and produced fresh streams of blood.

"Maybe we should just skip ahead to the *main event!*" Ankh was screaming in spite of himself. "I will get this thing ready for mailing. Then I will begin to peel your skin back inch by inch and watch it grow back. Afterwards, I will peel it off again." Ankh's eyes glowed with the prospect. "You know you are going to tell me where they are eventually. You will hold onto the vain hope that telling me will make me stop; but we both know it won't happen. Why don't you just abandon hope and tell me now? That way, you won't be disappointed when I continue to skin you alive."

"I suggest you get started," said Vigil through clinched teeth. "You have no intention of letting me live and it sounds like I have a better chance of saving the world if I don't tell you anything. Besides, I couldn't give you verbal directions to finding Adriel if I wanted to; and believe me, I *don't* want to! I would have to show you where he is; but you're smart enough to know you can't trust me. So quit yammering and get to it!"

"Have it your way," screamed Ankh. He moved the blade until it was positioned just below Vigil's testicles.

"You don't mind if I take *the boys* off at the same time, do you? I really don't want to touch it if I don't have to. Besides, if everything is in one piece when the package arrives in Scotland, I think it will make a better presentation. Don't you?" Ankh began to laugh uncontrollably. "Your *package* arriving in Scotland...get it?"

Vigil tried to think of some clever comeback, but his mind went blank. His amygdala was in overdrive and had robbed him of his sarcastic wit. The blade felt like fire on his naked skin, which Vigil thought was strange. He was sure the blade should have been ice cold.

"*You are so terribly funny,*" was all Vigil could come up with. His bleeding shin had already begun to heal and the incision closed up like a zip lock sandwich bag. In high risk situations, Vigil's healing processed sped up tremendously; but it took a lot out of him after the crisis was over.

Ankh waited to get the reaction from his brother that he

301

wanted. He flipped the blade over and ran it across Vigil's thighs, feigning a cut. Vigil wasn't fooled and even managed to give Ankh an impatient scowl.

Bracing himself for what was about to happen, Vigil defiantly said, "Do what you have to do and get on with it!" He had wanted to sound much calmer, but his blood chemistry had other ideas.

"I make the rules here," said Ankh.

Throughout the centuries, Vigil had suffered countless injuries and been subjected to nearly every conceivable form of torture. However, somehow he had always managed to evade castration. Fate, the bastard, had finally caught up with him it seemed. He closed his eyes and felt a thin line of cat-scratch pain begin across his scrotum. Ankh let out an almost girlish titter and instantly regretted it. If Vigil's situation had not been so dire, he would probably have laughed at him out loud. His eyes were closed tightly and his teeth were clenched and grinding into each other in anticipation of the pain and literal dismemberment. He convulsed violently as three rapid explosions rocked the room.

"Suka mat' ublyudok! I am planning to use that thing soon!" Ankh slumped awkwardly across his brother's midsection. Vigil cautiously opened one eye and surveyed the room. Bekka Dark stood in the doorway, supporting herself with the doorframe. She was naked and covered with lines of dried blood. Dried blood matted her hair into a grotesque case of *bedhead* and one eye was completely obscured by dried blood. Vigil thought she had never looked more beautiful.

"Such language," he said. "I am so turned on right now."

"I hope not," said Bekka. She crossed the room and pulled Ankh's body off of Vigil. After she checked the severity of the razor-like cut on his scrotum, she emptied the

302

rest of the clip into Ankh's brain.

"I am really getting sick of guys shooting me in the head," she said. Vigil noted her conviction and made a mental note to avoid ever shooting her in the head in the future.

"I know this might seem a bit odd," she said. "...but before anything else, I need to get this blood washed off of me."

"No...by all means," said Vigil. "I'll be right here if you need me."   After being one of the two people who had shot her in the head in the last twenty-four hours, he was not about to put up an argument.

Bekka Dark had caught enough of the conversation to know that Ankh had the same regenerative ability as she did. Until she could work on a more permanent solution to the problem, she bound him securely in a comic number of metal zip tie restraints. Then she gagged him...with Vigil's socks. She thought it seemed like poetic justice. She kissed Vigil for a long time. A moment or two later, he could hear the shower running. He would have liked to have cleaned up himself, but didn't want to be a problem; not after her going to so much trouble for him. He was hungry though and wondered if she ever finished preparing whatever it was she was making for him to eat.

Bekka didn't even dry off after she got out of the shower. She and Vigil bonded over the injuries they had both suffered at the hands of Ankh. She examined the wound to his shin and then slowly moved north. She tarried for some time around the *equator* and made sure everything was still in working order. She thoroughly addressed the small incision that Ankh had made. Once she was satisfied that Vigil was *fit for duty* as it were, she strung a line of kisses up his abdomen, to his chest, his neck and then finally settled in for long passionate kisses. All the while, Vigil was still helplessly bound to the bed and loving every minute of it. The soft attention Bekka was showering on him was a stark contrast to the torture he had endured only moments before.

"There is too much light in here," she said softly as she kissed him behind the ear. She rose up and walked across the room to the light switch. Her walk was graceful and seductive, whether she meant for it to be or not. She returned to bed with a pair of tin snips. Vigil had no idea where those had come from.

"I think we should perhaps both participate now," said Bekka. Her words were uttered in a breathy whisper. Vigil agreed. He couldn't show her the full breadth of his appreciation tied up like a hostage. Twists of her wet hair captured his fingers like a net as he pulled her in close for a kiss. Their embrace was such that for a while they seemed unable to separate. Finally, they settled in (under the covers for a change) and enjoyed an uninterrupted night of erotic passion. Then exhaustion finally won out and they fell asleep in each other's arms.

It was 4:47 in the morning when Vigil was awakened by heavy thuds and muffled cursing. That must have been how long it took for Ankh's regenerative powers to work. Vigil was pretty sure Ankh would have quite the headache until he was finally able to expel the full clip of Bekka's slugs from his brain. Being virtually immortal has its disadvantages as well. He leaned over the side of the bed and said in a low menacing voice, "Zuriel is safe. He's secured in a lockbox at an undisclosed location. Did I mention that I had him cremated? Sorry. It must have slipped my mind. You can visit him. You will be going to the same undisclosed location soon. Maybe you can share a lockbox together. For now, I could really use some more sleep."

Vigil took Ankh's head in both hands and with a skill

honed over the centuries, snapped his neck like a bamboo chopstick. His head fell to the floor and a thin trail of blood dripped from around his gag and pooled on the carpet.

"He was right," said Vigil softly. "There is no way I am getting my security deposit back."

Chapter Twenty-Six: Unresolved Issues

People who live only a single lifetime cannot possibly conceive of how complicated living for centuries can be. Even more so when working with other immortals and working for the government. Policies change every time the wind blows, yet life goes on. Vigil had seen governments and regimes rise and fall. Policies always seemed to be subject to the whims of the few. Vigil couldn't change it...usually. All he could do was work within the system and navigate his way through the bureaucratic *red tape*. He was pretty good at it. His success in eliminating targets gave him a considerable amount of latitude when it came to accepting assignments. That was why he barely ruffled a feather when he came back to the agency and reported that Bekka Dark had not been eliminated.

Bekka told Vigil she needed time to think. There was indeed a lot for her to think about. Knowing there were others like her in the world and that she might live for centuries was a lot to process. For the time being, she chose to return to the KGB and informed her superiors that Vigil had slipped through her grasp as well. She would get a verbal reprimand, but no real consequence. There was really nothing they could do to her anyway. They didn't know that, but her confidence always won out when dealing with her superiors.

Vigil needed information that only Ankh could give him. He had infiltrated so many levels of so many governments, he was too valuable to just *resolve*. Ankh was secured in the *undisclosed location* Vigil had spoken of...nearly intact. An agency transport had taken them across the ocean and about as far from D.C. as one could be taken in the continental United States. A concrete bunker on the west coast of Whidbey Island was one part of what remains of a coastal defense fort left over from World War II. There are hiking and biking trails on the island, along with campsites. It's a quite popular tourist destination.

The island is located northwest of Seattle and is only remote in the broadest sense of the word; but the best way to camouflage something is often to just hide it in plain sight. The bunker looks totally abandoned to the casual observer and vandals periodically spray graffiti on the walls. However, hidden inside is a covert entrance leading to an underground network comparable to that which exists beneath the Pentagon. There are multiple entrances to the concealed complex on the island; so landing near an isolated area is easily accomplished without arousing suspicion.

The agency wasn't aware they would be storing a living specimen. Vigil's report stated that the body he needed to be secured there was a high valued asset who needed to disappear for security reasons. The Whidbey Island facility was out of the way, but not where the highly classified experiments and examinations took place. Those types of research were done in Nevada; or if they were really covert, in a facility in Ohio. No one at Whidbey Island had a pay grade high enough to ask Vigil any questions about his missions.

He arrived at the facility with a long metal case about the size of a coffin. It was made of titanium and had a series of complex cypher and biometric locks securing it on every side. Inside, the body of Ankh was temporarily encased in a long block of polymer fitted with tubes for airways, feeding and (ugh) waste disposal. The polymer was chemically formed instead of injection molded so no unnecessary cruelty occurred, no matter how much Ankh might deserve it. He stayed in his capsule until the construction of his cell could be completed. Then the cell was chemically dissolved.

The cell was much like a doomsday bunker except that it was constructed completely from a titanium alloy. It was actually pretty nice, or so some might think. Not Ankh, of course. It had a living area with a wide selection of books, videos, gaming systems and art supplies. There was nothing electronic connected to the outside world; no communication in or out. The cell had a very nice steam shower, whirlpool tub and tanning bed. If Vigil had his way, it would be a long time before Ankh ever saw the sun again. The food preparation area would be the envy of the world's top chefs if they knew about it. There was also a wine cellar that was nearly second to none.

The one thing the cell didn't have was an exit. The reason construction took so long was that the cell was formed from only two parts; a top and a bottom. A construction crane was necessary to lower the upper part onto the titanium foundation. They were then laser welded together so that the seams no longer existed. Supplies were delivered through a dumbwaiter system no larger than a shoebox. It would take a construction crew and the necessary equipment more than a week to open the cell again. That was more than enough to insure that there would be no escape in the dead of night. In addition, Vigil had installed his own security measure into the ventilation system; well outside of the occupant's reach. It was a pair of disrupters like the kind Zuriel had used on him. They were set to go off if the any of the surfaces lost any integrity in any way. It wasn't perfect, but it was pretty close.

Vigil's superiors thought that the treatment of the prisoner was much too humane and they balked when they received the bill. They weren't aware that the confinement was the worst possible torture that could have been inflicted on Ankh. In essence, he had been buried alive, but still had to deal with a few of the inferior mortals he despised so much.

Vigil knew that Ankh would never divulge anything to anyone but him. That would be too much beneath him. That meant he would need to make regular visits back to the facility whenever conflicts heated up in some politically charged part of the world. At first, Ankh refused to say anything at all; but his tongue loosened up after a few zaps from the disrupter array. Vigil was glad he got a little use out of them after all.

Down a corridor from Ankh's massive cell, there was a plain vault set into a solid layer of lava rock. Only one person in the world could gain access to it. Inside, on a shelf on the north wall, was a row of identical metal containers marked with simple identification numbers. Each was the size of a coffee can and each had a biometric lock securing them. They contained the ashes of several immortals Vigil had *resolved* over the years. He used to think they were all his relatives. Now he didn't know for sure. He kept them at the facility for two reasons. One reason was that he didn't want to give anyone the opportunity to examine their DNA. If there was something someone could discover that could be used as a weapon against him, he couldn't take that chance...no matter how remote the possibility. The other reason was that he felt the need to give them some semblance of a final resting place. Vigil wondered what the afterlife might hold for them. In spite of everything, he hoped they found peace.

In time, he would resolve Ankh in the same way he had resolved the others. Ankh would then take his place on the shelf with the rest. Vigil already had a spot reserved for him. That could take decades though, even centuries. Ankh had been alive for a long time and wasn't going to go quietly. Vigil knew that.

* * *

Vigil would see Leslie on a semi-regular basis over the next couple of decades. As the years progressed, his visits would become less frequent and less physical. It would be his way of weaning the two of them from each other. He was determined to keep his promise to her and tried to do it in a way that would hurt the two of them the least. Hazel kept in touch with him and let him know she was seeing a fellow regularly from time to time. Vigil was glad.

"She's maintaining her independence though," Hazel would report. "...and he doesn't have your enormous...*charm*." Vigil laughed out loud and wished he could visit more without it being becoming awkward. *Hazel is never going to change*, thought Vigil. He really didn't want her to. That was the problem with the world; everything changed while he just went on as usual. Oh, he would change in time; but sometimes Vigil's life seemed to move exceedingly slow while the rest of mankind just sped by like angry commuters trying to get to work.

* * *

On one of Vigil's regular visits to the Whidbey Island facility, he decided to take a few days off for some rest and relaxation. God knows he needed it. The sun was about to come up over Seattle and the silhouettes of the buildings formed a jagged but uniform skyline. Vigil never tried to calculate how many sunrises and sunsets he had seen. There had been so many. They were all unique, yet all the same in one way or another. There was a thin tendril of fog accessorizing the dawn. He looked down from his hotel window and thought about the people down below; some coming home from night shifts and others rushing to get to their day jobs. Every one of them had a life story and each one was important to themselves and to the people they loved.

Vigil wondered if his regenerative ability was going to be unique, or maybe a new stage of human evolution. Bekka Dark had shown him that immortal bloodlines other than his own existed in the world. In the First Book of Moses, there were recorded births and names of a line of people who lived incredibly long lives by today's standards. They all supposedly came from the same bloodline...that of Adam. The children of Lazarus might just be following an old family tradition. Some religions believe in reincarnation. Vigil thought maybe he and a few other bloodlines had simply bypassed the reincarnation part of being born into a new body and just repaired the one they had.

Genesis stated that God was displeased with mankind after about fifteen hundred years. That led to the Great Flood. Perhaps they had the same mindsets that some of Vigil's brothers had. What if it was a world of *Adriels* and *Zuriels* who had become so jaded with their long lives that they cared nothing for their fellow man, or the suffering of others? He wondered if he might live long enough to see the evolutionary change or genetic advances that would allow mankind to once again live incredibly long. He wasn't sure he was ready to deal with that kind of world. He had enough trouble chasing down members of his own family tree. A world of people like them might just be too much to handle. He might have allies though. He wondered what Bekka Dark was doing at the moment.

Vigil liked Seattle. It was relaxing compared to most of the cities he was used to. It had most of the amenities of the bigger cities, but there was less hustle and bustle. He liked to walk the streets and usually found himself heading down toward Elliot Bay. There, he loved the ambience of the Pike Place Market. The market had a selection of arts and crafts made by people who loved to make them, so they were less commercial. The smell of the fish flying through the air at the Pike Place Fish Market reminded him of his sailing days...especially Madagascar and *Cinnamon*.

Vigil sat down at a French café table and sipped his cappuccino. He was enjoying a freshly baked croissant and decided to *people watch* for a while. He had new insights about people thanks to Bekka Dark. He now knew that any one of those people could be as immortal as he was. He tried to tell by looking at their faces. *Who in the crowd looks like they are an old soul?* This exercise proved fruitless. No one looked any different to him than before. That probably meant he couldn't be recognized for what he was. That thought gave him some level of reassurance.

Vigil spread a little butter on his croissant and sprinkled it with a touch of cinnamon. He closed his eyes and allowed the savory blend to captivate his senses.

"It really seems like you are enjoying that way too much," said a female voice. "Would you two like to be alone?"

"I thought you were on assignment in Croatia?" Vigil opened his eyes and Bekka Dark sat down at the table with him.

"As far as the agency is concerned, I am," she answered. "...and how sweet of you to keep tabs on me."

"I am nothing if not sweet," said Vigil smiling. "Besides, it's kinda my job."

"You are such a romantic," said Bekka sarcastically. "...and after I came all this way just to see you."

"So you are keeping tabs on *me* then?" asked Vigil.

"It is also kind of *my* job," she said. "...and I wanted to see you. I also wanted to know the status of our visitor we had in Israel."

"He is securely locked away for the moment," Vigil assured her. "...he will be resolved in due course."

"Why not just be done with him?" Bekka asked.

"Most of my leads have gone cold," said Vigil. "This information age allows too many of my targets to know what I am up to. I have decided to *go to ground* for a bit. It worries me that you found me so easily; though I am very happy to see you."

"I have a lot of connections others do not," said Bekka. "I also had an idea of your most recent destination. Once you leave here, I probably won't be able to find you until you surface again. Just be careful. I wouldn't want anything to happen to you."

"I will do what I can," said Vigil. "Now...since you are a guest in my country, what would you like to do?"

"How do you manage to make everything you say sound so suggestive?" asked Bekka.

"That's not my intention," said Vigil. "Maybe you are just a dirty girl...a dirty, dirty girl. Or maybe it *is* my intention, but not at the moment. I am serious. What would you like to do?"

"I don't know," said Bekka. "I was just having a bit of fun with you anyway. Maybe we could just see the sights, like a couple...you know?"

"Then we will just make a day of it and see what kind of adventures happen our way," said Vigil. Normally, this plan would seem a little reckless; but, not today for some reason. He felt very relaxed in Bekka Dark's presence. Maybe it was because he didn't have to worry as much about her safety.

They both were able to relax in a way neither was familiar with. Later they had lunch at an outdoor café. It began to rain, (it was Seattle after all) and it reminded them of Paris. The mountains in the distance made them think of Switzerland. Puget Sound reminded Vigil of some of the lochs in Scotland. He thought the reason he liked the area so much was that it combined some of his favorite sights around the world in one place. It was like a sanctuary to him and he could revitalize his system when he needed to. Bekka Dark had the same thought, but she didn't share it. She knew she could trust Vigil, but couples should keep some things from each other. Communication is the key to a good relationship, but too much information can do more harm than good.

Both of them knew they would wind up back in a hotel room. The question would just be whose. In the end, it was neither. For security purposes, they checked into a third hotel under assumed names. Dinner was delivered by room service. The young man who delivered the cart was shocked enough when Bekka answered the door wearing only a towel. He was even more shocked when she let it fall to the floor while searching for a gratuity. He refused any form of reward and quickly left the room, probably because he was embarrassed by the noticeable bulge in his pants.

"Did you really have to do that?" asked Vigil. He raised one eyebrow in a chiding kind of way.

"It is standard procedure," Bekka replied. "If he had been here to kill us, my actions would have been enough of a distraction to allow us the advantage. Besides, I got to keep the tip. I do not understand Americans and this *tipping*. They do not usually tip in Europe."

"Well…*when in Rome*," said Vigil.

"I do not think they tip in Rome either," said Bekka.

"Enough about tipping," he said. "Let's enjoy this meal while it is hot."

Neither of them dressed for dinner. Bekka Dark was not that far ahead of Vigil and he stripped off the rest of his clothes to match her dinner attire. It was one of the advantages of ordering room service. Since they were expecting no more visitors for the evening, he placed several security devices around the door and windows so they could feel safe and wouldn't be disturbed. For once, they weren't.

Vigil and Bekka didn't quite finish dinner before lust showed up early on the menu. They had planned it for dessert, but it couldn't wait it seemed. They didn't come up for air until after eight-thirty and it was dark. Bekka snuggled contently in the comforter and Vigil poured a drink from the minibar. He looked out over the city once more. To the north, the skyline had sharper lines than it had that morning. The sky was clear and only a thin layer of color could be seen at the distant horizon.

An explosion of light suddenly appeared before Vigil's face. Instinctually, he dropped to the ground and rolled over to where his automatic pistol hung on the back of a chair. He cautiously returned to the window to inspect the damage and assess the threat. He heard a barrage of explosions as light and color splashed across the wall opposite the window. Bekka Dark seemed undisturbed by the display.

"Have you never seen fireworks before?" she asked with her face half concealed by a pillow. "I thought you had seen everything."

Vigil felt pretty stupid; but he often overreacted when he let his guard down.

"I knew what it was," he said sheepishly. "I guess my humor is just too intellectual for this audience."

"Of course," said Bekka. "That's what it is." She muffled her humiliating laugh with the pillow. "Come back to bed."

"In a bit," said Vigil. "Someone went to a lot of trouble to shoot these things off. I should at least watch them for a little while." He wondered why there would be a fireworks display. There were no holidays near. *Someone must have some pull with somebody*, he thought. The skyline, especially the *Space Needle*, was clearly silhouetted as the grand finale exploded over Puget Sound. Vigil was reminded of his time in China. During the *Song Dynasty*, gunpowder had been used for displays before ever being used for warfare. Vigil thought about that because he wondered if his own ability might someday no longer be needed for warfare. He would probably have to wait a long time...centuries perhaps. He could wait if need be. He had been around a long time. Patience was one of his best virtues.

-END-

81399318R00176

Made in the USA
Lexington, KY
16 February 2018